THE GHOST

"Hi," I said again. "Yes, I'm talking to you. On the bench. Here. With me. Can you hear me?"

He turned to look at me, his eyes wide in surprise.

"Bet you're surprised," I said, smiling. "I know. It's weird. But I can see you. My name's Rory. What's yours?"

No answer. Just a wide, eternal stare.

"I'm new here," I said. "To Bristol. I was in London. I'm from America, but I guess you can tell that from my accent? I came here to go to school, and—"

The man bolted from his seat. Ghosts have a fluidity of movement that the living don't know—they remain solid, yet they can move like air. I didn't want him to go, so I bounced up and reached as far as I could to catch his coat. The second I made contact, I felt my fingers getting pulled into his body, like I had put them into the suction end of a vacuum. I felt the ripple of energy going up my arm, the inexorable force linking us both together now, then the rush of air, far greater than any waterside breeze. Then came the flash of light and the unsettling floral smell.

And he was gone.

OTHER BOOKS YOU MAY ENJOY

Devilish	Maureen Johnson
The Disenchantments	Nina LaCour
Hold Still	Nina LaCour
Let It Snow	John Green, Maureen Johnson, and Lauren Myracle
Looking for Alaska	John Green
The Name of the Star	Maureen Johnson
Nightshade	Andrea Cremer
On the Count of Three	Maureen Johnson
Ripper	Stefan Petrucha
Shelter	Harlan Coben
Spirit Walk	Richie Tankersley Cusick
Twisted	Laurie Halse Anderson
Wintergirls	Laurie Halse Anderson

THE

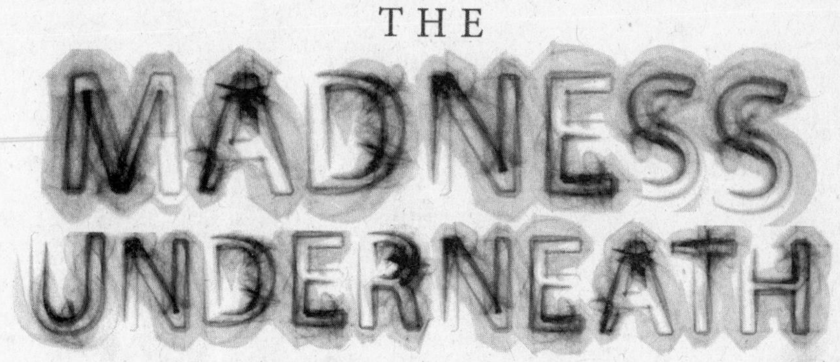

SHADES OF LONDON,
BOOK TWO

maureen johnson

speak
An Imprint of Penguin Group (USA)

SPEAK
Published by the Penguin Group
Penguin Group (USA) LLC
375 Hudson Street
New York, New York 10014

USA * Canada * UK * Ireland * Australia
New Zealand * India * South Africa * China

penguin.com
A Penguin Random House Company

First published in the United States of America by G. P. Putnam's Sons,
a division of Penguin Young Readers Group, 2013
Published by Speak, an imprint of Penguin Group (USA) LLC, 2013

THE LIBRARY OF CONGRESS HAS CATALOGED THE G. P. PUTNAM'S SONS EDITION AS FOLLOWS:
Johnson, Maureen, 1973–
The madness underneath / Maureen Johnson.
p. cm.—(Shades of London ; bk. 2)
ISBN 978-0-399-25661-5 (hardcover)
Summary: "After her near-fatal run-in with the Jack the Ripper copycat, Rory Deveaux is back in London to help solve a new string of inexplicable deaths plaguing the city"—Provided by publisher. [1. Boarding schools—Fiction. 2. Schools—Fiction. 3. Murder—Fiction. 4. Ghosts—Fiction. 5. London (England)—Fiction. 6. England—Fiction.] I. Title. PZ7.J634145Mad 2013 [Fic]—dc22 2012026755

Speak ISBN 978-0-14-242754-5

Printed in the United States of America

1 3 5 7 9 10 8 6 4 2

For my friend, the real Alexander Newman,
who would never let a tiny thing like having twelve strokes
get the better of him. When I grow up, I want to be you.
(Maybe without the twelve strokes? You know what I mean.)

THE ROYAL GUNPOWDER PUB, ARTILLERY LANE, EAST LONDON NOVEMBER 11 10:15 A.M.

Charlie Strong liked his customers—you don't run a pub for twenty-one years if you don't like your customers—but there was something about the quiet in the morning that pleased him to no end. In the morning, Charlie had the one cigarette he allowed himself daily. He drew on the Silk Cut slowly, listening to the satisfying sizzle of burning paper and tobacco. He could smoke inside when no one else was here. Good mug of tea. Good smoke. Good bacon on his sandwich.

Charlie switched on the television. The television in the Royal Gunpowder went on for only two things: when Liverpool played and *Morning with Michael and Alice,* the relentlessly cheerful talk show. Charlie liked to watch this as he prepared for the day, particularly the cooking part. They always made something good, and for some reason, this made him enjoy his bacon sandwich even more. Today, they were making a roast chicken. His barman, Sam, came up from the basement with a box of tonic water. He set it on the bar and quietly got on with his work, taking the chairs from their upside-down positions on the tables and setting them upright on the floor. Sam was good to have around in the mornings. He didn't say much, but he was still good company. He was happy to be employed, and it always showed.

"Good-looking chicken, that," he said to Sam, pointing to the television.

Sam paused his work to look..

"I like mine fried," Sam said.

"It'll kill you, all that fried food."

"Says the man eating the bacon sarnie."

"Nothing wrong with bacon," Charlie said, smiling.

Sam shook his head good-naturedly and continued moving chairs. "Think we'll get more of them Ripper freaks today?" he asked.

"Let's hope so. God bless the Ripper. We did almost three thousand pounds last night. Speaking of, they do eat a lot of crisps. Get us another box of the plain and"—he sorted through the selection under the bar—"cheese and onion. And some more nuts while you're there. They like nuts as well. Nuts for the nutters, eh?"

Without a word, Sam stopped what he was doing and returned to the basement. Charlie's gaze was fixed on the television and the final, critical stages of the cooking segment. The cooked chicken was produced from the oven, golden brown and lovely. The show moved on to the next segment, talking about some music festival that was going on in London over the weekend. This interested Charlie less than the chicken, but he watched it anyway since he had a cigarette to finish. When he was down to the filter, he stubbed it out and got to work.

He had just started wiping down the blackboard to write the day's specials when he heard the sound of breaking glass from below. He opened the basement door.

"Sam! What in God's name—"

"Charlie! Get down here!"

"What's the matter?" Charlie yelled back.

Sam did not reply.

Charlie swore under his breath, allowed himself one heavy post-smoke cough, and headed down the stairs. The basement stairs were narrow and steep, and the basement itself was full of things Charlie largely didn't want to deal with—broken chairs and tables, heavy crates of supplies, racks of glasses ready to replace the ones that were chipped, cracked, or stolen every day.

"Sam?" he called.

"In here!"

Sam's voice was coming from a small room off the main one. Charlie ducked down. The ceiling was lower in this room; it just skimmed his head. Many times he had almost knocked himself senseless on it.

Sam was near the wall, cowering between two shelving units. There were two shattered pint glasses, as well as a roughly drawn *X* in chalk on the stone floor.

"What are you playing at, Sam?"

"I didn't do that," Sam replied. "Those weren't there a few minutes ago."

"Are you feeling all right?"

"I'm telling you, those weren't there."

This was not good, not good at all. The glasses clearly hadn't fallen off a shelf—they were in the middle of the room. The *X* was shaky, like the hand that had drawn it could barely hold the chalk. No one looked healthy in the basement's faintly greenish fluorescent light, but Sam looked particularly bad. The color had drained from his face, and he was quivering and glistening with sweat.

Maybe this had been bound to happen. Charlie had always known the risks, but the risks were part of the agreement. He had gotten sober, and he trusted that others could as well. And you needed to show that trust.

Charlie said quietly, "If you've been taking something—"

"I haven't!"

"But if you have, you just need to tell me."

"I swear to you," Sam said, "I haven't."

"Sam, there's no shame in it. Sobriety is a process."

"I didn't take anything, and I didn't do *that*!"

There was an urgency in Sam's voice that frightened Charlie, and he was not a man who frightened easily. He'd been through fights, withdrawal, divorce. He faced alcohol, his personal demon, every day. Yet, something in this room, something in the sight of Sam huddled against the wall and this crude *X* and broken glass on the floor . . . something in this unnerved him.

There was no point in checking to see if anyone else was down here. Every business in the area had fortified itself when the Ripper was around. The Royal Gunpowder was secure.

Charlie bent down and ran his hand over the cool stone floor.

"How about we just get rid of this," he said, wiping away the chalked *X* with his hand. In cases like this, it was best to calmly get things back to normal and sit down and talk the issue through. "Come on, now. We'll go upstairs and have a cup of tea, and we'll talk this out."

Sam took a few tentative steps from the wall.

"Good, that's right. Now let's just get rid of this and we'll have a nice cuppa, you and me . . ."

Charlie continued wiping away the last of the *X*. He didn't see the hammer.

The hammer was used to pry open crates, to knock sticky valves into action, and to do quick repairs on the often unstable shelving units. Now it rose, lingering just long enough over Charlie's head to find its mark.

"No!" Sam screamed.

Charlie turned his head in time to see the hammer come down. The first time it did so, Charlie remained upright. He made a noise—not quite a word, more of a broken, gurgling sound. There was a second blow, and a third. Charlie was still upright, but twitching, struggling against the onslaught. The fourth blow seemed to do the most damage. An audible cracking sound could be heard. On that fourth blow, Charlie fell forward and did not move again.

The hammer clattered to the ground.

Out flew the web and floated wide;
The mirror crack'd from side to side;
"The curse is come upon me," cried
The Lady of Shalott.

—*Alfred Lord Tennyson,*
"The Lady of Shalott"

1

BACK AT WEXFORD, WHERE I WENT TO SCHOOL BEFORE ALL of this happened to me, they made me play hockey every day. I had no idea how to play hockey, so they covered me in padding and made me stand in the goal. From the goal, I could watch my fellow players run around with sticks. Occasionally they'd whack a small, very hard ball in my direction. I would dive out of the way, every time. Apparently, avoiding the ball isn't the point of hockey, and Claudia would scream, "*No,* Aurora, *no*!" from the sidelines, but I didn't care. I take my best lessons from nature, and nature says, "When something flies at your head—*move.*"

I didn't think hockey had trained me for anything in life until I went to therapy.

"So," Julia said.

Julia was my therapist. She was Scottish and petite and had a shock of white-blond hair. She was probably in her fifties, but the lines in her face were imperceptible. She was a careful person, well spoken, so achingly professional it actually made me itch. She didn't fuss around in her chair or need to change over and cross the other leg. She just *sat there,* calm as a monk. The winds might blow and the rains might fall, but Julia would remain in the same position in her ergonomic chair and wait it out.

The clock in Julia's office was hidden in plain sight; she put it behind the chair where her patients sat, on top of a bookcase. I followed the clock by watching its reflection in the window, watching time run backward. I had just managed to waste a solid forty-five minutes talking about my grandmother—a new record for me. But I'd run out of steam, and the silence descended on the room like a vague but ever-intensifying smell. There was a lot going on behind her never-blinking eyes. I could tell, from what now amounted to hours of staring at her, that Julia was studying me even more carefully than I was studying her.

And I knew about her relationship with that clock. All she had to do was flick her eyes just a tiny bit to the left, and she could see both me and the time without moving her head. It was an incredibly small move, but I had started to look for it. When Julia checked the time, it meant she was about to *do something.*

Flick.

Time to get ready. Julia was going to make a move. The ball was heading for my face. Time to dodge.

"Rory, I want you to think back for me . . ."

Dive! *Dive!*

". . . we all learn about death somehow. I want you to try to remember. How did you learn?"

I had to restrain myself. It doesn't look good if your therapist asks you how you learned about death and you practically jump off the couch in excitement because that's pretty much *your favorite story ever.* But as it happens, I have a really good "learning about death" story.

I wasted about a full minute, grinding away the airtime, tilting my head back and forth. It's hard to *pretend* to think. Thinking doesn't have an action stance. And I suspected that my "thinking" face looked a lot like my "I'm dizzy and may throw up" face.

"I was ten, I guess. We went to Mrs. Haverty's house. She lived in Magnolia Hall. Magnolia Hall is this big heritage site, proper antebellum South, *Gone with the Wind,* look-at-how-things-were-before-the-War-of-Northern-Aggression sort of place. It has columns and shutters and about a hundred magnolia trees. Have you ever seen *Gone with the Wind*?"

"A long time ago."

"Well, it looks like that. It's where tourists go. It's on a lot of brochures. Everything about it looks like it's from 1860 or something. And no one ever sees Mrs. Haverty, because she's crazy old. Like, maybe she was *born* in 1860."

"So an elderly woman in a historical house," she said.

"Right. I was in Girl Scouts. I was a really bad Girl Scout. I never got any badges, and I forgot my troop number. But once a year there was this amazing picnic thing at Magnolia Hall. Mrs. Haverty let the Girl Scouts use the grounds, because apparently she had been a Girl Scout back when the rocks were young and the atmosphere was forming . . ."

Julia eyed me curiously. I shouldn't have thrown in that little flourish. I'd told this story so many times that I'd refined it, given it nice little touches. My family loves it. I pull it out every year at our awkward get-together dinners at Big Jim's or at my grandmother's house. It's my go-to story.

"So," I said, slowing down, "she'd have barbecues set up, and huge coolers of soda, and ice cream. There was a massive Slip 'N Slide, and a bouncy castle. Basically, it was the best day of the year. I pretty much only did Girl Scouts so I could come to this. So this one summer, when I was ten, I guess . . . oh, I said that . . ."

"It's all right."

"Okay. Well, it was *hot.* Like, real hot. Louisiana hot. Like, over a hundred hot."

"Hot," Julia summarized.

"Right. Thing was, Mrs. Haverty never came out, and no one was allowed inside. She was kind of legendary. We always wondered if she was looking at us from the window or something. She was like our own personal Boo Radley. Afterward, we would always make her a huge banner where we'd write our names and thank her and draw pictures, and one of the troop leaders would drive it over. I don't know if Mrs. Haverty let her in or if she just had to throw it out of the car window at the porch. Anyway, usually the Girl Scouts got Porta Potties for the picnic. But this year there was some kind of strike at the Porta Potti place and they couldn't rent any, and for a week or so, they thought there was going to be no picnic, but then Mrs. Haverty said it was okay for us to use the downstairs bathroom, which was a really big deal. On the bus ride over, they gave us all a lecture on how to behave. One person at a time. No running. No yelling. Right to the bathroom and back out again. We were all excited and sort of freaked out that we could actually go inside. I made up my mind I was going to be the first person in. I was going to pee first if it killed me. So I drank an entire bottle of water on the ride—a big one. I made sure our troop leader, Mrs. Fletcher, saw me. I even made sure she said something to me about not wasting my water. But I was determined."

I don't know if this happens to you, but when I get talking about a place, all the details come back to me at once. I remember our bus going up the long drive, under the canopy of trees. I remember Jenny Savile sitting next to me, stinking of peanut butter for some reason and making an annoying clicking noise with her tongue. I remember my friend Erin just staring out the window and listening to something on her headphones, not paying any attention. Everyone else was looking at the crew that was inflating the bouncy castle. But I was on high alert, watching the house get closer, getting that first view of the columns and the grand porch. I was on a mission. I was going to be the first to pee in Magnolia Hall.

"My Scout leader was probably on to me," I continued, "because I had a reputation for being *that girl*—not the leader or the baddest or the prettiest, or whatever *that girl* is. I was *that girl* who always had some little idea, some bone to pick or personal quest, and I would not be stopped until I had settled the matter. And if I was gulping water and bouncing in my seat, claiming extreme need of the bathroom, she knew I was not going to shut up until I was taken inside of Magnolia Hall."

Julia couldn't conceal the whisper of a smile that stole across her lips. Clearly, she had picked up on this aspect of my personality.

"When we pulled up," I went on, "she said, 'Come on, Rory.' There was a real bite in how she said my name. I remember it scared me."

"Scared you?"

"Because the Scout leaders never really got mad at us," I explained. "It wasn't part of their jobs. Your parents got mad at you, and maybe your teachers. But it was weird to have another adult be mad at me."

"Did it stop you?"

"No," I said. "I'd had a lot of water."

"Let me ask you this," Julia said. "Why do you think you behaved that way? Why did it matter so much to you to be the first one to use the toilet?"

This was something so obvious to me that I had no mechanism to explain it. I had to be first to that bathroom for the same reason that people climb mountains or go to the bottom of the sea. Because it was new and uncharted territory. Because being first meant . . . being first.

"No one had ever seen the inside of her house," I said.

"But it was just a toilet. And you said this was a behavior you were aware of in yourself. That you come up with plans, ideas."

"They're usually bad plans," I clarified.

Julia nodded slightly and wrote a note in her pad. I'd given her a clue about my personality. I hated when that happened. I refocused on the story. I remembered the heat. Heat—real heat—was something I hadn't felt in England since I'd arrived. Louisiana summer heat has a personality, a weight to it. It wraps you entirely in its sweaty embrace. It goes inside of you. Magnolia Hall had never known an air conditioner. It was like an oven that had been on for a hundred years, and it felt entirely possible that some of the air trapped in there had been there since the Civil War, blown in during a battle and locked away for safekeeping.

I can always remember my first step through that doorway, that slap of dust-stinking heat. The stillness. The entrance hall with the genuine family portraits, the marble-topped table with a bowl of parched and drooping azaleas, the hoarded stacks of old newspapers in the corner. The bathroom was in an alcove under the stairs. Mrs. Fletcher had to supervise the unloading of the bus and make sure Melissa Murphy had her EpiPen in case she was stung by a bee, so she told me to come right out when I was done and not to touch anything. Just go to the bathroom and leave.

"I was in there by myself," I said. "The first person ever . . . I mean, first person that I knew, so I couldn't not look around. I only looked in rooms with open doorways. I didn't snoop. I just had to look. And there was this dog in the middle of one of the sitting rooms in the front, a big golden retriever . . . and I like dogs. A lot. So I petted him. I didn't even hear Mrs. Haverty come in. I just turned around and there she was. I guess I expected her to be in a hoop skirt or covered in spiderwebs or something, but she was wearing one of those sportswear things that actual senior citizens wear, pink plaid culottes and a matching T-shirt. She was incredibly pale, and she had all these varicose veins—her calves had so many blue lines on them, she looked like a road map. I thought I'd been caught. I thought, 'This is it. This is when I get killed.' I was so busted. But she just smiled and said, 'That's Big Bobby. Wasn't he beautiful?' And I said, 'Was?' And she said, 'Oh, he's stuffed, dear.

Bobby died four years ago. But he liked to sleep in here, so that's where I keep him.'"

It took Julia a moment to realize that that was the end of the story.

"You'd been petting a stuffed dog?" she said. "A dead one?"

"It was a really *well* stuffed dog," I clarified. "I have seen some bad taxidermy. This was top-notch work. It would have fooled anyone."

A rare moment of sunlight came in through the window and illuminated Julia's face. She was giving me a long and penetrating stare, one that didn't quite go through me. It got about halfway inside and roamed around, pawing inquisitively.

"You know, Rory," she said, "this is our sixth meeting, and we really haven't talked about the reason why you're here."

Whenever she said something like that, I felt a twinge in my abdomen. The wound had closed and was basically healed. The bandages were off, revealing the long cut and the new, angry red skin that bound the edges together. I searched my mind for something to say, something that would get us off-roading again, but Julia put up her hand preemptively. She knew. So I kept quiet for a moment and discovered my real thinking face. I could see it, but I could tell it looked pained. I kept pursing and biting my lips, and the furrow between my eyes was probably deep enough to hold my phone.

"Can I ask you something?" I finally said.

"Of course."

"Am I *allowed* to be fine?"

"Of course you are. That's our goal. But it's also all right not to be fine. The simple fact of the matter is, you've had a trauma."

"But don't people get over traumas?"

"They do. With help."

"Can't people get over traumas without help?" I asked.

"Of course, but—"

"I'm just saying," I said, more insistently, "is it *possible* that I'm actually okay?"

"Do you feel okay, Rory?"

"I just want to go back to school."

"You want to go back?" she asked, her brogue flicking up to a particularly inquisitive point. *You want tae go back?*

Wexford leapt into my mind, like a painted backdrop on a suddenly slackened rope crashing down onto a stage. I saw Hawthorne, my building, looking like the Victorian relic that it was. The brown stone. The surprisingly large, high windows. The word WOMEN carved over the door. I imagined being in my room with Jazza, my roommate, at nighttime, when she and I would talk across the darkness from our respective beds. The ceilings in our building were high, and I'd watch passing shadows from the London streets and hear the noise outside, the gentle clang and whistle of the heaters as they gave the last blast of heat for the night.

My mind flashed to a time in the library, when Jerome and I were together in one of the study rooms, making out against the wall. And then I flashed somewhere else. I pictured myself in the flat on Goodwin's Court with Stephen and Callum and Boo—

"We're at time for today," she said, her eye flicking toward the clock. "We can talk about this some more on Friday."

I snatched my coat from the back of the chair and got it on as quickly as possible. Julia opened the door and looked out into the hall. She turned back to me in surprise.

"You came by yourself today? That's very good. I'm glad."

Today, my parents had let me come to therapy by myself. This was what passed for excitement in my life now.

"We're getting there, Rory," she said. "We're getting there."

She was lying. I guess we all have to lie sometimes. I was about to do the same.

"Yeah," I said, stretching my fingers into the tips of my gloves. "Definitely."

2

I WASN'T GOING TO BE ABLE TO COPE WITH MANY MORE OF these sessions.

I like to talk. Talking is kind of *my thing*. If talking had been a sport option at Wexford, I would have been captain. But sports always have to involve running, jumping, or swinging your arms around. You don't get PE points for the smooth and rapid movement of the jaw.

Three times a week, I was sent to talk to Julia. And three times a week, I had to *avoid* talking to Julia—at least, I couldn't talk about what had really happened to me.

You cannot tell your therapist you have been stabbed by a ghost.

You cannot tell her that you could see the ghost because you developed the ability to see dead people after choking on some beef at dinner.

If you say any of that, they will put you in a sack and take you to a room walled in bouncy rubber and you will never be allowed to touch scissors again. The situation will only get worse if you explain to your therapist that you have friends in the secret ghost police of London, and that you are really not supposed to be talking about this because some man from the government made you sign a copy of the Official Secrets Act and promise never to talk about these ghost police friends of yours. No. That won't improve your situation at all. The therapist will add "paranoid delusions about secret government agencies" to the already quite long list of your problems, and then it will be game over for you, Crazy.

The sky was the same color as a cinder block, and I didn't have an umbrella to protect me from the dark rain cloud that was clearly moving in our direction. I had no idea what to do with myself, now that I was actually out of the house. I saw a coffee place. That's where I would go. I'd get a coffee, and then I'd walk home. That was a good, normal thing to do. I would do this, and then maybe . . . maybe I would do another thing.

Funny thing when you don't get out of the house for a while—you reenter the outside world as a tourist. I stared at the people working on laptops, studying, writing things down in notebooks. I flirted with the idea of telling the guy who was making my latte, just blurting it out: "I'm the girl the Ripper attacked." And I could whip up my shirt and show him the still-healing wound. You couldn't fake the thing I had stretching across my torso—the long, angry line. Well, I guess you *could,* but you'd have to be one of those special-effects makeup people to do it. Also, people who get up to the coffee counter and whip off their shirts for the baristas usually have other problems.

I took my coffee and left quickly before I got any other funny little ideas.

God, I needed to talk to someone.

I don't know about you, but when something happens to me—good, bad, boring, it doesn't matter—I have to *tell* someone about it to make it count. There's no point in anything happening if you can't talk about it. And this was the biggest something of all. I *ached* to talk. I mean, it literally hurt me, sitting there, holding it all in hour after hour. I must have been clenching my stomach muscles the whole time, because my whole abdomen throbbed. Sometimes, if I was still awake late at night, I'd be tempted to call some anonymous crisis hotline and tell some random person my story, but I knew what would happen. They'd listen, and they'd advise me to get psychiatric help. Because my story was nuts.

The "official" story:

A man decides to terrorize London by re-creating the murders of Jack the Ripper. He kills four people, one of them, unluckily, on the green right in front of my building at school. I see this guy when sneaking back into my building that night. Because I'm a witness, he decides to target me for the last murder. He sneaks into my building on the night of the final Ripper murder and stabs me. I survive because the police get a report of a sighting of something suspicious and break into the building. The suspect flees, the police chase him, and he jumps into the Thames and dies.

The real version:

The Ripper was the ghost of a man formerly of the ghost policing squad. He targeted me because I could see ghosts.

His whole aim was to get his hands on a terminus, the tool the ghost police use to destroy ghosts. The termini (there were actually three of them) were diamonds. When you ran an electrical current through them, they destroyed ghosts. Stephen had wired them into the hollow bodies of cell phones, using the batteries to power the charge. I survived that night because Jo, another ghost, grabbed a terminus out of my hand and destroyed the Ripper—and, in the process, herself.

The only people who really knew the whole story were Stephen, Callum, and Boo, and I was never allowed to talk to them again. That was one of the conditions when I left London. A man from the government really had made me sign the Official Secrets Act. Measures had been taken to make sure I couldn't reach out to them. While I was in the hospital after the attack, knocked out cold, someone took my phone and wiped it clean.

Keep quiet, they said.

Just get on with your life, they said.

So now I was here, in Bristol, sitting around in the rented house that my parents lived in. It was a nice enough little house, high up on a rise, with a good view of the city. It had rental house furnishings, straight out of a catalog. White walls and neutral colors. A non-place, good for recuperating. No ghosts. No explosions. Just television and rain and lots of sleep and screwing around on the Internet. My life went nowhere here, and that was fine. I'd had enough excitement. I just had to try to forget, to embrace the boredom, to let it go.

I walked along the waterside. The mist dropped layer upon delicate layer of moisture into my clothes and hair, slowly chilling me and weighing me down. Nothing to do but walk today.

I would walk and walk. Maybe I would walk right down the river into another town. Maybe I would walk all the way to the ocean. Maybe I would swim home.

I was so preoccupied in my wallowing that I almost walked right past him, but something about the suit must have caught my attention. The cut of the suit . . . something was strange about it. I'm not an expert on suits, but this one was somehow different, a very drab gray with a narrow lapel. And the collar. The collar was odd. He wore horn-rim glasses, and his hair was very short, but with square sideburns. Everything was just a centimeter or two off, all the little data points that tell you someone isn't quite right.

He was a ghost.

My ability to see ghosts, my "sight," was the result of two elements: I had the innate ability, and I'd had a brush with death at the right time. It was not magic. It was not supernatural. It was, as Stephen liked to put it, the "ability to recognize and interact with the vestigial energy of an otherwise deceased person, one who continues to exist in a spectrum usually not perceived by humans." Stephen actually talked like that.

What it meant was simply this: some people, when they die, don't entirely *eject* from this world. Something goes wrong in the death process, like when you try to shut down a computer and it goes into a confused spiral. These unlucky people remain on some plane of existence that intersects with the one we inhabit. Most of them are weak, barely able to interact with our physical world. Some are a bit stronger. And lucky people like me can see them, and talk to them, and touch them.

This is why in my many, many hours of watching shows about ghost hunters (I'd watched a *lot* of television in Bristol)

I'd gotten so angry. Not only were the shows stupid and obviously phony, but they didn't even make sense. These people would rock up to houses with their weird night-vision camera hats and cold-spot-o-meters, set up cameras, and then turn off all the lights and wait until dark. (Because apparently ghosts care if the lights are on or off and if it's day or night.) And then, these champions would fumble around in the dark, saying, "IF SPIRITS ARE HERE, MAKE YOURSELVES KNOWN, SPIRITS." This is roughly equivalent to a tourist bus stopping in the middle of a foreign city and all of the tourists getting out in their funny hats with their video cameras and saying, "We are here! Dance for us, natives of this place! We wish to film you!" And, of course, nothing happens. Then there's always a bump in the background, some normal creaking of a step or something, and they amplify that about ten million times, claim they've found evidence of paranormal activity, and kick off for a cold, self-congratulatory brew.

I edged around for a few minutes, taking him in from a few different angles, making sure I knew what I was looking at. I wondered what the chances were that the first time I came out and walked around Bristol on my own, I'd see a ghost. Judging from what was going on right now, those chances were very good. A hundred percent, in fact. It made a kind of sense that I'd find one here. I was walking along a river and, as Stephen had explained to me once, waterways have a long history of death. Ships sink and people jump into rivers. Rivers and ghosts go together.

I crossed in front of him, pretending to talk on my phone. He had a blank stare on his face, the stare of someone who truly had nothing to do but just *exist*. I stared right at him. Most people, when stared at, stare back. Because staring is weird. But ghosts are used to people looking right through them. As I suspected, he didn't react in any way to my staring. There was a grayness, a loneliness about him that was palpable. Unseen, unheard, unloved. He was still existing, but for no reason.

Definitely a ghost.

It occurred to me, he could have a friend. He could have someone to share this existence with. Something welled up in me, a great feeling of warmth, of generosity, a swelling of the spirit. I could share something with him, and in return, he could help me as well. Whoever this guy was, *I could tell him the truth.* He was part of the truth. No, he didn't know me, but that hardly mattered. He was *about* to get to know me. We would be friends. Oh, yes. We would be friends. We were *meant* to be together. For the first time in weeks, there was a path—a logical, clear, walkable path. And it started with me sitting on the bench.

"Hi," I said.

He didn't turn.

"Hi," I said again. "Yes, I'm talking to you. On the bench. Here. With me. Can you hear me?"

He turned to look at me, his eyes wide in surprise.

"Bet you're surprised," I said, smiling. "I know. It's weird. But I can see you. My name's Rory. What's yours?"

No answer. Just a wide, eternal stare.

"I'm new here," I said. "To Bristol. I was in London. I'm from America, but I guess you can tell that from my accent? I came here to go to school, and—"

The man bolted from his seat. Ghosts have a fluidity of movement that the living don't know—they remain solid, yet they can move like air. I didn't want him to go, so I bounced up and reached as far as I could to catch his coat. The second I made contact, I felt my fingers getting pulled into his body, like I had put them into the suction end of a vacuum. I felt the ripple of energy going up my arm, the inexorable force linking us both together now, then the rush of air, far greater than any waterside breeze. Then came the flash of light and the unsettling floral smell.

And he was gone.

3

THIS DESTROYING-THE-DEAD-WITH-A-SINGLE-TOUCH THING was even more recent than the seeing-the-dead thing. It had happened once before, the day I left Wexford. I'd found a strange woman in the downstairs bathroom where I'd been stabbed. She too had looked frightened, and I'd reached out, and she too had exploded into nothingness. I'd tried to tell myself that this had been a fluke, something to do with the room itself. The bathroom was where the Ripper had cornered me. The bathroom was where the terminus had exploded. I'd convinced myself that the *room* did it.

But no. It was me.

I walked home, an entirely uphill walk in every way, feeling queasy and shaky. Once there, I went to the "conservatory," which was really just a glassed-in porch. I sat with my head resting on my knees and replayed the scene again and again in my head. The inevitable rain came and tapped on the roof, rolling down the panes of glass.

I'd tried to make a new friend, and I had *blown him up.*

I'd been told to keep quiet, and I had. But it wasn't going to work anymore. I needed Stephen, Callum, and Boo again. I needed them to know what was going on with me. I had made a few efforts to find them in the last week. Nothing serious—I'd just tried to find profiles on social networking sites. No matches. This much I expected.

Today I was going to try a bit harder. I Googled each of their names. I found one set of links that were definitely about Callum. Callum had mentioned that he was good at football. What he didn't say was that he had been a member of the Arsenal Under-16s, a premier-level junior club. He'd been in training to become a professional footballer. And all of that ended one day when he was fifteen, when a malicious ghost let a live wire drop into the puddle Callum was stepping through. He survived the electrocution and recovered, but something in him was never the same. Whether it was physical or psychological, who knew, but he couldn't play football anymore. The magic was gone. Callum hated ghosts. He wanted them to *burn.*

In terms of contact information, though, there was nothing.

I moved on to Boo, Bhuvana Chodhari. Boo had been sent into Wexford as my roommate after I saw the Ripper. It was her first job with the squad. There were a lot of Chodharis in London, and even quite a few Bhuvana Chodharis. I knew Boo had been in a serious car accident, but I found nothing about it. Nothing about Boo at all, really. That surprised me. Of the three of them, I expected her to pop up *somewhere.* But I guess once you joined the squad, your Facebook days were over.

I searched for Stephen last. In terms of his past, I knew very little. I think he said once he was from Kent, but Kent was a big place. He went to Eton. He had been on the rowing team while he was there. I started with that, and managed to come up with one photo of a rowing team in which I could clearly see him in the back. He was one of the tallest, with dark hair and eyes fixed at the camera. He was one of the not-smiling ones. In fact, he was the least-smiling person in the photo. Like everyone else, he had his arms folded over his chest, but he seemed to mean it.

But again, there was nothing in terms of how to make contact.

I stared at the photo of Stephen for a long time, then at the ceiling of the conservatory, which was thick with condensation and fat drops of water. I knew that Stephen and Callum shared a flat on a small street in London called Goodwin's Court. I'd been there. I had never, however, looked at the building number. The few times I'd been there, I was following someone to the door, usually in a state of distress.

I pulled up a map and some images of the street. The trouble with Goodwin's Court was that it was very picturesque, and very small, and all of it looked more or less the same. The houses were all quite dark, with dark brick and black trim, so it was hard to see numbers. I found one pretty grainy picture that I thought was probably their house, but I couldn't see the number.

My phone rang. It was Jerome. He often called me on his break between classes. Jerome had been what I suppose I could call my "make-out buddy" at Wexford. But since I'd been gone, we had become something much more. I still couldn't talk to him the way I needed to talk to someone, but it was nice that I had someone in theory. An imaginary boyfriend I never saw. We were planning to see each other over the Christmas break in a few weeks, probably only for a day, but still. It was something.

"Hey, disgusting," he said.

Jerome and I had developed a code for expressing whatever it was we felt for each other. Instead of saying "I like you" or whatever mush expresses that sentiment, we had started saying mildly insulting things. Our entire correspondence was a string of heartfelt insults.

"What's wrong?"

"Nothing," I said quickly. "Nothing."

"You sound funny."

"You look funny," I replied.

I could hear Wexford noises in the background. Not that Wexford noises were so particular. It was just noise. People. Voices. Guys' voices.

He was talking quickly, telling me a story about some guy in his building who'd been busted for claiming to have an interview at a university, but actually he went off to see his girlfriend in Spain, and how someone had ratted him out to Jerome, and Jerome had the unwelcome task of reporting him. Or something.

I was only half listening. I rubbed at my legs and stared at the images of Goodwin's Court. I hadn't shaved in three weeks, so that was quite a situation I had going. For the first few days, I hadn't been able to bend over completely or get the injured area wet, so I couldn't shave. The hairs sprouted, and they were kind of cute. So I just let them go to see what would happen, and what had happened was that I had a fine web of delicate hair all over my legs that I could ruffle while I watched television, like some people absently pet their cats. I was my very own fuzzy pet.

The grainy picture told me nothing.

"Hello?" Jerome said.

"I'm listening," I lied. I guess the story had finished.

"I have to go," he said. "You're disgusting. I want you to know that."

"I heard they named a mold after you," I replied. "Poor mold."

"Vile."

"Gross."

After I hung up, I pulled the computer closer to stare at the image. I moved the view up and down the row of tiny, dark houses with their expensive gaslights and security system warning signs. Up and down. And then I saw something. There was a tiny plaque on the outside of one of the houses, right above the buzzer. That plaque. I knew it. That was their building. There was some kind of a small company downstairs, a graphic designer or photographer or something like that. The print was impossible to make out in the photo, but it began with a *Z*. I knew that much. Zoomba, Zoo . . . Zo . . . something.

It was a start, enough to search the Internet. I tried every combination I could with *Z* and *design* and *art* and *photography* and *graphic design*. It took a while, but I eventually hit it. Zuoko. Zuoko Graphics. With a phone number. I pulled up the address in maps, and sure enough, it was the same building.

Now all I had to do was call and ask them . . . something. Get them to go upstairs. Leave a note. I would say it was an emergency and that they needed to call Rory, and I would leave my number. So simple, so clever.

So I called, and Zuoko Graphics answered. Well, some woman did. Not the entire agency.

"Hi," I said. "I'm trying to reach someone else in this building. It's kind of an emergency. Sorry to bug you. But there are some guys? Who live upstairs? From you?"

"Two guys, right?" the woman said. "About nineteen or twenty?"

"That's them," I said.

"They moved out, about a week and a half ago."

"Oh . . ."

"You said it's an emergency? Do you have another way of reaching them, or—"

"It's okay," I said. "Thanks."

So that was that. I struck that off the list. They'd moved out. Because of me? Because I knew where they lived? Maybe they were really cleaning up their tracks so they could never be found again.

I heard someone come into the house. I quickly clicked on a link to BBC news and pretended to be deeply engrossed in world affairs. My mom came into the kitchen.

"We have chairs," she said.

"I like it down here. It's where I belong."

"Doing some work?" she asked.

My parents weren't stupid. They knew I hadn't really been keeping up with school stuff, but they hadn't been pressuring me. I was recovering. Everyone was very gentle with me. Soft voices. Food on demand. Command of the remote control. But there was just a little lilt of hope in her voice, and I hated to disappoint her.

"Yup," I lied.

"I just got a call from Julia. She's asking all of us to come in tomorrow for a group session. Is that all right with you?"

I ran my thumbs along the bottom edge of my computer. This wasn't right. We didn't *do* group sessions. Was this an intervention? It sounded like an intervention, at least like the ones I had seen on TV. They get your family and a psychologist, and they sit you in a room and tell you that the game is up, you have to change. Change or die. Except . . . I didn't drink or do drugs, so I wasn't sure what they could intervene about. You can't stop someone from doing *nothing* all time.

I thought about the man again . . . my hand reaching out in greeting. Maybe the first greeting he'd had in years. The hand that wiped him from existence. Or something.

"Sure," I said, slightly dazed. "Whatever."

The next day at noon, the three of us waited by Julia's door, staring down at the little smoke-detector-shaped noise-reduction devices that lined the hallway. That's how you could tell a therapist was behind the door. One of these little privacy devices would spring up naturally, like a mushroom after a rainstorm.

"So," Julia said, once we were all squeezed onto her sofa, "I want to talk to all of you about the progress we've made, and just a little bit about the process. Recovering from a trauma like this. There's no one method that fits everyone. I want you to know, and I want you to hear this, Rory . . . I think Rory is very, very strong. I think she's resilient and capable."

It was supposed to make me feel good, but I burned . . . burned with anger or embarrassment or resentment. I felt my cheeks flush. *This* was the worst of it. Right now, this. I'd survived the stabbing. I'd survived all of the other, much crazier stuff. But now I was a victim. I might as well have had the word tattooed on my face. And victims get strange looks and psychologists. Victims have to sit between their parents while they're told how "resilient" they are.

"In my opinion, I feel . . . very strongly . . . that Rory should be returned to Wexford."

I seriously almost fell off the sofa.

"I'm sorry?" my mother said. "You think she should go *back*?"

"I realize what I'm saying may run counter to all your instincts," Julia said, "but let me explain. When someone survives a violent assault, a measure of control is taken away. In therapy, we aim to give victims back their sense of control over their own lives. Rory's been removed from her school, taken away from her friends, taken out of her routine, out of her academic life. I believe she needs to return. Her life belongs to her, and we can't let her attacker take that away."

My dad had a look in his eye that I'd once seen in a painting at the National Gallery. It was of a man who was facing down an angel that had just come crashing through his ceiling and was now glowing expectantly in the corner of the room. A *surprised* look.

"I say this with full understanding that the idea may be difficult for all of you," she continued, mostly to my parents. "If you decide against this, that's absolutely fine. But I feel the need to tell you this . . . Rory and I have done quite a lot of work in our sessions. I'm not saying we've done all we can do. I'm saying the next logical step is to get her back into a normal routine."

She was lying. Julia, right now, was lying. And she was looking right at me, as if challenging me to contradict her. We both knew perfectly well that I'd told her nothing at all. Why the hell would Julia lie? Had I said things without even *realizing* it?

"She can have a normal routine here," my mom said.

"It's not her normal routine. It's a new routine based around the attack. Right now, keeping her away from the learning environment is punitive. I'm not talking about sending Rory out to live in a wild and dangerous environment—this is a structured one, with everything in place to allow her to resume her life."

"An environment where she was stabbed," my dad said.

"Very true. But that particular case was a true anomaly. You need to separate your fears from the actual risk involved. What happened will not be repeated. The attacker is deceased."

Their conversation became a low buzzing noise, like the background sound that's supposed to run across the universe. Of course I couldn't go back. My parents would never agree to it. It had taken me a week to convince them I could walk down the hill by myself. They were never going to send me back to school, in London, to the very place I'd been stabbed. Julia might as well have asked me, "Rory, do you want to go live in the sky? On a Pegasus?" It was not going to happen.

As ridiculous as this all was, if there is one thing that could sway my parents, it was a professional opinion. An expert witness. They both dealt with them all the time, and they knew how to take that knowledge and advice. Julia was a professional, and she said this was what I needed. They were still listening.

"I've been in touch with them," she went on. "There are new security measures in place. They have a new system that apparently cost a half a million pounds."

"They should have had that before," my dad said.

"It's best to think forward," Julia said gently, "not backward. The system includes biometric entry pads and forty new CCTV cameras feeding into a constantly monitored station. Curfew hours have been changed. And the police now include

Wexford on a patrol, simply because of all of the publicity. The reality is that it is probably the most secure environment she could be in right now. The school term is only going to last about two more weeks. This short period would allow her to reintegrate herself. It's an excellent trial run to get Rory back into a more normal routine."

Oh, the silence in that room. The silence of a thousand silences. I could hear that stupid clock ticking away.

"Do you really feel ready?" my mom asked me. "Don't let anyone talk you into feeling like you're ready."

It wasn't phrased as a question—I think it was more of an invitation. They wanted me to say I wasn't ready, and we would just go on like this, safe and secure and static.

This was happening. They were saying yes. Yes, I could go back. No, they didn't want me to, and yes, it went against every instinct they had . . . and possibly against every instinct I had.

4

I'M NOT SURE WHAT I EXPECTED TO SEE AS WE BUMPED along the cobblestone road that fronted Hawthorne. Maybe I thought Wexford would be covered in creeping vines, or part of it would have crumbled from age. This was maybe a bit extreme for three weeks, but three weeks is a *lot of time* in school time, especially when you live at said school. Miss three weeks, and you come back to a different world.

There were Christmas decorations on the streets, for a start. Christmas ads in the bus shelters. Christmas displays in windows. It was three in the afternoon, but the lights by the front door were switched on and the sky had taken on a dusky tint. Claudia, our hockey-loving, large-handed housemistress, met me at the front door, just as she had when I'd first arrived. This time, though, she came down the steps and gave me a car-crusher of a hug.

"Au*ror*a. It *is* good to see you. And your parents . . . Call me Claudia. I'm housemistress of Hawthorne."

Claudia managed the entire return and good-bye process, assuring my parents in every possible way aside from interpretive dance that all would be well and I would be looked after and coming back to school was very much the right thing for me. Before they left, my parents went through the personal rules we'd established. I'd call them every day. I would never take the Tube after nine at night. I would carry a rape whistle, which I'd already been given and which was already attached to my bag.

Claudia shepherded them back to the car. I finally understood why she was in charge of our building. She had *skills* with parents. She was like the parent whisperer.

"I want you to know," she said, when we were alone and back in the safety of her office, "I think what you are doing is exceptionally courageous, and all of us here at Wexford are behind you. Those events . . . are in the past. You're here to pick up where you left off, and you will have an excellent rest of term. I encourage you to take advantage of our health services. Mr. Maxwell at the sanatorium is an excellent counselor. He's helped many students . . ."

"I have someone," I said. "Back in Bristol."

"But you might want someone here. If you do, Mr. Maxwell would be happy to see you at any time. But enough of that. How are you coming along with your lessons?"

"I'm a little . . . behind."

"Quite understandable," she said, as gently as Claudia could say anything. "We have people to help bring you up to speed in all your subjects. Charlotte has already volunteered, and your teachers certainly know the circumstances. For the time being, we'll keep you out of hockey so you can use that time to catch up."

I tried to look sad.

"Don't worry," she said. "Next term, we'll have you back out there."

I would work on that one later. There was no way I was going back "out there."

"Now," she said, "we're almost to the end of term. Next week is the final week of classes. Then there's revision over the weekend and through Monday of the following week, with exams on Tuesday and Wednesday. Obviously, you've missed too much to take a full exam, but we've worked something out for you. All of your teachers will assess your current level, both through classwork and through some informal testing, and you'll be provided with modified versions of the exams. If necessary, we'll give you take-home exams that you can complete over the holidays. Your teachers are prepared to work with you if you are willing to put in the effort. All right?"

Claudia fished around in the top drawer of her desk and produced a small black box. She jacked this into her computer and pushed it across the desk in my direction.

"Are you right-handed?" she asked me.

I nodded.

"Just put your right index finger on the pad there and hold it still for a moment."

There was a square on the top of the box marked off in white. I put my finger on it, and she clicked the mouse a few times.

"Rotten thing," she mumbled. "Always takes a . . . ah. There we go. Now, let me show you how this works."

She led me back to the front door and pointed to a small touchpad.

"Try it now to see if your fingerprint was accepted."

I put my finger on the pad. A purple light came on, and there was a click.

"Oh, good. Sometimes it doesn't like the first time we take the impression. This is how you get in and out. It gives you ten seconds, or you have to do it again. The system monitors the whereabouts of all students. We know when you go in and out of this building. And *no one* goes in or out between eleven at night and five thirty in the morning. Now, why don't you go up and get yourself settled back in?"

The stairs of Hawthorne had a pronounced, musical creak as I walked back up to my room. My hall was much more narrow than I remembered, and I clunked along to my room with my last bag. Mr. Franks, our ancient custodian, had taken all my other things up at some point when I was in with Claudia. The room was weirdly bare. All of Jazza's things were over on one side. The two other beds—Boo's and mine—were stripped down to the mattress. I would have spread out in every direction, but Jazza had kept to her third with a devotion that made me tear up a little. It was like she refused to accept we weren't there. The only thing Jazza had added was a new floor lamp—a wobbly thing with a plastic upturned shade. It gave the room a warm glow when I switched it on.

I went to the window and looked out at the square. That's where the police had found the girl's body. That was the square I ran across when I met the Ripper. Everything had a Ripper memory attached to it. Julia had given me a whole talk about forging new mental connections to things. She'd said that after a while, the Ripper stuff would take on less significance, and when I looked around Wexford, I'd have new, more positive thoughts come to mind.

She also said it could take a while.

The building was freezing. During the day, they shut the heat down to conserve electricity. It came back up again at night and in the morning, but it was never *really* that warm. In Bristol, my parents had kept the house so hot, the windows would steam. This was considered very American, but in our defense, we are Southern. We get cold.

I was not going to be a baby about a little cold. I put on my fleece and set to work unpacking boxes and bags. I refilled my drawers, trying to remember the exact way I had arranged things before my untimely departure. I piled all my textbooks in order of subject. Further maths, French, English literature (from 1711 to 1847), art history, and normal history. I stepped back and examined my effort. Yup. Those were my books. Familiar, yet foreign, a wealth of information stashed behind every spine.

What I needed to do now was figure out how behind I was. That meant going through all the notes my teachers had been sending me while I was gone, marking off chapters, counting up assignments.

I pulled out the lists I'd been given: the pages I was supposed to have read, the essays I was supposed to have started, the problem sets I'd been given. I did the math. It didn't take long. Zero plus zero plus zero plus zero equals zero. When should I tell my teachers that I *hadn't actually done anything* since I left?

I flipped to the front of my binder and looked at the term schedule. Just about two weeks. That's all that was left of the term. So what if the exams started in . . . twelve days?

I shut the binder. One step at a time. Today's step was just getting back to school. No need to take it all in at once.

I turned my mind to other matters. I still had no idea where Stephen, Callum, and Boo were, but now that I was back in London, it seemed like I'd have a much better chance of finding them. Possibly. I wasn't exactly sure how. They didn't really have a beat or a known routine. The only one who was ever in the same general place was Callum. He covered the Underground network. I guessed I could ride the Tube for hours and hours, trying to catch a glimpse of him at some station. That wasn't much of a plan. London is a very big place—one of the biggest cities in the world—and the Underground went on for hundreds of miles and had dozens of stations and millions of riders.

I would think of something. In the meantime, I needed something to do, someone to talk to. And there *was* someone here I could have a chat with. But to do that, I needed to put the uniform back on. Back on with the gray skirt and the white blouse. I could feel myself becoming a Wexford person again through the feel of the fabric—the slight polyester squeak of the skirt, the stiff collar of the shirt. But it was always the tie that did it for me. I looped it around my neck and fumbled with it for a moment until I had it right. I was Wexford property again.

Alistair spent most of his time in the library because he thought Aldshot smelled bad. His favorite spot was up in the stacks, in the romantic poetry section, in a dark little corner by a frosted glass window. This was where I found him, spread out in his usual way.

Alistair died in the 1980s, when overcoats were big and hair was even bigger. He was used to people walking past him, or over him, or through him, so he didn't really pay any attention when I stood by his Doc Martens.

I was careful to leave a lot of distance between us. Blowing up one potential friend by accident, well, that can happen. Blowing up another would be carelessness.

"Hey," I said, "Alistair."

A slow drawing up of the head.

"You're back," he said.

"I'm back," I replied.

"Boo said they took you to Bristol. That you wouldn't be coming back, ever."

"I'm back," I said again.

Alistair wasn't the hugging type, but I took the fact that he hadn't already started reading again as a sign that he welcomed my presence. I slid down the wall and took a seat on the floor, tucking up my legs so we didn't tap into each other.

"One thing," I said. "Never touch me. Don't even get near me."

"Nice to see you too."

"No, I mean . . . something's gone wrong with me. And now I am bad for you. Really. No joke."

"*Bad* for me?"

It's really hard to tell someone you can destroy them with a touch. It's not the kind of thing that should ever come up in conversation.

"I'm unlucky," I said, in an attempt to cover. "I attract nut-jobs and trouble."

"So why'd you come back?"

"Why wouldn't I?"

"You got stabbed," he said.

"I got better. I was bored sitting around at home."

"And you came back here? Why didn't you go back to America?"

"Someone's renting our house," I said. "And my shrink said I needed to come back to get my normal life back."

"Normal life?" That got a dark little laugh.

It was good to see Alistair was the same cheerful entity that I'd left behind.

"So the Ripper," he said. "The news says he died, that he jumped off a bridge. That's a lie. They covered it all up. Typical. The press lies. The government lies. They all want to keep people in the dark."

He scraped the rubbery sole of his shoe against the library floor. It made no noise.

"I don't think that many people in the government actually know what happened."

"Oh, they know," he said. "Thatcher and her kind always know."

"It's not Thatcher anymore," I said.

"Might as well be. They're all the same. Liars."

I heard footsteps approaching. The library wasn't very populated during the day, and not many people made a point of coming to this corner of the second floor. This is why Alistair liked it. It was the literature corner, full of works of criticism. It was also a bit dim and cold.

Whoever was coming seemed to really want some criticism, because the footsteps were sharp and fast. The person hit a switch, waking up the aisle lights, which reluctantly flicked on one by one.

"I thought you might be here," he said.

I recognized Jerome, obviously, but there was something very strange, something almost a little foreign. His hair had gotten just a touch shaggy and was falling into a center part. His tie was a bit loose. He seemed about an inch taller than I remembered, and slouchy shouldered. And his eyes were smaller. Not in a bad way. My memory had screwed everything up and adjusted all the measurements.

"Oh, God," Alistair said. "Already?"

I'd gotten used to not being around Jerome, and strangely, this had made us closer. We'd definitely gotten more serious in the last two weeks, but we'd done it all over the phone or on a screen. I'd grown accustomed to Jerome as a text message, and it was somewhat unsettling to have the actual person sliding down the wall to sit next to me. Unsettling, but also a bit thrilling.

"Welcome back, stupid," he said.

"Thanks, dumbass."

Jerome shifted a bit, moving closer to me. He smelled strongly of Wexford laundry detergent. He looked down at my hand, which was resting on my thigh, then reached out and touched it, gently tapping the back of my hand with his fingers. We both looked at this gesture, like it was something our hands were doing of their own accord. Like they were children putting on a show for us, and we, the indulgent parents, were watching them.

"On the way here, I saw someone pissing on a wall," I said. "It reminded me of you."

"That was me," he replied. "I was writing a poem about your beauty."

"I hate you both," Alistair said, from his side of the dark corner.

I ignored him as Jerome brushed my hair away from my face. When anyone touches my hair, I basically turn to slush. If a friend does it, or if I'm getting my hair cut, I fall asleep. When Jerome did it, it sent an entirely different sensation through my body—warm and wibbly.

The lights in the aisle clicked out. They did that automatically after about three minutes. I flinched. Actually, it was a bit more than a flinch—it was a full-body jerk and a small, high-pitched noise.

"It's okay," Jerome said, raising his arm and making a space for me to lean against him. I accepted this offer, and he wrapped his arm around my shoulders.

Here's something I do that's really great: when I get nervous, I tell completely irrelevant and often very inappropriate stories. They just come out of my mouth. I felt one coming up now, rising out of whatever pit in my body I keep all the nervous tics and terrible conversation starters.

"We had this neighbor once," I said, "who named his dog Dicknickel . . ."

Jerome was somewhat familiar with my quirks by now, and wisely took my chin in his hand and directed my face toward him. He nuzzled me with the tip of his nose, drawing it lightly against my cheek as he made his way toward my lips. The wibbliness got wibblier, and I craned my neck up. Jerome kissed it lightly, and I let out a little noise—a completely involuntary and small groan of happiness. Jerome rightly took this as a signal to kiss a bit harder, working up to the back of the ear.

"How long are you two going to sit there?" Alistair said. "I know you're not going to answer me, but if you're going to start kissing, can you leave?"

The only reason I opened my eyes was because Alistair sounded a little too close. This turned out to be a good call because he was, in fact, standing over us—I mean, *right* over us. Many people would be put off of a good make-out session by the sight of an angry ghost looming directly overhead, all spiky hair and combat boots. What terrified me, though, was the fact that Alistair was just about an inch or so away from my foot. I immediately yanked my legs away from him. In the process, I very nearly kneed Jerome in the groin, but he reflexively tucked and covered the way guys do.

"What is the *matter* with you?" Alistair said.

It looked like he was going to come even closer to see why I was convulsing.

"Stay back!" I said.

"What?"

Honestly, I have no idea which one of them said it. Could have been either. Could have been both. Alistair backed off a bit, so I achieved my immediate goal of not killing one of my friends. By this point, Jerome had crab-walked back a bit and then scrambled to his feet. He was scanning the aisles and generally looking freaked out. I had just yelled "Stay back!" pretty loudly. Anyone nearby would come and check to make sure I wasn't being assaulted in the dark of the stacks. It's one thing to have a girlfriend who gets startled by the automatic lights and then cuddles close to you for a kiss. It's another thing entirely when said girlfriend curls up like a shrimp in a hot pan when you try to kiss her, nearly nailing you in the nuts in the process. And then to have the aforementioned girlfriend scream "Stay back!" . . .

The moment, to put it as gently as possible, had passed.

"I'm sorry," Jerome said, and he sounded genuinely *alarmed*, like he'd hurt me. "I'm sorry, I'm sorry . . ."

"No!" I said, and I forced a smile. "No. No, no. It's fine. It's good! It's fine."

Alistair folded his arms and watched me try to explain this one away. *Jerk.* Jerome was keeping toward the wall, in a stance I recognized from goalkeeping—knees slightly bent, arms at the sides and ready. I was the crazy ball that might come flying at his head.

"I . . . didn't sleep much last night," I said. "Not at all, actually." (A massive lie. I'd slept for *thirteen hours straight.*) "So, I'm like . . . you know how you get? When you don't sleep? I *really* did not mean to do that. I just heard a noise and . . . I'm jumpy."

"I can see that," he said.

"And hungry! It's almost time for dinner."

"I know how you are about dinner."

"Damn straight," I replied. "But . . . we're okay?"

"Of course! I'm sorry if I—"

"You didn't."

"I don't want you to think—"

"I definitely do not think," I said. And that was the truest thing I'd said in a *long time.*

"Dinner then," he said. "Everyone will be excited to see you."

He relaxed a bit and moved away from the wall. Jerome took

my hand. I mean, it was a grip. A grip of relationship. A statement grip. A grip that said, "I got your back. And also we are, like, a thing." The incident was over. We would laugh about it, if not now, then by later tonight.

"You have the whole campus," Alistair called as we left. "The whole city. Do you really have to keep coming here to do that? Really?"

The sky was a particularly vibrant shade of purple, almost electric. The spire of the refectory stood out against it, and the stained-glass windows glowed. It had gotten pleasantly crisp out, and there were large quantities of fallen leaves all around. I could hear the clamor of dinner even from outside the building. When we pushed open the heavy wooden door, all the flyers and leaflets on the vestibule bulletin board fluttered. There was another set of doors, internal ones, with diamond-cut panes. Beyond those doors, all of Wexford . . . or at least . . . most of Wexford.

This was it, really. My grand entrance back into Wexford, and it started with the opening of a door, the smell of medium-quality ground beef and floor cleaner. Aside from those things, it really was an impressive place, housed in an old church, made of stone. The setting gave our meals a feeling of importance that my high school cafeteria couldn't match. Maybe we were eating powdered mashed potatoes and drinking warm juice, but here it seemed like a more important activity. The tables were laid out lengthways, with benches, so I got a side view of dozens of heads as we stepped inside and I made my way past my fellow students.

And . . . no one really seemed to notice. I guess I'd been imagining a general turning, a hush in the room, the single *clang* of a fork being dropped onto the stone floor.

Nope. Jerome and I just walked in and proceeded to the back of the room, where the trays were. The actual food line was in a small separate room. I got my first welcome from the dinner ladies, specifically Helen, who handled the hot mains.

"Rory!" she said. "You're back! How are you?"

"Good," I said. "Fine. I'm . . . fine."

"Oh, it's good to see you, love."

She was joined in a little cheer by the other dinner ladies. When we emerged, heads turned in our direction. I didn't exactly get a round of applause, but there was a mumbled interest.

"Rory!"

That was Gaenor, from my hall. She was half standing, waving me over. She and Eloise made a space for me that I didn't quite fit into, but I pressed butt to bench as best I could and turned my tray. Jerome sat on the other side, a few seats down. My hall mates generally swarmed. Even Charlotte poked her big red head over my shoulder just as I was shoveling a particularly drippy chunk of sausage into my mouth.

"Rory."

I tried to get the fork away from my mouth, but I had already inserted said sausage, so all I could do was accept the weird back-shoulder hug that she gave me. It was quite a long hug too. With something like this, I would have expected a little squeeze—maybe you could count to three, and then it would be over. This hug lingered and settled in, at least ten seconds. This was no handshake hug. This was a contract. A bond. I made haste with my chewing and swallowing.

"Hey, Charlotte," I said, shrugging loose.

Then I heard the squeal and I knew Jazza had arrived. I turned to see her tearing up the aisle toward us. Jazza always reminded me a little of a golden retriever. I mean that in a good way. Just the way her long hair (which was always bizarrely smooth and shiny) flopped joyfully as she hurried to greet me, the genuine happiness she exuded. She almost flipped me backward off the bench when she embraced me.

"You're back!" she said. "You're back, you're back, you're back . . ."

And I was.

5

I WAS DEAD ASLEEP WHEN MY PHONE BUZZED. I REACHED OUT automatically and slapped it silent. Then I grabbed it and held it right in front of my face. It was 1:34, and I had one text message. It read:

Come downstairs -s

I blinked.

Stephen? I wrote back.

The reply, a few seconds later: Yes. Wear shoes.

I knelt on my bed and looked out the window, but I couldn't see anyone. Just the empty square, the empty sidewalk. Empty London, all tucked in for the night. This emptiness didn't fill me with confidence. I was in no mood for weird text messages telling me to go outside in the middle of the night, especially when I couldn't see anyone outside the window.

This didn't mean I wasn't going, of course. Because, Stephen.

I got up as silently as I could, grabbed my sneakers from the foot of my bed, plucked my fleece from the hook by my door, and crept out, closing the door quietly behind me. Jazza didn't stir at all. Downstairs, the hall lights were on, even though no one was around. They used to be off at night. Maybe this was part of the new security plan—always look awake, always look at home, always keep the public areas lit. There was no noise from Claudia's room as I passed by. I remembered the alarm as I stood by the front door. If I tried to get out, it would go off. Stephen was nodding at me. He held up his thumb in a thumbs-up gesture. I smiled and thumbs-upped back. Then he shook his head no and typed something into his phone.

Open the door.

I can't open the door, I typed. Alarm go boom.

He shook his head again and typed another message.

Just open it.

I took a deep breath and pushed. The door opened with no fanfare, no screech and flash, no metal bars slamming down. I stepped into the cold night. A great plume of my breath fogged up in front of my face.

I was used to seeing Stephen in his police uniform, but today he was wearing a black sweater and a pair of jeans. He had a scarf thickly knotted around his neck in the way that all English people seemed to tie their scarves (a tie that eluded me no matter how I tried). And although it was very cold, he wore no coat. I think some English people think coats are for the weak.

I'd forgotten just how tall he was, and how *worried* he always looked. He had very thin and straight black eyebrows that were perpetually pushed slightly toward his nose in a worry wrinkle, like he'd just been told something mildly problematic—not terrible or tragic, just annoying and difficult to fix. He turned this vaguely troubled gaze on me, the newest and most immediate problem.

"Hey," I said. "You heard I was back, huh?"

My relationship with Stephen had been a strange one from the start. He wasn't, for many reasons, the most open person. But he was here. I think I'd known he would come. My initial inclination was to grab him around his long, skinny middle and hug him until his head popped off, but Stephen was not really a hugger.

I decided to hug him anyway. He tolerated this reasonably well, though he didn't reciprocate. I guess I expected a smile or something, but smiling also wasn't his thing.

"Your roommate," he replied. "Julianne. Is she asleep? Your lights have been off for a half an hour."

Nor was conversation, really.

"You've been looking at my window for a half an hour?"

"That's not an answer to my question."

"She's asleep," I said. "At least, she's quiet. She didn't say anything when I got up."

"Would she normally say something?"

"It's good to see you too," I said. "They said that's a really good security system, but not so much, huh?"

"It is quite a good system."

"So why didn't it go off?"

"Disarming the alarm system of a school building isn't exactly the trickiest thing the security services has ever had to do."

"Security services . . ."

"We should move."

"What?"

"Come on."

"But . . ."

He had already slipped a businesslike arm across my back and was ushering me down the cobblestone path and around the corner. Stephen was the only person in the world I would tolerate this kind of thing from, because there was one thing I did know—if he dragged me out of bed and ushered me through the dark, there was a reason. And I would be safe.

There was a red car, and I heard the doors unlock when Stephen pointed the remote at it.

"That's not a police car," I said, pointing out the obvious.

"It's an unmarked vehicle. Get in."

"Where are we going?"

"Let me explain inside the car."

There was a figure sitting in the front passenger seat. I recognized the head of white hair at once, and the altogether too young face that went with it. It was Mr. Thorpe, the government official who'd come to visit me in the hospital. The one who told me I was never allowed to say anything.

"What's he—"

"It's all right," Stephen said, opening the back door for me. "Get inside."

Stephen held the door open until I acquiesced.

"Aurora," Mr. Thorpe said, turning around. "Good to see you. Sorry to pull you out in the middle of the night like this."

"What are we doing?" I asked.

"We need to talk."

Stephen started up the car.

"Where are we going?" I asked.

"Do you enjoy being back?" Thorpe asked.

Thorpe didn't exactly seem like the kind of person who cared whether or not I was adjusting well to my circumstances, and Stephen was suddenly very focused on his driving.

"It's okay," I said. "I just got here. As I guess you know."

"We do."

"Why do I feel like my being back has something to do with you?"

"It does have something to do with us," he said. "But I hope that you're happy about it."

"Where are we going?"

"We're just going to take a short ride," Thorpe said. "Nothing to be worried about."

Stephen looked at me through the rearview mirror and gave me a reassuring nod. I wrapped my arms around myself and shivered. He turned up the heat.

The first few turns, I knew basically where we were—in the Wexford neighborhood, going south. Then we were lost in a warren of tight little streets for a few moments, reemerging near King William Street, where the old squad headquarters was, where we'd faced down the Ripper. We turned off that quickly enough and were on a road that ran along the Thames Embankment. We were definitely heading west. West was the way to central London. The black cabs got more numerous, the path along the Thames thicker with trees and impressive buildings, the lights on the opposite bank shinier. I caught sight of the London Eye, glowing brightly in the dark, then we were going right, into the very heart of London.

We pulled up into the circular drive of what I first thought was a hotel. It was a moment before I noticed the sign for the

Tube, the distinctive red circle with the blue bar across it. We were at Charing Cross station. Stephen pulled the car up right in front of the doors. Thorpe got out at once, and Stephen released me from the back.

"Come in," Thorpe called. "This way. Come inside."

There was a female police officer standing by one of the front doors. She pushed it open as we approached. She moved fast, like she'd been waiting for us and her most important job of the night was to open that door.

Charing Cross was a large central hub for both trains and subways. It had a large central area full of shops and ticket counters, with a glass roof crisscrossed with metal latticework. A woman in a black suit waited for us in the middle of the concourse.

"The CCTV is off?" Thorpe asked her quietly.

The woman nodded.

"Stay in the control room. No one comes down."

I gave Stephen a what-the-hell-is-this look, and he responded with a it's-fine-no-really-it's-fine stare.

"We're just going to go down to the platforms," Thorpe said. "This way."

He began walking toward the opening marked **UNDERGROUND**. We followed him down the steps. Gates had been opened, allowing us to proceed. Charing Cross Tube station was a somewhat grim place, with brown tiles on the floor and tiled walls done in variations of brown; the ticket machine walls were an alarming electric lime green. The escalators were shut off, so we had to walk down to the platforms, Stephen in front of me and Thorpe just behind. It was unnerving to be in a Tube station after hours. There was no body heat from the thousands of people who usually rushed around, no sound of musicians playing or talking or laughing or trains roaring along. Every one of our footsteps on the slated metal steps was clearly audible as we descended.

"Bakerloo?" Thorpe asked.

Stephen nodded.

I looked up at the sign, with the brown lettering that indicated the Bakerloo line. The Bakerloo line at Charing Cross . . . that meant something to me. But it wasn't until we got down to the platform that the significance became clear.

"Do you see someone?" Thorpe asked me.

At the far end of the platform was a woman. Her hair was a silver-blond, swept back in heavy wings. She wore a black cowl-neck sweater and a gray skirt—ordinary enough clothes. I think the shoes told me she was from a different era. They were just a bit too chunky, too platform. She stood right at the edge of the platform, her gaze fixed on the opposite wall. The last time I'd spoken to this woman, all she could say was "I jumped" over and over in a brittle whisper. She was vulnerable and pale and, frankly, depressing to be around. Just getting near her made my spirits sink.

"The woman," I said, glancing at Stephen. "I've met her before."

Thorpe nodded to Stephen, who gently cleared his throat.

"Let's go and talk to her," Stephen said.

"Why?" I whispered. "What are we *doing* here?"

"Something important, I promise. I wouldn't have brought you here otherwise. I just need you to talk to this woman."

I looked down the length of the empty platform, where the

woman stood by the gaping maw of the silent tunnel. She had turned toward us, expectant. Stephen started to walk toward her, slowly, allowing me to follow. The woman could do me no harm—I knew that. I wasn't frightened of her. It was more that she was so obviously sad—beyond sad, to some terrible point of existence. She was a palette of grays, and I didn't want to get anywhere near her.

"It's you," she said when we reached her.

"Yes," Stephen replied. "I was here a few days ago."

"You came back. You brought her."

"I did, yes. Rory, this is Diane."

"Hello," I said. I kept a foot or two behind Stephen, eyeing the woman.

"He said you would help me." There was desperation in Diane's eyes. "Will you help me?"

"Help you what?" I said.

"Make it stop. He said you could make it stop."

At first, I refused to accept what I'd just heard. It made me vaguely sick. Stephen wouldn't have brought me down here for that. Stephen didn't even *know* I could do that . . .

"You don't have to do it if you don't want to," Stephen said. "But she's suffering."

Except he clearly *did* know.

"Please," Diane said again. "Please. Please. I can't go on like this. Please. Please. I never wanted to be here. I thought it would be quick. Jumping is quick. But I never went away. I jumped . . . but I never went away."

I had used a terminus before, so it wasn't that I was entirely opposed to the idea, in general. And if anyone needed a terminus, it was probably this poor woman, trapped on a train platform for thirty or forty years, constantly stuck in the place that she'd killed herself. This gray and sad woman . . .

And yet. I'd been brought here all cloak-and-dagger. Stephen knew things that he shouldn't have known. Thorpe stood down at his end of the platform and watched the show. That's what it felt like—a show. I stepped away from Diane a bit and waved Stephen closer. His chin was down toward his chest, and he couldn't look directly at me.

"How did you know?" I said, low enough so that Thorpe couldn't hear.

"I kept an eye on you in Bristol," Stephen said quietly.

"An eye on me? You followed me? And didn't say anything?"

"I wanted to make sure—"

"And you told Thorpe? You told this woman I'd fix things for her? You brought me here to test me or something?"

"You don't have to do anything you don't want to do," he said, lifting his head a bit. "If you want, we walk away right now."

"Oh, sure," I said.

"I mean it. We leave right now if you say so."

I looked back at Diane for just a moment, but I had to turn away. She was the embodiment of depression, of desperation. Releasing her would be fair. It would be right. I could come back and do it some other time, maybe. But not now. Not when I'd been brought here like this.

"Okay," I said, drawing myself up as tall as I could. "We leave. Now."

He blinked slowly.

"If that's what you want."

"That's what I want."

Stephen examined my face for a moment and rocked back and forth on his heels ever so slightly. We stood practically toe to toe, and I could smell the cold on his coat.

"Right," he said.

Diane must have been listening, because she let out a wail. It was unpleasant to hear, so I blocked it out. I walked back down the platform toward Thorpe and left Stephen to try to talk to her. This was his fault. He'd made the promise. He could explain to her why it wasn't going to happen.

"What's going on?" Thorpe called.

"Nothing," I replied. "I'm leaving."

"Is it done?"

"Nope," I said.

"Are you unable to . . . do what she asks?"

"I'm not—"

"Rory!" Stephen yelled.

This is when I felt something at my back. It felt like the wind—a cold and strong wind. There was a zing of electricity up my spine, and I couldn't move, couldn't talk.

It wasn't unlike that feeling you get at the top of a roller coaster, just when you hear the clanking noise that pulled you up there stop, and something lets go, and you know the feeling is about to get much more intense and extreme. Everything goes up—your pulse, the blood to your head, even your organs seem to leap as it all falls away. The air comes into your lungs faster than you can process it, so you choke on it for a moment.

My ears filled with the sound of my own heartbeat, my blood

being forced through my veins. The world went white. Then everything settled just as fast as it had stirred, and I could smell the smoky flower smell, and the world came back into focus.

I fell to my knees on the platform surface, just managing to keep myself from going headfirst over the edge by grabbing at it. Then I felt hands at my waist, holding me steady, pulling me back into a seated position.

"You're all right," Stephen said. "You're all right. She came up behind you. She grabbed you. She was too fast. I couldn't stop her."

Thorpe hurried up to us.

"Did something happen?" he asked.

In reply, I got down on my knees on the bumpy yellow section at the very edge of the platform, leaned over the side, and began to throw up on the tracks. Someone—Stephen, I guessed—held me from behind to make sure I didn't lose my balance. The sickness didn't last long, and it cleared my head instantly. I pushed back and sat on my heels and wiped my mouth.

"I didn't do it," I said, once I caught my breath.

"What?" Thorpe asked.

"It happened," Stephen said. "The woman touched Rory, not the other way around. That's what she means."

"But you *are* sure."

"There's no mistaking it," Stephen said, a little sharply. "It's not subtle."

"Then get her back to her school and make sure she's all right."

"Come on," Stephen said to me softly. "Can you stand?"

I didn't answer, and when he tried to help me, I pushed his

hands away and walked down the platform. I knew Stephen was a few steps behind me, quiet, nervous. I saw several mice dash along the edges of the corridors or along the steps as we approached, put out by our appearance. The Tube belonged to them at night.

I stood outside Charing Cross station for a minute, taking deep, heavy breaths of cold air. The policewoman watched me from a distance—impassive. She couldn't have had any idea why I was here or what I'd just done. I was trying to figure out what I was feeling. It wasn't anger, but it was something related to it. Was it exhaustion? Maybe even relief? It was all those feelings, maybe, and I didn't feel like having any of them, so I decided to ignore them all and concentrate on breathing nice and slow.

Stephen exited the station a minute later. He went right to the car and held the passenger's door open for me.

"Don't we have to wait for Thorpe?" I asked. There was a bit of a growl in my voice, mostly from the vomiting. It made me sound very angry. I was fine with that.

"He can ride with the other officer. He said I should take you."

I got into the car, and Stephen shut the door. He turned on the engine and turned the heat on full blast. Gusts of warm air roared out of the vents and directly into my face. I reached over and turned it down.

"I thought you might be cold," he said.

"I am. It feels good. I just threw up."

"She was too fast for me to stop her," he said. "Sometimes they move quickly, more quickly than us. I couldn't stop her."

I'd seen it. I knew that was true. There was nothing he could have done to stop her if she'd been moving as fast as she really wanted to go. Ghosts are quick when they want to be.

Still, I wasn't letting him off the hook that easy. I maintained a steely silence for a few moments.

"Be mad at me if you want," he said. "But everything I've done has been for good reasons."

"Like what?"

He took off his black glasses and rubbed them on his leg. His leg bounced a little with tension.

"Rory, I just . . . it's . . . it's very complicated."

"Try me."

"Rory . . ."

"What's Thorpe doing?" I said. "Over there, by the door?"

Thorpe wasn't over by the door. I'd just said that to distract him. I yanked the keys out of the ignition.

"Tell me," I said, shoving them down my shirt and holding them against my chest. "Tell me, or we go nowhere. Tell me or I'll start screaming. Do you want me to draw lots of attention to what's going on here? I'll totally do it."

A deep sigh from Stephen. He banged his head gently against his headrest and stared up at the car ceiling.

"They were going to shut us down. They were happy with the results of the Ripper case, but without a terminus, they didn't know how we could still function."

"You still have one," I said. "What about the one in the bathroom? The one Jo used on Newman?"

He reached into his pocket and removed a small plastic vial, then he switched on the interior light so I could look at it. It contained a gray stone.

"That's it," he said. "It's gone cloudy, as you can see. It doesn't work anymore. We've tried. It's like a blown lightbulb."

"What about the two in the river?" I asked. "Can you get them back? You can get things out of the Thames—guns and evidence and stuff, right?"

"Guns, maybe, on a good day. But not two extremely small stones. The Thames is a powerful tidal river. Presumably the stones drifted a bit before they sank, and now they're mixed in somewhere in the millions of tons of sediment and sludge. So you are the only terminus. Then I saw what happened to you . . . I needed to show Thorpe that there was one terminus left. I also needed a good reason to bring you back. I was never comfortable with you being sent away like that, on your own, with no support. This solved both problems. We'll be allowed to keep going for a while now that he's seen."

Stephen was right. I couldn't have stayed there on my own, with no one to talk to. He reached over and took the vial and put it back in his pocket.

"And how did you do it?" I asked. "How did you bring me back?"

"Thorpe did that. I honestly don't know how he set it up. I only know he made a very strong suggestion to your therapist that you should be returned to London. He didn't give me any details."

Of course. Now it all made sense. Julia's sudden decision that I should return to Wexford. Her obvious lie about all the work I'd done in therapy.

"It was up to you," Stephen said. "You were asked if you wanted to return. You said yes."

"But I didn't say I would just . . . put on some freak show for Thorpe, or blow up some woman. You could have told me where we were going."

"I wasn't sure if you'd agree to just . . . doing it. But I thought if you saw the pain Diane was in . . . it was appropriate use, Rory. She was in agony. Now, I've told you everything. Give me back the keys. Now."

The keys were sweat-stuck to my chest. I knocked them loose and they fell gracefully into my crotch. I picked them up and handed them over. He started the car again and was putting it into reverse, then stopped.

"Boo and Callum," he said, his voice smooth and quiet again. "They know you're back. I can take you to see them now, and we can talk about it. If you want. We can go right now, or we can do it some other time. I don't know how you're feeling."

The rapid change in emotions, the way he wasn't looking at me . . . he was still feeling very guilty. His reasons may have been good, but he still felt bad about using me like that, about keeping things from me.

I did want to see Boo and Callum. Truth be told, I was still glad to see Stephen. And to tell even more truth, it was just a little bit fun to play with his guilt. And he did feel guilty. And after the last few weeks, I deserved whatever fun I could get.

"We can go now," I said in a low voice, rubbing a clear patch in the fog on the window.

6

IN JUST A FEW TURNS, WE WERE HEADING TOWARD THE YELLOW glowing eye of the clock at the top of Big Ben. The Houses of Parliament were lit up for the night, and the London Eye loomed just across the water, a neon bluish-purple circle revolving slowly. Everything in this part of London was alight. We crossed the bridge by the Parliament buildings and headed over to the south side of the river.

We turned past Waterloo station and onto the fairly quiet residential streets beyond. He drove down a street with a chip shop on the corner and pulled the car into the only empty space along the street and turned off the engine.

"We have a new flat—" he began.

"I know," I said.

This seemed to surprise him. He knew something about me, but I knew something about him as well.

"Oh. Right. Well, the owner of our old flat decided it was time to start charging three thousand pounds a month again.

So that was that, really. Since we did such a good job with the Ripper, Her Majesty's Government has given us a proper office and somewhere to live. It's just here."

He pointed at one of the many largely identical buildings along the road—plain brick houses in a row, the kind found all over the city. Definitely not as fancy as the old place.

"There's one more thing," he said. "I told Callum and Boo there was a meeting tonight, but not what it was about. For two reasons. One, I didn't know what would happen. It was possible that you wouldn't go through with it or it wouldn't work. And two, Boo. She would never have stood for it. And I couldn't tell Callum without telling Boo. They never knew how close we were to being shut down."

"Sounds like you've been keeping a lot of secrets," I said.

"It goes with the job. Come on."

We entered a very narrow hall, stepping on a pile of mail and flyers as we passed inside. There was weird textured wallpaper in the hall, and a light that didn't quite do the job it was meant for. It glowed down, making a puddle of light in the vestibule, but the stairs were shrouded in darkness. There was no handrail, and the carpet on the steps was slippery from being trod on too many times. I put my hands on the walls and supported myself as I went up, my fingers running over the Braille of the wallpaper. Another jingle of keys. I heard voices inside the apartment on the landing—one low, laughing. The other high-pitched and insistent. I knew that last voice very well. I had lived with that voice.

When he opened the door and I poked my head inside, I recognized a lot of the furniture from the old flat, including the two old sofas and the unstable kitchen table with mismatched chairs. The other flat had been larger, so everything was crammed in, leaving barely enough room to get around. Books were piled on the floor, all along the walls, piles and piles of them in varying heights. There were also document boxes and piles of thick folders. Maps and notes were taped all over the walls, which were covered in more textured wallpaper, this time in a mustard yellow. It was particularly jarring when combined with the red Scotch plaid curtains that were drawn tightly shut over the front windows.

A head popped over the top of the sofa, then the rest of Callum appeared as he climbed over the back of the sofa to get to me.

"Hey!" he said. "Look who it is!"

Callum gave me a big hug, wrapping me in his extremely impressive arm and chest muscles. Boo was on the other sofa, her leg in a cast, stretched out. Boo had been trying to protect me from the Ripper, and he had thrown her in front of a car.

"Get off her, you perv!" she yelled at Callum. "Come here!"

I crossed over and gave her a hug. Boo had touched up her hair in exciting new ways. She'd previously had a sharp-cut black bob, kind of a Louise Brooks look, with a deep red streak. She had added a touch of violet to the edge of her bangs, so that there was a strong purple line running right above her eyes. It looked like a fashionable lobotomy scar.

"How long will that be on?" I said, pointing at the cast.

"Just a few more days, but I'm getting used to it. I have to crawl up the stairs on my bum . . ."

"It's very entertaining," Callum said.

"Make us some tea," Boo commanded. "Mine's gone cold, and Rory needs some."

"I cannot wait until that thing is off your leg," Callum muttered.

"Make one for me too," Stephen said.

Boo pulled on my arm, causing me to fall onto the sofa next to her.

"How are you?" she asked.

"Okay."

"Really?"

"I'm okay enough. What about you?"

"You know," she said, shrugging. Boo and Jo had been best friends, and Jo's death—or her after-death death—had been a terrible blow. The pain of that blow was still evident in her expression, but like me, she was shuffling onward.

"I'm doing some research," she said, patting some folders that sat next to her on the sofa. "As soon as this cast comes off, I start my training. I'm either going to go in as an Underground employee, like Callum, or I'll do an apprenticeship at British Gas."

Boo told me some more about her future job prospects, showing me glossy brochures of people in coveralls looking intently at pipes and wires and going down ladders into dark underground places. The prospect really did seem to delight her. Stephen went to a desk by the window and poked at his laptop in a way that suggested he was just trying to stay out of our conversation for a moment.

"Gas company workers can get in anywhere," she said, "all the good underground spaces. I'd look good with a safety helmet, yeah? Toolbelt?"

"You don't even need tools," Callum said, passing by with some cups of tea balanced on a large book. "You've got those talons. You could probably pry open a manhole with those things."

Boo stretched out her fingers, displaying her long, fake purple nails, then slashed playfully at Callum's hip. She accepted the teas, passing one to me, and Callum moved on to Stephen.

"That's my atlas," Stephen said, observing the object Callum was using as a tray.

"Sorry, love."

"I've told you about that."

"No one needs an atlas," Callum said, passing him the last mug. "What with the Internet and all. Here's your tea."

Stephen came over to join us, and the atmosphere in the room settled instantly.

"Right," Stephen said. "So, tonight, we had a meeting with Thorpe . . ."

"I still don't understand why you had to have a meeting at two in the morning," Boo said.

"That's when it had to happen," Stephen said.

Callum glanced over at Boo.

"And we have official clearance to continue," Stephen finished.

"Clearance to continue?" Boo asked. "They were going to shut us down?"

"It was being discussed."

"And you didn't *mention* this?" Boo said.

"They were concerned because we don't have the termini anymore," Stephen said.

"And so am I," Callum said, his voice edged with anger. "Please tell me this solution involves getting some new ones."

"It does," Stephen said. "It involves Rory."

Callum and Boo looked at me expectantly. Stephen cleared his throat a bit.

"She . . . is a terminus."

I can't fault Callum and Boo for not knowing what to say to that.

"You're shitting me," Callum said, after a moment.

"I'm not," Stephen said. "I can only assume that it happened at some point after the final Ripper attack. Which is why you need to tell us everything that happened to you from the minute of impact."

Now the focus was back on me. Julia had been trying for weeks to get me to this very point—the point of the knife as it went in, those minutes when I was slumped on the floor, when I saw the blood coming out of my own abdomen. When the Ripper—his name was Alexander Newman—told me that I was going to die.

It was not something I felt like talking about. But there did seem to be a compelling reason for me to do so—there was a logic to telling them.

"He cut me," I said. "He said he did it in such a way that I would bleed and die slowly. He gave me the terminus."

"He *gave* it to you?" Callum said.

"I couldn't move. He said he had this theory that if someone with the sight died connected to a terminus, that person might come back . . . because he had died holding one. He wanted to see what happened when I died. And then . . . Jo came through the door."

"The door was locked," Stephen said.

"She went *through* the door."

"That would have hurt her," Boo said quietly. "She told me that hurt. She said it felt like being ripped apart."

I paused for a moment out of respect for that. I didn't know Jo could feel pain, or that she'd felt it coming to get me.

"And once Jo came into the room?" Stephen prompted.

"She took the terminus from me, and she went after Newman with it. That's when . . . everything blew up. There was a really bright light, and the mirrors smashed. And then they were gone, and I passed out."

"When did you first know what you could do?" he asked. "Was it on the bench, in Bristol?"

Callum and Boo looked over in confusion, but I guess they decided to let me keep talking. This story was full of weird surprises.

"No," I said. "There was one before that, on the day I left Wexford. I found a woman in the bathroom where it all happened. I went down there before I left school, just to look at the room, and I found her in a stall."

"Had she been there before?"

"No," I said. "I'd never seen her before. I have no idea where she came from. She was hiding in the bathroom stall, and she looked really scared. She didn't speak. I don't think she could. I just reached out . . . I was telling her it was okay. I didn't know. I just touched her. And it happened."

"Did you have to touch her in any special way?" Callum asked. "I mean, did you have to keep your hand on her?"

"I don't know. I just touched her on the shoulder. It happened right away, I think."

"Any physical effects after that?" Stephen asked.

"My arm tingled."

"Nothing else?"

"No."

"Does it hurt?"

"No," I said. "It's not pain. I sort of feel like my arm is being sucked into something, and then it starts to shake. It feels . . . electrified, I guess. The rest of it is like normal terminus stuff. There's a light. There's a burning smell. But that's it."

"But tonight you were physically ill," Stephen said.

"Tonight?" Boo cut in. "*That's* where you were? I mean, what if it's dangerous? What if it hurts her?"

"I thought about that," Stephen said. "But it's doubtful we could ever find that out. Much like our sight, it may not come up on any kind of examination. I suppose we can schedule a full physical workup . . ."

But now that Boo had brought it up, this new possibility was going to be on my mind. What if it did hurt me? What if having an internal terminus was like having cancer?

Or what if it made me super healthy?

God, I was tired.

"Stop," I said, holding up my hand. "Can we just . . . stop? I've had enough medical stuff in the last few weeks, so . . . just, don't."

That ended that part of the conversation and they all looked very uncomfortable. Even among my freaky friends I was a freak.

"Let me make one thing clear," Stephen said. "Rory is not a weapon. How she uses her ability is entirely up to her."

"And that's fine," Callum said, "but we aren't police if we have no power to do anything. This is still the problem, even though Rory is a terminus. If she isn't around, and if she isn't—don't take this the wrong way, Rory—willing or able, where does that leave us?"

"It leaves us exactly where we've been for the last few weeks," Boo said. "We can still do our jobs, just without weapons. Regular police don't carry guns."

"But they have units with guns if they need them. Don't they? There are armed response units."

"Callum is making a valid point," Stephen said, "but I agree with you, Boo. The squad long predated the terminus. According to what records I have, they didn't get them until the seventies."

"Where did they come from?" I asked.

"That's unclear," Stephen said, scratching his jawline.

"They must have come from somewhere," I said.

"They clearly did come from *somewhere,* but that somewhere isn't known to us. Diamonds come from a range of places. Africa. India. Russia. Canada."

"It doesn't matter where they came from," Callum said. "We don't have them now, and we need them. For weeks, I've been getting calls. All kinds of problems on the Tube. Trains being delayed, dangerous situations where people could be hurt or even killed."

"The Tubes ran for years without us zapping anyone," Boo countered. "They don't need us to make the Tubes run. And if there are problems, we go and we deal with them. By *talking.*"

"And if they don't listen? Was the Ripper going to listen? And whoever comes next?"

"None of this is for tonight," Stephen said, and there was finality in his tone. "It's late. I have to take Rory back before anyone misses her. We'll deal with our procedural problems some other time."

I said my good-byes. There were more long hugs with Callum and Boo while Stephen stood by the door, keys in hand. And then we were back in the car, going to Wexford.

"So what happens now?" I asked.

"You get on with your life," he said. "You go back to school."

I tapped my fingers against the car window.

"You're saying if there was something out there, something bad, like the Ripper, no one would force me to go after it."

"The Ripper is gone. Newman is gone."

"But something like that."

"It's very unlikely that there would be something like that, but yes. That's what I'm saying."

"But Thorpe would," I said. "He'd make me."

"Forget about Thorpe. He's seen what he needed to see."

"He didn't *see* anything," I pointed out.

"He saw your reaction. That wasn't faked. He knew that. Anyway, Thorpe is my problem, not yours. Whatever's happened to you . . . it's up to you how you use it. It has to be your decision."

"Thorpe could make your life miserable."

"You're suggesting my life isn't already miserable," he said, with a slightly too weak effort at a smile. I think he was making a joke. It was very hard to tell with Stephen.

We were almost back to Wexford when we stopped at a red light just outside of a pub that was still doing Ripper specials—Bloody Marys ("Jack's drink of choice") were two for one. It was all a joke now. People had been murdered, but it didn't matter. It was just Jack the Ripper, and he was dead now, so it was funny to have Bloody Marys and have your picture taken lying on the ground of the crime scene.

"So," I said, "all the Ripper stuff. How did that work?"

"What do you mean?"

"How did they keep it all quiet?"

"It wasn't that difficult," he said. "No one saw what *actually* happened, except for us. Only you saw how it all ended."

"How did they explain the bathroom being smashed up?"

"The assumed a fight went on—a struggle. The attacker must have broken the mirrors and the window."

"But they said the police chased him," I said. "They pulled a body out of the water."

"That was all staged," he said. "Some cars were sent to chase a potential subject."

"And the body?"

"A John Doe from the mortuary. They assigned it a name and an identity. It was all done very high up. Most of the people involved thought they were part of an actual chase."

"But what if people try to write about him?"

"That was all taken care of," Stephen said. "The story is that he was just a loner—someone who lived on the street. No neighbors. No living relatives. No one to interview. Just a very unfortunate person with a mental condition."

"And all of the CCTV footage that had no one in it?"

"The footage was all fake. That was proven."

"No it wasn't," I said.

"Well," Stephen said. "It's fake now."

"What about the crack in the floor?" I asked.

"What?"

"How did they explain that? I mean, you can break a window or a mirror in a fight, but you can't crack a tile floor, can you?"

"You're telling me that crack wasn't there before?"

"No," I said. "It happened that night. It was a big explosion."

"Well," he said, "we're just very lucky you survived."

We had reached Wexford. He stopped the car at the far end of the cobblestone road.

"I'll be able to see you all the way to the door from here," he said. "It should be open. We unlocked the building and had someone stationed there to make sure no one got in until it was secure again. I'll be here until you get inside."

It felt like we should have a more meaningful good-bye than that, but I wasn't sure what to say. I'd already hugged him once tonight.

"Sure," I said, unfastening my seat belt. "Right. Okay. So, I'll see you around, or?"

"You can always reach me," he said. "If you need me."

"Right. Okay. So . . ."

I walked up the road alone. The door opened, just as promised, and I looked back down the lane and raised my hand as a final good-bye. I couldn't really see him—the road was too dark at the end where the car was parked. But it was still there. I could see the headlights, two glowing eyes pointed at me, waiting for me to get to safety.

7

"Right," Mark said, switching the lights out in art history the next morning, "let's get started. John Constable, English Romantic painter, lived from 1776 until 1837 . . ."

Art history was a long class—three hours, with two ten-minute breaks that were really more like fifteen minutes, but still. Long. I wrote down the names of paintings and stared at the slides, but my mind was completely elsewhere. It was on the platform at Charing Cross. It was in the car with Stephen and at the flat with Callum and Boo.

I'd felt something last night, aside from nausea. Something real. Something . . . exciting? Something that made me feel complete again. Plus, Jerome was pressing his leg against mine—not hard. But it was there. John Constable, English Romantic painter, didn't stand a chance. (Also, for the record, if someone is called a Romantic, it should mean some sexy times, I think. Instead, what it really means is people in puffy shirts who probably had a lot of real-life sexytimes, but produced almost exclusively pictures of hillsides or people in dramatic poses, like pretending to be Ophelia dead in a swamp. I definitely call shenanigans on this.)

We emerged, three hours later, our brains swollen with images of sky and damp and moping. Once we got outside, Jerome swayed side to side a bit, like he was standing on a teetering top.

"What?" I said.

"What were you going to do today?"

"Work," I said. "I guess . . . work. Because I'm kind of behind."

"I have things this afternoon as well, but I was thinking . . . we could go out? Properly? On a date. Tonight?"

"A date?" I repeated.

I'd never been on a real date. I'd ended up going places with people—guy people—but it was always kind of, well . . . kind of crap. "Dates" seemed to be something that existed in movies or television shows or a more domesticated past where you were wooed in high school and got married upon graduation and immediately gave birth to ten children. They were not something for people like me. But here I was, quasi-boyfriend saying he wanted to take me on an actual date, and I was just staring at him impassively, like a horse watching a mime pretending to walk against the wind.

"Yes," I said. "Date. Yes."

"Okay," Jerome said. "Good. So, maybe, instead of dinner? We'll go out?"

"Yeah. Sure."

"Would you like to go to dinner, or to a film?"

"Sure."

"Which one?"

"I don't know," I said. "Whichever."

"Okay, well, we can figure it out."

"Okay," I said.

"Okay."

We shuffled apart, nodding.

I was going on a date, a date, a date. I repeated the word in my head as I pressed my finger on the keypad, as I tripped up the steps of Hawthorne. The word beat in time to the creaking of the wood. A date, a date . . . I shoved open the first fire door and breathed in that strange, clinical carpety smell that lived only between the fire doors . . . open second fire door . . . a date. A date with my man. My boy. My guy. Boyfriend? Whatever. My future activity had a word, and that word was *date.*

Jazza was out, so I had the room to myself. I sat at my desk and looked at my pile of books. I listened to the radiators hiss and clank lightly. I heard people coming back to the hall, doors opening and closing, bits of conversation. All the familiar Wexford noises and smells, and this new one . . . date.

I was interrupted in my reverie by a knock at the door. I called for the person to come in, and Charlotte appeared and drifted in. I guess this was the first weird thing, because Charlotte did not drift. Charlotte moved from place to place decisively, like a high-speed train. She walked to class with purpose. She walked to dinner with purpose. She walked to the bathroom with purpose and brushed her teeth with purpose and ran her hands through her hair with purpose.

"Hello," she said.

She sat on Jazza's bed, drew her knees together, and put her hands on them. She looked at her hands, and then at me. It appeared that we were going to have some kind of talk. I had never had a talk with Charlotte, and I wasn't sure if I was ready or willing to have a talk with Charlotte. But the one thing I had learned about living at school—you don't always get a choice in these matters.

"I don't know if I could have come back," she said.

"Oh, well," I said. "You know."

Charlotte took that empty statement as a profundity and shook her head in understanding. I started to wonder if she was feeling quite right. The Ripper *had* nailed her in the head with a lamp on the night of my attack.

"Are you okay?" I asked.

"I wasn't at first," she said. "I didn't sleep at all for a week. I was exhausted and crying a lot. I was having anxiety attacks. I'd shake all over, and my thoughts would race. My parents thought they might have to take me out of school for a while . . . Then I met this amazing woman. She changed everything."

For one terrible second, I thought Charlotte was going to tell me that after getting hit on the head with a lamp, she now saw ghosts. That would not be funny.

"She's a therapist."

"Oh," I said, sinking in relief. "I have one of those. It didn't do much."

"She's really special, though. She changed my life. She's the only reason I was able to go on with the term. I genuinely feel better after talking to her. I just came from her office, actually. I feel really good."

Strangely, I could see how good Charlotte felt. It was something about her eyes, the relaxation in her body.

"She knows about you, and she says you're welcome to call. She's a private practitioner, but she doesn't charge."

"Doesn't charge?"

"I think she's independently wealthy. She only takes clients by referral, and she specifically treats victims of violence. I met her through a friend of Eloise's."

The door opened, and Jazza came in, dragging her cello case.

"Oh," she said, seeing Charlotte sitting on her bed. "Hello . . ."

Jaz hung by the door, clutching her cello for protection. Charlotte stood slowly and stretched.

"It really is good to have you back," Charlotte said. "Here. I just wanted you to have her card, in case you needed it."

There was one toss of the red hair and a nod to Jazza as she let herself out.

"What was that?" Jazza asked.

"The name of her therapist." I held up the card. Jazza snorted. Actually snorted.

"She's been *quite the victim,*" Jazza said. "She's probably furious you're back to steal the spotlight."

It was oddly comforting that the attack had messed someone else up—apparently, much worse than it had messed me up. And yet it was also a little annoying. If anyone had a right to be messed up, it was me. Unless I too was acting like that—seeming wounded at one second, utterly confident in the next, my personality flickering on and off like a yard sale lamp.

"Did she look weird to you?" I asked. "Like, relaxed?"

"I have no idea." Jazza pulled her cello into the room and tucked it into the corner by her closet. Jazza had time for everyone except Charlotte. There was an old feud there, one that predated my arrival. Charlotte was the full moon that brought out the werejazza.

I looked at the card. Clearly, this woman had talent if she had fixed Charlotte, but in the end, she was just another therapist I couldn't talk to. I dropped the card into my top desk drawer.

"I have a date tonight," I said. "An actual date."

"This seems to surprise you."

"No." I reclined back on the bed. "I just . . . a date. It's so formal-sounding."

"Is it formal?"

"I think we're getting dinner," I said.

Dinner and . . . perhaps we could have a redo on the making-out fiasco. I spent a pleasant few minutes visualizing what that might entail. I got to the part where the imaginary hand was just sliding under my imaginary shirt . . .

Where it encountered my scar. My terrible, nasty, jagged, ugly scar. The imaginary hand withdrew in horror. My actual hand reached up under the bottom of my shirt to see if the scar felt as bad as it looked. It could definitely be felt. What was my boyfriend going to do when he saw my scar? My newly labeled boyfriend, who had only tentatively ventured into that territory anyway. My shirt had never come off. I had no idea when we would get to the shirt-off phase. Maybe now we never would, because we'd both know what was under there, aside from the customary attractions.

"I need to show you something," I said to Jazza. "And I need you to be honest with me. Can you be honest with me?"

"Of course."

"No, I mean *actually* honest."

I stood up and lifted my shirt, pulling it up to just under my chest, revealing my abdomen. I had grown used to the scar. It had to be a shock to see it for the first time, all Frankensteiny with the hash marks across the cut line where the sutures were made.

"It looks bad," I said, poking at it to show her. "But it doesn't hurt anymore."

"It doesn't look . . . that bad. It's not that bad."

It was totally that bad. Her pained expression and wide eyes and massive lie told me that. It was time to stop talking about it.

"Actually," I said, lowering my shirt, "I've seen worse scars. I told you about the time my grandma got a questionable boob job in Baton Rouge a few years ago?"

"No?"

"She got the boob job because she had a coupon for it. *Twenty percent off.* She had a surgery coupon. She got her boobs on sale. Those scars were worse."

This was a partial lie. My grandma really did get her boob job with a 20 percent off coupon from the local paper. We were pretty horrified when we found out, but we found out pretty late, after the surgery was over and she'd been recovering for two weeks. I don't think there was any bad scarring, though. That was the part I was lying about.

"They definitely don't seem real," I went on. "They don't move. But they're real-ish. They're bigger, and they stick straight out. She calls them 'my new front porch' whenever she talks about them, which is a lot. She wears these low-cut tops and says, 'Just getting some sun on my new front porch.'"

That part was entirely true.

"What I think," she said, as she repositioned herself and straightened up, "is that you are very brave. And it looks fine. It's *not* bad. It's not. It's just—a line."

"But my bikini modeling career is over," I said. "Unless it's for pirate bikinis. They don't mind it if you have a bitchin' scar when you wear a pirate bikini. That would be amazing. A little skull and crossbones on each boob—"

Jazza held up a hand, possibly because I was saying "boob" too often.

"You don't have to make jokes," she said. "Have you been downstairs? To where it happened?"

"I skipped that," I said.

"Do you want to go now? You and me," Jazza said, offering her hand. "Together."

There was something about Jazza Benton that just made the world stable and right. She could rock a sensible sweater and mutter at you in German. I'd missed her face, with her big cheeks and small-animal-of-the-forest eyes.

I went downstairs with her.

The bathroom was at the end of the short hallway, just a few doors down from the common room. Even as we walked just a few feet in its direction, it was like we were in a different world, a world where I descended into somewhere quiet, where my fears lived. The door was new. I'd heard that the last door had been broken down when the police came in, ripped right off the wall. I pushed it open.

The light was on. The bathroom used to have an on-off switch, but it appeared that it would now be illuminated at all times.

There it was. Just a bathroom. The smashed window had been replaced, as had the shattered mirrors. There was a faint tang of fresh paint as well. The crack in the floor was still there, though an attempt had been made to fill it in with some kind of white substance. The spot where I'd been stabbed was over by the sinks. I went over and stood there, running my hand down the wall. I'd slumped here. I'd slid down. I remembered looking around this room and thinking that this was where I was going to die.

But I didn't.

I walked across the room, to the toilet stall where I'd seen—and accidentally blasted—the woman. I pushed the door open.

There was a toilet. Nothing more.

"Just a bathroom," I said.

"Just a bathroom," Jazza repeated.

I looked at the crack in the floor. It was a lot like my scar. The room and I had been broken, and we had a similarly shaped reminder of what had happened to us. And if the Ripper came back, which he wouldn't, I would blast him into a giant ball of white light and smoke. One brush of my hand, and that was all it would take. I was *empowered,* literally. That's what I had to remember. I was bigger and badder than any ghost that crossed my path. That hadn't occurred to me before. They needed to *fear* me. I'd never been fearsome before.

"Better?" she said.

"Yeah." I nodded, giving her the best smile I could manage under the circumstances. "I think so."

8

THAT EVENING, AFTER JAZZA HAD GONE OUT TO SOME KIND of German language immersion meeting at a pub, I prepared myself for my date. This mostly involved deciding which of my small selection of similar outfits to wear and putting my hair up and taking it down again.

When I was ready (hair up, wearing jeans), I spent fifteen minutes staring out the window, waiting to watch Jerome cross over from Aldshot. I didn't want to stand outside. It seemed much cooler to come sweeping down the stairs like Scarlett O'Hara in a sweater, with an "am ah late?" (I had noticed that I had one thing going in my favor—my English friends seemed to love it when I amped up the Southern thing. If anyone at home had heard me talking, they would have wondered why I was suddenly talking like someone who lived on a plantation and had servants weaving magnolias into her hair at that very moment. My English friends couldn't tell the difference between real South and cartoon South, and this, to me, was adorable.)

He appeared at six fifty-five, his curly head bobbing along, his scarf looped casually around his neck. I waited out the five minutes, even though I could see him right below.

"So I was thinking," he said, rocking back on his heels, "a meal, and . . . I don't know. We can go anywhere you like."

"Where do people go?"

"I have no idea. Do you want food? Are you hungry?"

"I'm always hungry," I said.

"What kind of food?"

"Whatever you'd like."

"I'd like whatever," he said. "Whatever you want to do."

"Are *you* hungry?"

"I'm hungry," he said.

Once we had established that we were both in the mood for food, it took five more minutes to establish that food should be Italian food, and another ten of looking at Jerome's phone for possible places to obtain said Italian food. The restaurant we'd decided to go to was near Spitalfields Market, which is pretty much where everyone goes on a Saturday night. Every pub was filled to capacity, and people spilled out into the streets. We dodged around a giggling and very drunk band of women wearing fascinators that looked like tiny top hats, except for one in a tiny bridal veil.

The place was very small, with about ten tables. Small restaurants, I realized, were scary. Small restaurants watch you. Small restaurants expect something of you. You have to be a better sort of person, and I wasn't sure if I was that person yet. They seated us like we were together, which we were. When I was asked if I wanted a glass of wine to start, I laughed out loud, and the guy just looked at me and wandered off. A small plate of bread appeared between us, and the waiter took away our wineglasses in a snatching motion that felt a little judgmental.

I'd been planning on ordering the cheapest or close-to-cheapest thing on the menu, which turned out to be spaghetti and meatballs. Jerome ordered risotto, which just sounded cooler. Mine sounded like food you get for children. Maybe I would get crayons as well.

"How is it so far?" he asked. "Being back?"

"It's good," I said.

"Yeah?"

"Yeah," I said. "Well, I haven't done any actual work yet, so I guess I'll see."

Though I'd talked to Jerome every day, I had never told him that I wasn't doing any work from school. We never discussed my work from school. It was like my work, or lack thereof, was my dirty little secret—as opposed to the mushy and sometimes vaguely graphic things we'd said to each other. It was my secret shame.

"What about you?" I asked.

"The Oxford and Cambridge UCAS was due back in October. I didn't apply. For Bristol and Durham, it's due in January, but . . . I think I'm going to take a year and try to run my own business, just to see what happens."

"Business?"

"Tours," he said. "I started giving Ripper tours when you were away. I didn't want to say, because . . . I mean . . . I didn't talk about you. There were just so many people around, all the time. And they wanted tours of the area, so . . ."

"It's okay," I said. And it was okay. Jerome had been obsessed with the Ripper from the start.

"What I was thinking," he said, "was that I could stay in London for my gap year and do walking tours and freelance work. My uncle has a spare room in his house in Islington he'll let me stay in. I could make all the money I need to pay the university fees. It's not the most exciting gap year, but it will keep me from being destitute. What about you?"

"I guess . . . I go home, and . . ."

At this point, I was interrupted by the arrival of a plate that contained very little spaghetti and three suggestively large meatballs.

College applications. I was supposed to start collecting those. I was supposed to have taken the SAT at a remote testing center in November. I was supposed to start asking for recommendation letters. A lot of things hadn't happened. The gaping hole called "my future" gaped a bit more.

Maybe I would go home and just repeat school. Maybe I would work at the grocery store for Miss Gina and save up money for a year, like Jerome was doing. Maybe I'd be assimilated back into the crazy quilt that was Bénouville, Louisiana, and never, ever, ever leave again. It was, after all, a swamp. And swamps suck people in.

"I'm freestyling it a little right now," I said, poking at my spaghetti.

The waiter futzed around us, moving our bread basket and hovering pointlessly, demanding updates on our enjoyment levels while we had mouthfuls of food. If dates were like this, then dates were kind of weird. I felt like every move I made was being watched. I think Jerome felt equally uncomfortable, so we skipped dessert, paid up, and decided to take a walk around the market. Then we looped through the crowded streets, hand in hand. Jerome was talking about some things going on in his building, and it was nice just to listen for a change.

We took the long way back to school, walking down Bishopsgate, through the throngs of people coming in and out of Liverpool Street station. We turned onto Artillery Lane, which is a very narrow, very Dickensian street running along the Wexford campus. There was no one around, and this was about as close as we could get to Wexford without actually being back on the grounds. We both came to a stop by a little recessed spot next to one of the buildings, a stump of an alley off of the alley where they kept the trash bins. A sub-alley used for trash is also a fine spot to kiss. I mean, people talk about the top of the Eiffel Tower and tropical beaches at sunset—but those places sound demanding, like they expect something from you. That's just too much backdrop. A dark London trash alley is real privacy, and it doesn't judge you. It's probably just glad that you're there to kiss, because those alleys probably see far more unpleasant things on a nightly basis. The small pile of empty vodka bottles and discarded T-shirt and single sneaker in the darkest corner spoke to that.

I leaned up against the wall, feeling the cold of the bricks against the back of my neck. Jerome brushed my hair back from my face, because the wind had kicked up a bit and blown a few strands into my mouth. (Oh, the ongoing love affair between hair and mouths. Hair always goes for the mouth. The mouth opens, and hair says, "I'm going in! I'm going in!" like a manic cave diver.)

"Is this all right?" he asked. He was using that very low, somewhat husky universal kissing voice.

"Huh?" I said, because I am sexy.

"This," he said. "Are you . . . all right?"

"Oh. Yeah. No. Yes, I mean, fine. I'm fine. We can do this."

Now it was awkward. Never get stabbed—it makes *everything* awkward.

He leaned in slowly, and I found myself caught somewhere between two very different emotions. One was the gushy warmth and general excitement, the tingling. And the other was the bald awareness that kissing is kind of weird. The half closing of the eyes. The O shape of the mouth. Seeing that little bit of the inside of the lips when someone purses in preparation for the kiss.

He stopped just short of my face.

"This isn't all right," he said.

"It is," I said. "It is. Come here."

I pulled him forward and pressed his mouth to mine. I think he liked the forcefulness of it—although maybe I was a bit too forceful, because I felt the delicate clink of tooth on tooth. After a moment or two, I started to relax and closed my eyes fully, sliding my hand up into his hair, feeling the general warmth of the whole thing. It was all going well until a couple of guys from Jerome's building passed by and started to snicker, and then one of them interrupted to say his door handle was broken.

"I suppose we should get back," he said.

On the way to Wexford, we passed the local pub, the Royal Gunpowder. The sidewalk surrounding the pub was covered in flowers and candles stuck into liquor bottles.

"What's all that?" I said.

"Oh. Yeah. That happened after you left."

"What happened?"

"One of the staff murdered the owner," he said.

"There was a murder next to Wexford?"

"It's not connected. The guy who did it had a drug problem. The press made a big deal about it because of the Ripper stuff and the timing, but it was just one of those things."

"Just one of those things" is probably not the best way to describe a murder, but I knew where he was coming from and what he was trying to do. A murder around the corner was freaky and unwelcome. Julia had mentioned that I might hear about other violent things on the news and imagine connections or have unpleasant memories. But I understood—these things do happen. They're not good, but they're also not all connected. I was calm about it.

I think. I may have walked away kind of quickly, but aside from that, I was calm about it.

We could have stayed out a bit longer; it wasn't curfew yet. But the night felt over. Going to the restaurant and talking—that had been exhausting. The kiss had been good while it lasted, but it had taken a bit of effort to get it going. And we'd concluded the night by walking past a murder scene. It was jimjam time for Rory.

We had a quick kiss in front of Hawthorne—not a full-on one, but enough to catch the attention of anyone around. It was a statement kiss. Then I let myself back in and took the creaking steps back upstairs. Jazza was still out making Teutonic merriment, so I had the room to myself for a little bit. I put on my pajamas and tucked myself into bed.

Why had tonight been so *weird*?

I had a very uncomfortable thought—I wasn't actually sure *why* I liked Jerome, aside from the fact that he liked me. And he was English. And he was cute. Mostly cute? What was "cute"?

His head was kind of large.

Where did that thought even *come* from? By what standard was I supposed to judge? His head was *fine.* Did looks matter, anyway? I liked making out with him. I liked that we were together, that people saw us together. I liked the general feeling of it all.

Maybe that's what relationships were.

I was overthinking this. I hadn't accomplished much in my time with Julia, but she had told me that I might react weirdly in "emotionally and physically intimate situations." Things might feel weird at first. All things considered, I was doing well. (Also, I had clearly been paying a lot of attention to what Julia said. She had gotten in my head.)

I got out of bed and trundled next door. Gaenor and Angela were around. Gaenor and Angela were easily the two loudest people on the hall, possibly the building. Possibly the world. They never minded me coming into their room and shooting the breeze for a while. That's how I would dispel the creeping darkness—be normal.

Just be normal. That's all I had to do.

9

When I woke up on Sunday, Jazza was gone. This was because I woke up at noon.

At home, I'd been getting up at noon on the weekends, but I'd never done that at Wexford. Nobody did, unless they were sick. There was something unspeakably decadent about it. I felt wanton, like I should stroll around Wexford in the creepy silky-polyester robe my grandmother had bought me for my birthday. My grandmother basically wears whatever the Disney star of the moment is wearing, and she tends to buy me matching items. These things include the aforementioned silky robes, matching pajama sets of shorty-shorts and tank tops, see-through lace body suits, and fishnets. I hadn't brought that robe to Wexford, because I didn't think the good people of England really needed to see the poly-silk outline of my thighs as I shuffled along in the morning.

Also, I realized I was alone yet again. Before—the great

before, which seemed so long ago and so very different from the now—I never felt like I had any privacy. There was always someone else in the room. Often Jazza, and definitely Boo, who shadowed me everywhere I went. But now Jazza was gone a lot. It was the week before exams, after all, and her calendar was full of study groups and rehearsals. Room 27 was all mine. It was big and lonely and cold. I put on my fleece, which served as my bathrobe, my jacket, and my safety blanket.

As I walked down the hall, I noticed how quiet it was. A few people had their doors cracked open, and when I peered inside, I saw them hard at work, bent over computers and books. I was the only one swanning down the hall, freshly awake. I showered and dressed and tried to slide into the rhythm everyone else had set. I left the door open just a crack and settled in at my desk. (The slightly open door was to invite visitors, and also I felt I was more likely to work if everyone could see me.)

And I did work. I did some reading. I did a little French. I did a few problem sets.

I paused when I noticed it had gotten darker—not dark, but there was a dim quality to the daylight, a low fade made worse by the overcast sky. Three in the afternoon, and already it seemed like dusk. I reviewed what I had accomplished, thumbing through pages read and counting up assignments completed. I had done reasonably well, better than anything I had done in previous weeks, but it wasn't even in spitting distance of enough.

It dawned on me, perfectly and clearly, that I was going to fail everything. I'd known this. I'd even said it out loud. But I'd never really breathed that fact in. Smelled it. Tasted it.

This was failure. Doing all you could and yet knowing that it just wasn't going to cut it.

I shut my door to panic alone.

Why was I here? They'd brought me back, and now what was I supposed to do? I felt like I was faking all of this, like I was playing the part of a student. I had the costume and the props, but I didn't really belong here. I'd pinned notes on the stupid corkboard backing of my desk, and I'd highlighted things . . . But it was all so *meaningless*.

For about an hour, I had an overwhelming urge to grab my bag, stuff in a few things, and take the next train to Bristol. I could be back on my parents' couch that night if I got moving. I could admit that I wasn't ready for this, that the semester was a wash. My parents would be thrilled, I was sure. Not about the semester being a wash—but certainly about having me back where they could keep me safe and sound. It would be so easy to do. The very idea made me warm inside. It was okay to give up. I'd been brave. Everyone would say so.

And yet . . . even as I opened a dresser drawer and figured out which things I would take with me in this hypothetical scenario, I remembered the problem.

There would still be ghosts.

I would still have a future.

I would still go back to school *eventually*. You can't curl up on the sofa and deny life forever. Life is always going to be a series of ouch-making moments, and the question was, was I going to go all fetal position, or was I going to woman up? I went into fetal position on the bed to think about this. Fetal position turned out to be very comfortable.

Someone had to help me.

I slithered to the end of the bed and stretched my arm as far as I could to reach around in the top drawer of my desk and find that business card. Jane Quaint. The therapist who had changed Charlotte into the shiny New Charlotte. The one who made her unafraid of school and life. I flicked the card with my nail a few times and rubbed the edge under my chin. I'd had a therapist, and that had been a pointless exercise. A time-suck. A total pain in the ass. But this woman had done some kind of magic with Charlotte, and now Charlotte was fully functional. Maybe she could make me fully functional.

The gloom accumulated outside. God. So dark. So early. My books, so thick. My confusion, so total.

It couldn't hurt to call.

I would call.

Now. I would call now.

English phones have a double ring that I still found strange and charming, kind of like the chirping croak of a little frog. The call was on its third ring-ring and I was just about to hang up when a surprisingly deep yet clearly female voice answered.

"Hi," I said. "My name is Rory, and—"

"From Wexford?" said the woman.

"Oh. Yeah."

"I know who you are, dear. A friend of Charlotte's, yes?"

That might have been stretching things a bit, but I wasn't going to split hairs.

"Right," I said.

"Well, I'm very glad you've called. I was hoping you would."

"You were?"

"It was no small thing you went through," she said. "And from the tone in your voice, it sounds like you aren't having the best day."

I cleared my throat. "No," I said. "I guess not."

"Why don't you pop round?"

"What, now?"

"Why not?" she said. "It's a quiet Sunday around here. Why don't you pop round, and we'll have a nice chat?"

I could see, even from this brief exchange, what Charlotte was talking about. Julia was nice, but she was clinical. When you spoke to her, she was clear and firm. You didn't "pop round" to Julia's. You had an exact time, to the minute. This Jane sounded more like a friend. She gave me an address in Chelsea, and when I asked her what Tube stop that was, she was dismissive.

"Oh, just get in a taxi, dear. I'll pay for it when it arrives."

"What . . . really?"

"Really. Just come over now. I have some time."

I regretted making the call already. I had agreed to see this strange woman, and now I really had to go. She was even paying for my ride, which was just . . . incredibly odd. But health stuff was different in England. Well, I'd done it. I'd called, and now I had to go see this woman. I told myself that doing something was better than having this dithering breakdown.

While I was in the cab, winding across London, it began to pour rain. Chelsea was on the west side of the city, far, far from Wexford. And London is a very sinuous place. I don't think there is a straight line in the entire metropolitan area. Water ran down the cab windows, so much that I couldn't even see where we were. I just caught the glint of signs and the red of buses. By the time the cab stopped, the downpour was so fierce, I wasn't sure how I was going to make it from the curb to the house. This is why English people do not leave home without umbrellas. I was an idiot.

The cab ride came to thirty-six pounds. That was an incredible amount of money to have to pay for a ride across town, and I felt a twang of panic. I didn't have that much on me. I'd gotten in this cab on the word of some person on the other end of a phone. I looked at the house, wondering what happened now. The house that was set back from the road and gently guarded by a brick wall with a black iron gate. Through this gate came a woman carrying an industrial-sized umbrella. I presumed this was Jane, as she went right to the front window of the car. As she spoke to the driver and gave him the fare, I heard her voice. This was Jane.

Jane Quaint looked like she was somewhere around sixty. Her hair was a furious orange-red, which stood out in stark contrast to her very pale, very delicate skin. The color couldn't have been natural—that kind of pulsating orange rarely exists outside of fruit and tropical birds. She had on an outfit that consisted of many wraps and folds and layers of fine gray wool that looped around and around from about five different directions. I couldn't tell if it was a shawl or a sweater or a dress. It bagged down to the knees, where it seemed to turn into pants. The whole thing was bound together at her right shoulder by a long silver pin in the shape of a twisted arrow.

I opened the door carefully as Jane reached over, making room for me under her umbrella.

"*Wretched* day," she said. "Come inside. Let's get ourselves out of this."

The gate surrounded a small square of brick-paved ground, with a few small potted trees. The house was certainly large by London standards—three stories high, three windows across. It was completely detached, an impressive pile of bricks with a porticoed entryway.

Jane set her umbrella in a stand in the large entry hallway, which was very dark. It was papered in a rich black wallpaper with a recurring fan pattern in metallic gold. All the decorations were generally dark, lots of black with gold accents. I fixed my eye on a life-sized porcelain leopard in the corner, colored silver and black.

"I'm still very fond of the tastes of my youth," she explained. "I was a bit of a rock-and-roller back then. After that phase was over, I went into psychology. But I kept the decor. I find if you keep things, they tend to come back into style eventually."

"I like it," I said.

"That's very kind. One friend of mine describes it as looking like a Victorian brothel on Mars. I've always found that description rather pleasing. Do come through to the kitchen. I think we need a cup of tea."

The house was very warm, which I appreciated. And the kitchen was warmer still, and huge. This room was not black. Unlike the sharply Deco feel of the hall, this was a cheerful green, with a big farm table and lots of plates on display. Jane busied herself with the kettle, and I sat on a stool and tried to figure out how to deal with the most awkward part of this entire affair. I decided I just had to ask.

"Charlotte said, about paying you—"

"I don't charge," she said, cutting me off. "I'm a woman of

independent means, and I do this because it's my calling. If you can afford to provide a service to society, you should do so. That's what I think. Now. Tea or coffee?"

"Coffee?"

"Right, then. Oh, and here . . ."

She indicated the counter by the window, on which there were several plastic containers of what looked like baked goods. Many, many baked goods.

"One of my clients is a baker," she said. "I don't accept money, but some people bring things, little presents. She always makes sure I'm fully supplied with baked goods. I hope you're not one of these girls who doesn't eat."

"Oh, I eat."

"I'm glad to hear it. There's a reason they call it comfort food. I'm not saying you should eat these sorts of things all the time, but food does provide a bit of comfort. And if you're having a bad day, a brownie might be just what you need. Give yourself a little kindness and perk up the old blood sugar. Here you go."

She presented me with a brownie on a beautiful little china plate in a rose and white willow pattern.

"Have a taste of that," she said. "Angela's quite good. She uses all kinds of exotic things in her baking, curry powder, tea, chilies, herbs. Things you'd never think should go into baked goods. She's frightfully clever with that sort of thing. I think she's going to be on a baking show on television . . . must remember to look out for that."

She filled a tray with coffee- and tea-making equipment—proper loose tea for herself, and a fancy single-serve French press for me.

"All right," she said, picking up the tray. "Come this way. And could you get the door?"

She led me through a set of double doors. Unlike the all-black room, this room was white and silver, absolutely stark. There was a fuzzy white rug, white leather chairs, a white sofa. The walls here were bare except for a few diplomas. I could make out the names of Oxford University and King's College. At one end of the rug was a gleaming silver ball chair, like a big egg that you could climb inside. A cocoon. A cocoon was precisely what I wanted right now.

"Go ahead," she said, nodding to the chair. "People love sitting in it."

She took a seat on the sofa and poured herself a cup of tea.

"Right, then," she said. "I'll tell you what I know about you, and you can tell me the rest. I know your name is Aurora, or Rory, and I know you were stalked and stabbed by the Ripper."

"That's me," I said.

"And I imagine people have been asking you a lot about how that makes you feel. I can guess at that—I think it makes you feel not good. But looking at you, you seem to be someone who's gotten on with things."

"I do?"

"Well, you returned to your school, where I've heard—in the most conversational terms—that you seem to be getting on very well with things. Charlotte thinks very highly of you."

"She does?"

"Absolutely."

I took another big bite of the brownie.

"The thing is," I said, "I've had therapy before, and I didn't really . . . I don't really like talking about the attack."

"Understandable. But I'm sure you know that talking about it is often the way of dealing with it and processing it?"

"I know that. But . . . I can't."

Julia would have latched on to that and dug in, mining her way into my soul. But Jane shrugged, took off her shoes, and tucked her feet under her on the sofa.

"Some people want to talk about what happened to them, to break it down bit by bit. Other people do not. Why don't we just talk about how things have been going since your return? We can talk about whatever you like. Why did you ring today?"

"I was doing homework and studying," I said. "And I realized I was dead."

"Dead might be overstating the case."

"Not really," I said.

"Why don't you tell me about it?"

So, I did. I told her about school and having all my assignments in Bristol but never looking at them. I told her how I had piled my books up and how I had kind of felt nothing about them for a while, and then all of a sudden, I felt everything about them. I told her my fears of falling behind and generally not being a part of Wexford. And if I fell behind at school, I would have no place in the world, and how my future seemed so blurry to me right now, like I was driving in heavy rain. I might be on the right path, but more likely I was heading for a wall or into a rushing river.

I told her I was homesick, but had no desire to go home. I told her I was excited about having a boyfriend, but sometimes I didn't even know why I liked him.

God, I talked a lot. Even for me, I talked a lot. I saw what Charlotte meant by feeling better around Jane—you just felt like you could say things around her. And she wasn't checking a clock. She just listened. She didn't try to get me on any track or on any subject. She only stopped me when I said, "I wish I was normal."

"Let me say this . . ." Jane leaned forward and adjusted her long-empty tea cup. "There is no normal. I've never met a normal person. The concept is flawed. It implies that there is only one way people are supposed to *be,* and that can't possibly be true. Human experience is far too varied."

"But I've met normal people," I said. "I swear I have."

"You've met people who get on well with life, and some of the people who get on with life with the most skill are far from what most people would call *normal.* So I never worry about normal. I *do* find that there are generally two types of people, though—there are people who have seen death up close and people who have not. People who survive, people like us—"

"Like us?"

"Oh, yes." She nodded. "I'm like you. I've gotten close to death as well. That's why I'm here. That's why I do what I do. Because I *know.*"

She settled herself back in the sofa a bit and adjusted the folds of her complicated outfit.

"Where I grew up, in Yorkshire, there was a man who lived down the road from us who ran a television repair shop. I never liked him. I always felt like he was looking at me strangely when I walked past. I never actually thought there was something wrong with him, just that I didn't like the feeling I got when he looked at me. One night, around this time of year, it was late, and I was walking back from a friend's house. I took a shortcut across a bit of field. That sort of thing never worried me.

Nothing bad happened in our village. Then I realized I wasn't alone. He was walking behind me. I asked him what he was doing. He said he'd seen me and followed because he wanted to make sure I got home safely. And I think I knew then. I think I knew that if someone follows you at a few paces, you're in trouble. It's our animal instinct. When I heard him speed up, I ran. There were woods on the edge of the field, and I went for those. He overtook me.

"I'll tell you, he didn't expect me to fight like I did. There was a thick bit of downed tree branch on the ground, and I picked it up and gave him a right old thumping. I'll never forget it, because the moon was so bright that night, and I was beating a man with a tree branch, using a strength I didn't even know I had. I almost had him, too. But he managed to get the branch away from me. I ran and started screaming. The other houses were fairly far, but I think my scream must have carried over those fields. It certainly gave the sheep a start."

Time was moving very strangely. My absorption in her story was total. It was like I was there. I knew what it was like to run across that field in the moonlight.

"Oh, he hit me good," she said. "Knocked me right on the back of the head. I was quite dazed. I think he was in a panic by then, because he was swearing and panting for breath. He dragged me across the field, through the mud and the dung, then he gave me another good whack and rolled me into the small pond there, the one the animals drank from. It was only a few feet deep, but that was deep enough. I was unconscious for a few moments, I think, but some part of me said, 'Stay awake.' And I did. I fought, and I stayed awake. I was a good swimmer, and I could do a dead man's float, so that's what I did. I made him think I was dead. He ran off in terror, and I pulled myself out of that water and fell on the grass, and I looked up at the sky . . . and everything was different. After that, I felt like I had two lives. There was the me I had been before the attack, the one people knew and wanted to relate to. The one people wanted to comfort and fix. And there was another me, a hidden me that no one ever saw. There was a me who had tasted death. That me knew things other people didn't know. Do you know this feeling?"

I could only nod. There was a gentle throbbing in my mind—I needed to get back. It was getting late.

"I should really go," I said. "I . . . I feel better now."

"I'm glad," she said.

Jane walked me to the door. The rain had slowed to a light drizzle, and the sky was dark and bright. The streetlights glimmered and refracted the light. London was beautiful, it really was. And it smelled so clean after the rain.

"I'd like to speak again," she said. "I have a policy. Once I've taken someone on as a client, I make myself available. You can always come here if you're having a bad day."

"Thanks," I said.

"I mean it. I hope to see you again. Take a cab back."

She put two twenty-pound notes in my hand.

"I can't," I said. "You don't have to."

"I know I don't have to, Rory. I want to." She put her hand on my shoulder. "Let me tell you one more thing. After the night of my attack, I was never the same, but in a good way. I left home. I came to London. I did the things I dreamed of doing. I met rock stars. I met wonderful people. I've had a wonderful life. And all because on that night, in that field, I saw something very powerful. I *felt* something very powerful. I survived. And so did you. What most people will never tell you, or might never understand, is that what happened to us can have a very positive effect. It can make us strong."

A strange thing happened as I walked away from Jane's house—I was finally thinking *clearly*. I could see what Charlotte meant. Jane knew how to fix people. Now that I'd talked through some of my issues, I'd blown the dust and garbage out of my brain and I could think for once. I could smell the rain, heavy with iron. The cold woke me, but it didn't sting. My breath puffed out in front of me in a great white plume, and I laughed. It was like I was breathing ghosts. I wasn't in the land of long highways and big box stores and humid, endless summers. I was in London, a city of stone and rain and magic. I understood, for instance, why they liked red so much. The red buses, telephone booths, and postboxes were a violent shock against the grays of the sky and stone. Red was blood and beating hearts.

And I was strong.

10

THE NEXT MORNING WAS THE WETTEST I HAD EVER SEEN IN my life, and I've been through a few hurricanes. I don't know if there is actually more rain here in England, or if it was just that the rain seemed to be so deliberately annoying. Every drop hit the window with a peevish "Am I bothering you? Does this make you cold and wet? Oh, *sorry.*" The square was now a mud pool, and the cobblestones were slick, so I almost killed myself about six times just getting to class.

My first class was further maths. Further maths had gone further into some incomprehensible zone of mathyness. From there, French, where I discovered that my class had started reading a novel. A *novel.* In French. Not only hadn't I started the novel—I didn't have the novel. So I sat there while everyone else went through a book I didn't own. Gaenor sat next to me and shared her copy, but this wasn't much help. I hadn't read the story so far, and I couldn't translate fast enough without a dictionary. I sometimes drift a bit in class on the best of days, but today I was tired, it was raining, and people were reading something I didn't understand. The words oozed together on the page, and the rhythm of the rain beat in my head. The room was so warm . . .

I woke when Gaenor nudged her elbow into my side. She actually nailed me right in scar territory, and I think she realized that, because she clapped a hand over her mouth. It was fine—it didn't hurt me. Our teacher was looking directly at us. She had to have seen. I rubbed at my mouth and tried to act like that had never happened. Maybe my eyes had never closed.

Who was I kidding? I'd been *out.*

"Feeling all right?" Madame Loos asked at the end of class.

"I had to . . . um, painkiller," I said. "I had to take one. I'm sorry."

I was such a liar. It was disturbing how quickly it came. But *painkiller* was the magic word. I got a terse nod, and nothing more was said. No one was going to ask stabby girl about her painkillers.

Then I went to English literature and had the same experience all over again. I was so far behind in all the reading, I couldn't get any of the references. I thumbed through the anthology that was our main textbook and counted how many pages I seemed to be behind. It looked to be about 150 pages. There was only one solution: I would have to read. I would have to read and read and read until my eyes went dry. Because reading essays and poetry written in 1770 is not quite the same as blowing your way through a novel written in the last few years. It requires more concentration, more stopping to figure out what they're talking about.

So I nervously doodled a picture of a horse farting a rainbow and tried to look deep in thought. I was going to have to start drinking a lot more coffee. All day, every day.

What was strange, though, was that I really *did* feel better about my general situation. Jane had done something. The facts had not changed, but my feelings toward them were more positive. So I was tired and behind. Big deal. I had survived. I was getting on with things. I would take my laptop and drink coffee and embed things into my brain. Coffee was supposed to make you smart. And I had the afternoon to work. You could do a lot in an afternoon if you put your mind to it.

I walked down Artillery Lane on my way to get the coffee. I paused by the Royal Gunpowder and looked at the various tributes that had been left to the dead man. There were bottles, but there were also notes and some dead and dying flowers mixed in with a few fresh ones. Just inside the window, facing out to the street, was a photograph of a man. He looked middle-aged, big and friendly, with a very red face. There was an unlit votive candle next to the picture. On the brick wall, just under the window, someone had written in what looked like black Sharpie JUSTICE FOR CHARLIE.

The rain picked up a bit, and I hurried along so my computer wouldn't get wet. It was in my bag, and I was under an umbrella, but I always get paranoid about things like that. Once I was safely in the coffee shop with a large cup in front of me, I logged on to their Wi-Fi and decided to look up some articles about what happened at the Royal Gunpowder. There were plenty of these to choose from.

England has some pretty seedy newspapers, and there were several headlines like this:

PUB OWNER PAYS PRICE FOR CHARITY

Charles Strong knew about the dangers of drink. A recovered alcoholic, fifteen years sober, he managed to maintain his pub without touching a drop of his wares. "He believed that the pub was the centre of the community," says daughter-in-law Deborah Strong. "It didn't matter that he didn't drink. He was there for the customers. He was there for the people."

But Charles never forgot what it was like to recover from an addiction. He made it a policy to hire people in recovery, to give them a chance to get back into the working world. He was proud of his employees, many of whom went on to other jobs. But it may have been Charles's altruistic nature that caused his death. On the morning of 11 November, Charles was beaten to death with a hammer by his employee, Sam Worth, a former drug addict with a history of violence. Worth called the police and led them to his employer's body. Worth claimed innocence at the scene but, in the face of overwhelming evidence, changed his plea to guilty. He has offered no explanation for his actions. No motive has been determined, but the suspicion is that it was an argument about money.

All of this has come as a shock to an area of East London still reeling from the Ripper murders. Only two days before the death of Charles Strong, a student at the Wexford School was attacked on school property, just one street away from the Royal Gunpowder. The Metropolitan Police have increased their presence in the area. A Met spokeswoman offered this comment: "While these two unfortunate events are unconnected . . ."

The BBC offered something a little less sensational in tone.

NO MOTIVE IN PUB SLAYING

> Police are still searching for a motive in the murder of Charles Strong, 56, owner of the Royal Gunpowder public house. Strong was murdered on 11 November by one of his employees, bartender Samuel Worth, 32, of Bethnal Green. Worth had previously been convicted for GBH and possession of narcotics, but had been clean and sober for over a year. There was no known argument between the two men, and police have found no evidence of a criminal motive in the attack.
>
> Worth is currently under observation at the Royal Bethlehem Hospital following a suicide attempt. Worth initially denied any role in the murder, but changed his plea in custody. He is now being evaluated to determine whether or not he is fit to stand trial . . .

When Jerome had explained it, it sounded much more straightforward: a man had killed his boss. These articles painted a slightly different story. A man killed his boss *with a hammer* for no apparent reason. Maybe I was a little paranoid, but I knew things now—I knew, for instance, that an entirely fake story had been built around the Ripper to explain the whole thing away. And sure, maybe this guy was just unstable. But . . . *two days* after the Ripper and just around the corner from Wexford? What were the chances? London was a big and bustling place, but people generally didn't go around murdering each other at rates like this.

I took Artillery Lane on the way back, stopping in front of

the pub. I walked around the two exposed edges of the building. The pub was closed for business and dark inside. I peered in the windows, but there was nothing other than tables and chairs and a bar all waiting in the dark. Such an ordinary place, too. Table tents advertising a drink special, a trivia machine in the corner, quietly waiting for a player.

As I made my way back around to look at the photograph in the window, something on the ground caught my eye. I knelt down and pushed some of the flowers and bottles away, revealing the edge of the building and the sidewalk.

A hairline crack ran across the sidewalk and butted into the side of the building. The crack was narrow near the street and widened as it hit the wall. I positioned myself against the wall and turned in the direction it pointed, just across the street, slightly to the right. There was another building in the way, but there was no mistaking it.

The crack pointed right toward Hawthorne.

A crack in the sidewalk is nothing to get excited about. London is full of cracks. It's got a lot of sidewalk. It's old. But that creepy old rhyme kept running through my head, "Step on a crack, break your mother's back . . ." (Who even thought of that? Why would stepping on a crack break anyone's back? Why specifically your mom's? Was it an early, failed attempt at a "your mom" joke?)

But there was a crack in the sidewalk, and there was a crack in the bathroom floor.

I thought about it all night. I zoned throughout all of dinner, excusing myself early to walk back around the corner to the Royal Gunpowder afterward. It was too dark to see the crack now, but a sign had appeared in the window saying **REOPENING TOMORROW LUNCHTIME**.

I got my phone out of my pocket. My finger hovered over Stephen's number, which was now safely back in my phone after he had texted me. I was just about to press the button to call, when my brain played out the conversation as it was likely to go. "I just want you to know? There's a crack? In the sidewalk?" After the awkward silence, he would probably say something like, "I see. Well, thank you for informing me."

Yes, the crack in the bathroom floor had appeared the night of the explosion, because there had been an explosion. Or a power surge. Whatever it was, it had broken glass. Sure, it takes a bit more force than that to crack a tile floor, but . . . in any case, the crack in the sidewalk had probably been there already. I was making connections where there were none, and to what end? So what if there was a crack?

If I called Stephen with this, I would look like an idiot. And that was unacceptable.

I put the phone away.

I may have mentioned that when I get an idea in my head, I sometimes can't let it go.

I do try. If it really seems to be pointless or bad for me, I try to shake it loose—but these ideas, they cling. It's like I'm shackled to them with an iron chain. They rattle along behind me, dragging against the ground, always reminding me of their presence. The crack, the crack, the crack. Step on a crack, break your mother's back.

It haunted me all through Wednesday, distracting me in class (not that difficult, to be fair). I considered going over to the library to talk to Alistair about it, but then I remembered how I'd almost killed him the last time I was there, purely by accident. Maybe it was best to avoid him until I got this new little trick of mine under some kind of control.

Why was I so hesitant to call Stephen? Who cared if he thought it was dumb?

I sat at my desk in my room that afternoon, puzzling this over until dinner, accomplishing nothing. It occurred to me only right before it was time to go to the refractory that I didn't have to tell Stephen, but Callum and Boo had also put their numbers into my phone.

Callum would like to go out, do a little investigating. Callum would come out in a second. He wouldn't even ask why. Why did I always think Stephen had to be called?

So I texted him.

Want to come out and play tonight?

I heard nothing back, even though I stared at my phone for fifteen minutes. I went back to my room and sat at my desk and tried to do some more problem sets for maths, but I kept checking and checking. Dinner came, and there was still no answer. I found it hard to engage in conversation. It didn't help that much of the conversation around me was about exams, and I did not want to talk about exams. They started this time next week, and everyone was beginning to lose it a little. My normally cool and in-control friends were fraying around the edges. People were starting to look sleepless and get snappy. Doors slammed with regularity. And here, at dinner, people were talking, but there was a moodiness. Some people ate three helpings, while others could barely eat at all. Some people studied as they ate.

I just ate. And waited. My phone buzzed right as I was getting up for dessert.

Was underground, couldn't reply. Does that mean what I think it means? I'm not too far from you. Liverpool Street? How about 7:15?

That was only twenty minutes from now. I typed a quick OK and put my phone away.

11

I'M NOT GOING TO LIE," CALLUM SAID. "I AM VERY, VERY HAPPY right now."

I met Callum just inside the station. Making my escape from dinner and explaining where I was going—that had required a little bit of fast thinking. I'd said I needed to go to Boots, and Jazza said she would come with me, so then I had to say that I was going to call my parents on the way and have a long talk. And I did give my parents a *very* quick call as I ran over, just to make myself a little less of a liar.

"I have a whole list of you-know-whats that need dealing with," Callum said. "Let's go make boom booms."

"Okay," I said, holding up my hands. "But first there's something I have to show you."

I led Callum back down Artillery Lane to the Royal Gunpowder.

"Did you hear about the man who was murdered here?" I asked.

"Oh, yeah. This was big news. The hammer murder. Very nasty."

"Just a few days after the Ripper attacked me. It's so close to my building." I pointed in the direction of Hawthorne. "I mean, that's, like, yards. Or something. Or a few hundred feet. It's not far. And it happened just two days after the Ripper. And there's a crack. Look!"

I had to explain my crack theory. Callum listened, putting his hands in the pockets of his jacket and rocking back on his heels a bit.

"Trust me," he said, "I'd be thrilled if that was one for us. But that's just a straight-up murder. A man killed his boss. He confessed."

"But the crack—"

"This is London," he said. "We have a lot of cracks in a lot of pavements."

"But there is also a crack in the floor of the bathroom. And this crack . . . Look, it looks kind of like it's coming from the direction of Hawthorne."

"Is it a new crack?"

"I have no idea," I said. "But isn't it weird?"

"If the guy hadn't confessed, then maybe?" Callum said apologetically. "But he did. They know he did it. He had blood all over him. He'd done this kind of thing before. We can go in and look, if you want."

"It opens for business tomorrow. But maybe we could *get* in?"

"That's breaking and entering," he said. "I like where you're going with this, but I really think maybe this isn't one to worry about."

"But don't you think . . ."

"Look," he said, not unkindly, "when you first get your sight, it's hard to understand it, yeah? Like I got mine after getting a bad shock with a live wire in a puddle, and I was terrified of electricity and puddles . . . puddles. Do you know how hard it is to walk around and be scared of puddles?"

Callum didn't look like someone who would be scared of anything. Maybe it's a bad assumption to think that just because people have broad shoulders and big muscular arms that they aren't afraid of things.

"The Ripper stuff, it was really bad. And you went through a lot, so . . . I'm just saying. You can make yourself crazy thinking that everything has a meaning, or that it could happen again. Like, I knew I wasn't going to get electrocuted again, but it took over a year before I wasn't terrified of everything . . . like using my phone if it started to rain. I thought all water, all electricity wanted to kill me."

I could see what he was saying. I could make myself sick thinking that all these things had significance.

"I'm not saying it's not weird that someone was killed here," he went on, "but people were tense, yeah? The Ripper scared people. And this guy who killed his boss was on all kinds of drugs. But they know he did it, so don't let it scare you. We can do some real work, yeah? I got a whole list of things I want to deal with, so let's go do it."

Since I had asked Callum to come out with me, it only seemed fair that I follow through with it and go with him to where he wanted to go. And the first ghost he wanted me to see was apparently right there at Liverpool Street.

"There's been one here for a few weeks," he said as we

headed down on the escalator. "I've been dying to get rid of this one."

Callum scanned the platform, which was packed with people all the way to the wall. It was still London rush hour.

"Next train in three minutes. You'll see him then."

Sure enough, the train came in. People poured off, and more people tried to cram on as the others came off, and then the platform was clear for a few moments. Except for one guy. One guy who wore only a dirty sheet. He was thin and bearded and laughing. And he was doing some kind of dance, a hopping sideways dance. He leaned into the opening of the door and shouted something inside. It wasn't English. I'm not sure it was any language. It sounded like *loopgallooparg.*

The doors bounced back open. He laughed harder and did it again.

"He's an idiot," Callum explained. "And doesn't seem to understand anything I say. Doesn't like it when I do this."

Callum slapped the ghost's head. He wasn't quite solid, not like Jo or Alistair, but he did flinch and hop away a few feet. The doors closed, and the train glided away.

"So I do that," he said. "I slap ghosts in the head. That's what I'm reduced to."

He looked at me expectantly. I looked at the strange, hopping man.

"Is he really doing anything wrong?" I asked.

"Holding up the trains causes huge chaos."

"But I mean, *wrong* wrong. Like, *really* wrong."

"Train chaos isn't wrong enough?"

The platform had already started filling again, so we had to lower our voices.

"Too many people," I said, looking around. "I can't do it with so many people. I get sick. I throw up."

"Sure," Callum said. "All right. Well, there are some others I know of in some less public places. I just really wanted to take care of this one. But that's all right. Another day. Let's take a ride."

So we got on the train. I looked out into the darkness. Through the Tube windows, I could just about see the walls of the tunnels mixed in with our reflections. The Tube rocked me gently back and forth.

"Been thinking," Callum said. "I was saying to Stephen that you should, you know, be one of us. Properly one of us."

From the way he said it, I think he was trying to sound casual on purpose, like this was just a little something he wanted to slip into the conversation. But, of course, there was nothing casual about that statement.

"What did he say?" I asked.

"He said you were American and in school."

"Why do those things matter?" I asked.

"The American part means it's hard to be hired to join what's essentially a secret service. But they can get around that."

I wasn't exactly sure what joining would really mean. Probably living in England for a long time, and not being traceable, and lots and lots of lies . . . I had no idea what went into it all. But the idea fit. It was a future I could see.

"I don't know," I said. "I never thought about it."

"It's not easy," Callum said. "But, you know, if *anyone* was right for the job, it's you. You should start leaning on Stephen before it's too late."

"Too late for what?"

"I don't know how long this takes, and you're not here forever, are you? And he needs convincing. I don't know why he's being so difficult. It's just common sense. Anyway, this is our stop."

Another station, another ghost. This one was much less entertaining than the last, another pathetic creature, barely visible. She looked to be about my age. I couldn't even tell what she was doing wrong, but Callum claimed that she was probably responsible for a signal disturbance. I didn't see how. She sat in the corner, just behind the safety barrier, looking generally terrified by everything, especially us.

"Callum," I said, "I don't think I can do this. I—"

"I already figured that much out," he said, looking deflated.

"I'm really sorry. I mean, she's just not doing anything. I can't."

"No," he said. "I understand."

He tried to sound like it didn't bother him, and I appreciated the effort.

When we were back on the train, I nudged him.

"Maybe let me get used to it for a while," I said.

"Don't take this the wrong way," Callum said, "but I wish it had been me. What I wouldn't give to be what you are now."

"I know. Sorry."

"I don't know how much longer I can do this," he said. "Not without a terminus."

"You're going to quit?"

"I probably would have quit, but . . . Boo. And Stephen. I don't think he could cope. We're like his family, you know? But maybe . . . maybe I won't have to. Maybe it'll all shut down on its own."

"But you just got permission to keep going."

"For now," Callum said. "We still can't really do anything. You're the terminus. We're just some sods who see ghosts and can't do anything about it. And Stephen should have told us we were in danger of being shut down, but that's Stephen. Keeps it all to himself. Won't delegate. It's driving Boo and me mental. It's hard, you know? I was good at football. Then I got hurt and got the sight, and I couldn't play anymore. Then I got this job, and I got a terminus, and everything made sense again. I had control again. I hate to say it, but I *get* why Newman wanted one so much. I don't think he should have *killed everyone he worked with,* but I get him wanting one."

I curled up in my coat a little. I'd pushed that aspect of Newman's story out of my mind. Newman had been in the Shades, but when they'd found out he was unstable, they fired him and took away his terminus. Desperate to get it back, he'd confronted the other members of the squad in their old headquarters, in the abandoned King William Street Tube station. He killed them all in his attempts to get a terminus and was himself killed in the process.

It was weird to have the sight. It was weird to be a Shade. It had driven him insane.

"What was it that Newman said to you that night," Callum asked. "About dying with a terminus?"

"He had some theory that if someone with the sight died holding a terminus, they'd come back. As a ghost, I mean."

"And he knew this how?"

"I have no idea if he knew it at all," I replied.

"Stephen is convinced there's more information that we've never been allowed to see. An archive. Maybe he's right. Maybe Newman had access to things they don't let us see anymore, but . . ."

"But?" I said.

"I don't know. I don't think they care enough about us to hide anything. And what would be the point of hiding stuff from us? I think he's being a little paranoid. He hides things from us, and he thinks people are hiding things from him. I mean, if there was a method of making people into ghosts, I guess I could see the point in holding on to that but . . . no. I don't know."

He shook his head and scratched his arm.

"You know they think we're freaks," he went on. "You know Thorpe hates dealing with us. And can you blame him?"

We arrived back at Liverpool Street, both of us quiet and pensive. Callum walked me out and down Artillery Lane.

"Really," I said when we reached the back of my building, "I'll try harder. Just don't give up yet, okay?"

"Forget it," he said, slapping me reassuringly on the shoulder. "I'm just glad you're back. Things always get interesting when you come around."

12

I was sitting in history on Thursday, listening to my teacher go through the list of everything that the exam might possibly cover, when it occurred to me, in a dim and distant way, that I had no idea what he was talking about. I was listening to words, and I recognized them as words, but they were arranged in a way that had no meaning. This is possibly due to the fact that all the people in English history have the *same names*. William. Edward. Charles. James. Henry. Richard. George. Elizabeth. Mary. Or that there are people with titles that rotate through all these stories. A Prince of Wales here, a Duke of Gloucester there. A Richmond and Buckingham and Guildford and on and on and on.

And when you take English history in England, they sort of assume you know where the hell they're talking about—that you understand what's up north and what's down south and what's near the water. This is stuff I get when we have to do the Civil War at home. I can picture where Philadelphia is, and South Carolina, and Virginia. These things make sense. I don't have to look everything up on a map, or try to figure out which of the nine million Duke of Buckinghamshiremond-lands they're talking about, or who was who in the War of the Roses, or why roses? Just, why roses?

Anyway, he was saying words that I was supposed to know, and I was probably supposed to be writing them down. I took a stab at this, writing "Edward" and "James" and "battle of . . ." It occurred to me I should be more concerned about the fact that I had no idea what was going on, but I felt nothing in particular. At home, I was a top student. Wexford was a much more challenging school, and when I'd first arrived, I was panicked all the time because I couldn't keep up. Then I was panicked because a murderous ghost was after me. Now I was back, there was no murderous ghost after me, the crack, at last, had passed from my thoughts, and I was so behind as to be out of the race. I felt nothing but a pleasant sleepiness when I looked at my books.

"Aurora," my teacher said. "A word."

My history teacher was not, in my experience, an unreasonable person. I was pretty sure he wasn't going to yell at me for looking spacey. And he didn't. He did, however, present me with a large, sealed envelope.

"I'm going to have to assess where you are so I can determine what exam questions to set for you next week. This is a short pretest. Take it over to the library. There's a proctor over there who will monitor your progress and take it from you when you are finished. It's just thirty minutes. Keep the answers very short and simple—I just need to know where you are in basic terms."

I felt like I was carrying my own death sentence . . . or, if not a death sentence, maybe instructions for my own torture. Our librarian, Mrs. Feeley, was indeed expecting me. I was seated by myself at a table. There were only three questions on this pre-exam, with space enough to write a paragraph or two of answer.

Explain the origins of the Bishops' Wars of 1639 and 1640.

Give the basic timeline and the major events of the English Civil War of 1642 to 1651.

List three immediate repercussions of the Great Fire of London.

These were not unreasonable questions, and should have been easy to anyone following along in class. The third one I could do. The second one I could kind of do. The first one, I had completely forgotten. I'd been given a half hour to do the whole thing. I dithered for a few minutes, trying to figure out if I wanted to start with the one I knew or the ones I didn't know. Maybe the fact of forcing my brain on to those questions would jog some knowledge. So I jabbed at question two for a bit, penciling some dates in the margins, trying to string them together, adding whatever I could recall. The result was such a broken, spotty timeline that I had to erase it completely. I had wasted time. On to question three.

Three immediate repercussions of the Great Fire. In 1666, a fire starts on Pudding Lane, the most delicious sounding of lanes. London is crowded—the buildings built so far out that they practically touch each other across the street. It spreads quickly, burning for days. It burns down a large portion of the east section of the old city, the one contained within the city walls. Those city walls had stopped just outside of Wexford. This area had been preserved from the fire.

"Five minutes," Mrs. Feeley said.

Five minutes? How had that happened? I'd just started. Three immediate repercussions . . . The buildings were rebuilt more safely, in stone and brick, with wider streets. And the fire destroyed many of the rats that spread the plague . . .

This area had not burned.

The crack was back in my brain.

I recalled the woman I'd seen, and accidentally destroyed, in the bathroom. Could she have been from around that time? It was possible. I'd been looking at a lot of paintings from the mid-1600s in art history and they looked very similar, but peasant dress in the Middle Ages and Renaissance probably didn't change all that much. I was going to have to start studying clothing history if I was going to see these people.

But if this area hadn't burned, what had been here? What was underneath Wexford? Maybe that was where I should start. There had to be maps.

"Time's up," she said.

I had only written part of the answer to one question.

"Can I ask something?" I said, passing back the paper.

"Of course," Mrs. Feeley said.

"What used to be here?"

"Can you be more specific?"

"On this site."

"Wexford was originally built as a workhouse."

"No, I mean further back than that. I mean this whole area."

"Well, I don't know the entire history of the site, but what period are you wondering about?"

"Around the Great Fire. Maybe just before and after?"

"Well," she said, "in that period, this area would have been just outside the boundaries of the London Wall. Quite literally just outside of. Bishopsgate was a boundary street. There would certainly have been a number of fields. Henry the Eighth also used the area to store artillery and train soldiers. That's why the streets have the names they do—Gun Street, Artillery Lane."

"Are there maps?"

"We don't have much of a cartography section, but there is quite a collection at the British Library."

"Is that far?"

"Not at all. It's just next to King's Cross station."

Having tanked my pretest, I still had three hours left to kill in the afternoon. If I hurried, I could probably be there within a half an hour or so.

The words *British Library* call to mind something ancient. I was expecting a grand old building. Instead, it was a modern place, with lots of interactive screens, weird tables with "stand-up chairs," which were essentially boards you could lean against and work standing up, and swish cafés.

It turned out there were multiple map rooms, but to access them, I first had to go downstairs to a room full of lockers, where we had to leave our coats, all liquids, and all pens. Everything we were going to carry with us (money, computers, paper, pencils) had to go in a clear plastic shopping bag. Then I had to get a library ID card. Then I had to go online and spend half an hour trying to figure out what I needed. Then I had to order it. I put in the request and was told that my maps would be available in about an hour to an hour and a half, so I walked around for a while and watched other people study. I obsessively checked my status, waiting for the message telling me that my map had come. Finally, it arrived. I was handed a stack of massive, flat portfolios, like huge folders, which I gingerly carried over to one of the nearby tables. I opened up all the flaps of the first one, revealing a single page inside. It looked almost new, yet it was from 1658, and they were letting me *touch* it.

It was a close-up view of London back when London took up mostly just a single mile along the Thames, encased by a wall. The artist had drawn ships sailing down the Thames, rows of houses, and arches all along the London wall. (These were the actual "gates" of the wall, and their names still existed: Bishopsgate, Aldgate, Moorgate . . . I knew all of these places.) I had to look close, but I could see windmills and trees and even tiny little people. There were fields in places I knew to be bustling parts of East London.

And there was Artillery Lane, spelled here "Artillerie Lane," the very street that ran along Wexford, where the Royal Gunpowder was located. It was next to something called the Artillerie Garden. I looked this one up quickly online—it was a munitions storehouse and training ground for the military. Just across Bishopsgate, in a little warren of buildings, I saw the word *Bedlam.*

I'd heard that before. My grandmother used it a lot to mean insane. Like, when her two little dogs heard the can opener going, her kitchen became Bedlam.

I looked up Bedlam. Bedlam—the Bethlehem Royal Hospital. One of the world's first psychiatric facilities, except what all the information described hardly sounded like compassionate medical care. There were manacles and chains and all forms of restraints, buckets of water, cold and terrifying cells. The public could even come in and pay to see the patients. It was a human zoo. Mad preachers shouted from the windows and gained devoted followings. Brilliant but sick patients drew elaborate diagrams of mind-controlling machines. The hospital had been in several locations, but for quite a while, it was that tiny tower with the flag, which sat where Liverpool Street station is now.

Wexford was practically on top of it.

Now my mind was moving swiftly. If the hospital had been there, presumably many people had died there. Presumably they needed to be buried. I looked up "Bedlam burials" and was rewarded instantly with many hits. *Current Archaeology* had a front cover story called "Bedlam Burials." There was a picture of a skeleton neatly packed in the dirt, being unearthed. I turned up more articles on lots of skeletons being uncovered. They'd found them in 1863, when they were building Broad Street station, which was long gone, but had been close by. And in 1911, they found piles and piles more when they were tunneling their way to Liverpool Street.

We were sitting right on top of the graveyard of the world's most infamous mental institution, which is arguably many hundreds of times worse than being on top of the old haunted burial grounds that things are always being built on in America. Loads of mad ghosts . . . who might be disturbed by, say, a major explosion that might have, quite possibly, opened up some kind of crack that they could pass through? And they might, for instance, kill people with hammers . . .

Now I had a reason to call Stephen.

Stephen wasn't answering his phone. I tried several times as I ran back to the Tube and wound my way through the insane

King's Cross rush-hour traffic in an attempt to get back to Wexford before anyone noticed I had gone. I got home fifteen minutes before dinner. Jazza was sitting on her bed, looking like a small child who'd just seen a wolf eat her pet bunny.

"Hey," I said. "How's my favorite roommate?"

"Have I told you that I'm wretched at German?"

"You tell me that daily," I said. "But I don't believe you."

"Well, I'm not good enough for someone applying to study German."

"But you're good enough for *me,* and isn't that what counts?"

"Not really. I'm going to fail."

I had no idea how she was doing in German, but I doubted she was going to fail. I was going to fail. I was the failure of our room.

"Do you have any Cheez Whiz?"

Things had to be bad if she wanted predinner Cheez Whiz.

"Do I have any Cheez Whiz? She asks stupid questions, my roommate. Heater or microwave?"

"Microwave."

While I was in Bristol, I had been sent three jars of my favorite substance on earth. I took one of them from my bottom desk drawer. I was carrying the cheezy goodness back down the hall when Charlotte materialized from the direction of the fire doors.

"How are you doing?" she asked.

"Fine," I said.

"Are you keeping up with everything okay?"

I couldn't say yes to this and keep a straight face. Plus, from the way she curled up the question at the end, I got the distinct impression that Charlotte already knew the score.

"It's an ongoing process," I said, sticking the jar into the microwave.

"That's a great way of looking at it. I heard you saw Jane. She's great, isn't she?"

"She's good," I said.

We both watched the jar revolve slowly.

"Is she helping you?"

"I just went the once."

"Well, she's really great, I think. I think you already look better."

The microwave beeped, and I opened it up.

"I'm glad," I said. I smiled and maneuvered around her to get back to my room. I liked Jane too, but there was something deeply unnerving in the way Charlotte liked her. Charlotte liked Jane *too* much. I didn't even know what that meant, or why it was a problem.

Maybe I had therapy jealousy.

I stuck my finger into the container and helped myself to a bit of the cheez, only to scald myself. I quickly put it in my mouth and bounced open the door with my elbow.

"Is Charlotte kind of creepy?" I asked Jazza, kicking the door shut behind me.

"Creepy how?"

"Just . . . creepy. I don't know. Creepy."

"It's not the first word I would use to describe her."

Jazza was digging around in her tuck chest for a suitable snack with which to consume the Cheez Whiz. Cheez Whiz is a very forgiving food—you just need something slightly more stable than Cheez Whiz to eat it with. I have been known to eat it with slices of actual cheese.

"Is she different, though? Since the attack?"

"Definitely different," Jazza said. "A little nicer, but in an unctuous way. She wants to *help* all the time. I don't need her *help.* Is that what you mean by creepy?"

"I think so," I said.

"I suppose that's good," Jazza said, sighing a little. She could never be mean for more than a minute or two at a time, then something clicked inside her. "I know she's going to therapy. It must be helping. I mean, I know she was hurt. But you were hurt worse."

That was true. I really was. I was holding on to the title.

My phone was ringing, and Stephen's name came up. I had to answer this, but I couldn't answer it in front of Jazza, and this was going to be a problem. We didn't leave the room to answer phone calls. But I had no choice in the matter, and bounced up with a quick "Be right back!"

"Where have you been?" I said.

"Doing my job. What's wrong?"

I hurried down the hall and stood in the vestibule between the fire doors. This was as close to privacy as I was going to get.

"I don't have long," I said. "I'm in my building. People around."

I launched into what I had discovered. He didn't interrupt me. I went through all my notes. The location of Bedlam, how far it was from Wexford, the burial pit discovery. He listened to it all, and somehow, though he was totally silent, I knew I was catching his interest. Stephen liked research. He liked map reference numbers and dates and the word *cartography.*

"All right," he said. "You're right. It's worth knowing."

"What would you normally do next?"

"Talk to the suspect."

"Okay. So let's do that."

"The suspect in question is in a mental health facility under close guard."

Jazza waved to me and began to approach.

"Have to go," I said. "Can you just . . ."

"All right," he said, sighing a little. "I'll look into it."

I was in French on Friday when my phone vibrated in my pocket. I managed to slide it out and hide it in my lap, in the folds of my skirt. It was a message from Stephen.

Going to speak with suspect in Royal Gunpowder incident tomorrow morning.

I had long mastered the art of typing texts with one finger without really looking. Well, without looking much.

What time are you picking me up?

His response was quick:

Picking you up for what?

I'm going with you.

Out of the question.

My teacher was looking in my direction now. I quickly pressed the phone between my thighs, vanishing it.

"Let me just cover the things you've been able to do so far," I said. The minute I got out of class, I had called Stephen. I was not giving up on this. I paced the green with the phone to my ear. The middle of the green was actually the safest place to talk. Too many people along the edges. "You convinced my therapist that she had to let me come back to school. You busted into my school's security system. You arranged for me to be taken to a Tube station in the middle of the night to do a show for Thorpe—"

"Rory—"

"Not to mention all the stuff I don't know about. Oh, and covering up the entire Ripper case with a fake dead body?"

"I didn't do that," he said.

"You know what I mean. You can arrange it so I can go."

"Rory, this is a facility for the criminally insane. A medium secure unit. This man has confessed to murder. This is serious."

"And the other things we've dealt with weren't serious?"

"Of course they were serious," he said. "But—"

"Let me ask you *this,*" I cut in. "If there is something in that basement, and it needs to be taken care of, who's going to do it? Who's the terminus? Me. And if you want the terminus to behave, you have to take me."

I surprised myself with this last one. It was very blunt. I think it shocked him into silence.

"I'll get in touch with you later," he said.

And he did. The reply came as I was walking home from dinner.

I'll pick you up around the corner from Wexford at 9:45 tomorrow. Sharp. Wear plain white shirt and black trousers or skirt. -s

13

THERE WAS ONLY ONE SMALL PROBLEM WITH THIS OTHERwise flawless plan: I was supposed to be in art history at the same time we were going to the hospital. I am not, as a general rule, a class skipper. I'd only ever done it once, and that was entirely by accident. It had happened the year before, back at home. I was running late for school and didn't have time for coffee. No coffee in the morning makes Rory a stupid girl. For all of first period, I battled to keep my eyes open. In second period, I thought it was third period. So instead of going to second-period French, I went to third-period study hall and went to sleep in the corner of the library, where they have this deflated fuzzy beanbag that no one wants to use because someone claimed there were bed bugs in it. I woke to find myself being shaken by the librarian. They'd realized I was missing from French and put out one of those school-wide Amber-alert things my school does. They track you down. I got a moron reprimand.

Wexford was a different sort of place. They didn't follow you around. For my own conscience, I justified this in several ways: 1. Saturday art class was kind of a weird add-on class that wasn't quite like the other classes. It wasn't an extracurricular, but it didn't have that "real class" feel. I may have entirely made this one up, but that was the way it appeared to me. 2. No idea what was going on anyway, so missing one more class would not hurt. 3. Mark was a cool guy and would probably figure I was getting some kind of treatment or therapy. He wasn't regular faculty, so he wouldn't have known my whole story or hung out much with the other teachers. 4. I had better things to do: namely, go to a mental hospital and talk to a murderer. That had to be way more important than me examining the works of the puddles and puffy clouds painters.

I should explain myself to Jerome, at least. He would wonder. He would worry. Would he worry? That was cute.

Or he'd think I had overslept and missed class. Much more likely.

I would worry about excuses later.

I cobbled together an outfit with one of my uniform shirts, and I planned on stealing a skirt out of Jazza's closet the second she left the room. All I had to do was get out of the building and around the corner without being seen by the wrong people. The wrong people, in descending order of importance, were Jerome, Jazza, my teacher Mark, most of the people on my hall, and my art history classmates. I couldn't go too early—Jazza would notice if I woke up and left before her (and I needed the skirt). The perfect time, I decided, was nine thirty. Most people went to breakfast then. I could slip out and no one would be the wiser.

Except that morning, everyone decided to switch things

up. Jazza lingered in our room. Gaenor came over to borrow shampoo. Eloise came by to talk. And then, when the coast was finally clear, I found my escape route blocked by Claudia, who felt that this was clearly the moment when the bulletin board in the lobby needed cleaning off. She *would not move.*

9:30 came and went. Then 9:35. Then 9:40. By 9:41, I went into a slight panic, which set off a brain wave. We had a house phone on every hallway, with emergency numbers listed next to it, along with Claudia's office phone. I called her, left the phone off the hook, and when she went into her office to answer, I ran through the lobby and out the door. At this point, I was in real danger of being seen by people heading to class, but there was nothing I could do about that. I could only hope that by running and by not being in a uniform, I would confuse people enough that they wouldn't realize it was me. This seemed extremely unlikely, but I am prepared to lie to myself on occasion to make life more palatable.

I hate to run, as I think I have mentioned, but I ran that morning. I ran like a thing that runs, almost running directly into people as I took the corner onto the busy shopping street. For a moment, I thought Stephen had left without me or not come at all, because there was a smug little red Smart Car in his usual spot, but then I saw the police car across the street. I continued my run right across the street.

"Made it," I said, getting in and clicking the seat belt triumphantly into place.

I don't think Stephen considered successfully getting into a car by nine forty-five—well, nine forty-seven—in the morning to be a major triumph. He just didn't understand how complicated my life was.

"Don't look so happy to see me," I said.

"Put this on." He handed me what looked like a black bowler hat with a white-and-black-checked band around it. There was a fluorescent-yellow police jacket as well.

"Why?"

"Because you're riding in the front. You have to look like you belong. Put it on."

I slapped on the hat and put on the jacket. They were both just a touch large, but not too bad. At least these were for women. I'd worn Callum's before, and those were huge. There was a heady plasticky-rubber smell coming off the jacket, and it still had square folds all over it, like it had just come out of a package. I examined myself in the side view mirror. I looked . . . not exactly like a policewoman, but not entirely unlike one.

"I like this. Can we turn on the siren?"

"Stop it," he said.

There was a stiffness to his whole demeanor that suggested he had not liked my ultimatum. He was taking me, but he was angry.

"Do you realize the sort of place we're going to?" he said.

"I realize we're going to a mental hospital."

"To meet a murderer."

"I've met a murderer before."

"I know," he said. "That's probably why I agreed to this. I think. It's a good thing Callum's taking Boo over to the hospital to have her cast removed—I didn't have to make any excuses about where I was going."

It was a miserable morning, overcast as ever. The car's windows had fogged up from the moisture, and the windshield wipers beat back the gloom and the almost imperceptible rain.

"I understand you and Callum went out the other night," he said.

"He told you?"

"He didn't. Boo did."

"He wasn't supposed to tell Boo either," I said.

"He didn't. Boo just knew."

"How?"

"Boo is very observant," he said. "She always seems to know what we've been doing. She said Callum was 'glowing,' which I suppose means that he looks very happy after he's been patrolling."

"Or he's pregnant," I said.

Stephen let this pass.

"Well, since you're going on official business, here is the background: The victim, Charlie Strong, was a recovered alcoholic. He continued to run his pub after he stopped drinking, but had a policy of hiring people who were in recovery as a way of supporting the process. Sam Worth, the suspect, had such a history, and a recent one. History of Class A drug use, two charges of possession. He was jailed for two years for beating a man half to death with a metal chair. He was high on acid at the time and thought the man was trying to steal his ears."

"Steal his ears?"

"Apparently Sam took quite a lot of drugs. So he has form."

"Form?"

"Form . . . a past. A criminal record. History of drug use, history of violence. No drugs were found in his system at the time of arrest, though. He claimed innocence at the scene, but changed his plea once he was in the cells. A week ago, he attempted self-harm or suicide by beating his head against a wall until he was bloody and concussed. That's when he was transferred to a mental health facility. What they're trying to determine now is whether he's fit for trial. So that's where things stand."

On that cheery note, Stephen went silent. There was a throbbingly pink advertisement on the bus in front of us for a musical called *Foot-tastic.* It featured a photo of a man and a woman who were smiling so hard, I had the feeling that their skin might just unzip and fall off their skulls.

"I'm going to fail everything," I said, just for a change of subject.

"You don't sound overly concerned about that."

"Just keeping it in perspective," I said coolly. "I've dealt with worse recently."

"True," he said. "But you have to move on."

"I have moved on."

"I mean, you need school."

"Are you giving me a stay-in-school lecture? Is that what's happening here?"

"I'm not giving you any lecture—your marks are your problem."

Maybe it was best if we didn't talk right now. The occasion wasn't really one that invited carefree banter, and when I just keep talking, things often got weird fast. It was time for quiet now.

The Royal Bethlehem Hospital didn't look like a mental hospital, not that I have much experience on the subject. It was brick, very American looking, like an administrative building on a college campus or something from Main Street, Anywhere, USA. Big windows, red roof, tiny square turret on top. It was cheerful and efficient, even if it was draped entirely in cobwebs of fog. We parked right out front, in a space reserved for official vehicles.

"Here is how this will work," Stephen said, turning the car off. "This man is accused of murder. Remember that. I will do the talking. Are we clear?"

"Crystal," I said.

"Even if people ask you questions, you do not answer. They can't hear your accent."

"Got it."

"Close up the coat and keep the hat on. Look like you're meant to be here. Technically, you are impersonating a police officer, so we have to do this right."

Everything was fine until we actually went through the front door.

I call it "water park feeling." I always think I want to go to water parks. The idea of going on a water slide always seems like a good one. I like pools; therefore, it follows that I should like a park made of pools. And every summer, without fail, I make this mistake and end up going to Splash World, where I remember that I hate water parks, because they are not about pools—they are about slides. They are about heights. They are often about slides that reach to great heights that are enclosed, and as any shipwreck survivor would be happy to tell you, water and enclosed spaces are bad combinations. Add to that the free-fall aspect, and you have a combination that the reptile part of the brain abhors. The brain says *no*. The brain says *bad*. The brain says *you will fall and then you will drown, or possibly both at the same time*.

I know it the minute I approach the turnstiles and buy a ticket, because that's when you can smell the chlorine. As soon as it hits my nose, my reptile brain wakes up, checks the files, and sends up the warning. And this is why I always end up claiming I have cramps and holding the towels while gleeful children run around me, totally unafraid.

On this particular morning, it wasn't chlorine I smelled. But as we walked through the front door, I caught the faint bite of antiseptic and the strange and false odor of recycled air that comes from a place with no open windows. Hospital smell.

We started at the front desk. From there, we were taken to a series of stations through a series of doors that had to be opened with swipe cards. Stephen had to show something called a warrant card, which turned out to be his police identification. He signed documents on clipboards.

I could tell, as we progressed through the building, that we were moving to more and more serious levels. In the beginning, there were paintings on the walls, paintings done by the patients. At first, the paintings just hung. Then they were bolted. Then they were gone and the walls were a plain off-white and everything else was a soothing light green. Everything was calm, orderly, and official.

Finally, after some last papers were signed, we were taken to a room with a heavy door, with large, very serious bolts on the outside and a tiny window just big enough to peep in. We were let inside, and the door was locked behind us.

My first impression of the man at the table was that he was big. He had a few days' scraggly beard, which was blondish-gray. He was dressed in the hospital-issued clothes, which looked like scrubs. His hands were cuffed together on the table, but this didn't feel necessary. He slumped in his chair, looking feeble and defeated. There were cuts and bruises on his forehead from where he'd banged it into a wall.

The room was bare except for a few bolted-down chairs and the bolted-down table. There was a CCTV camera in the corner of the room, behind a protective coating of thick plastic, with just a circle cut out to expose the lens. Stephen looked at the camera for a moment. The red light on the side suddenly blinked and went off. No cameras. This was a private interview.

There were two chairs on either side of the table, but I wasn't sure if I was supposed to sit next to Stephen, or if this was his job and I was supposed to hang back.

"I'm Constable Dene," Stephen said. "And this is WPC Devon."

I guess my real last name, Deveaux, was too distinctive, and Devon sounded more English.

Sam raised his head slightly.

"Constable?" he said.

"I realize you've probably been talking to a number of people of a much higher rank."

"Done talking. I've told you lot already."

"And I realize you might not want to tell your story again," Stephen went on. "I realize you've had to tell many people, but we're going to need you to tell us again."

"You afraid to sit down?" Sam asked me.

Actually, yes. I was terrified of sitting down. How nice of him to notice.

"PC Devon," Stephen said, without turning around, "why don't you sit down?"

Now all the attention was on me, and it was possible that

nothing would go forward if I didn't peel myself off the wall and sit in the chair. I was, I reminded myself, not a trained police officer or mental health professional or anything like that. I was a high school student, a foreigner, and someone who had gotten into all of this completely by accident, and it was not my responsibility to be big and brave here. But I had demanded to be here.

I unstuck myself from the wall and planted myself in the plastic chair. I put my hands in my lap, where they were safe from germs and whatever else it was I feared in this room.

Now we could continue.

"I know this is difficult for you," Stephen said, "but it would be helpful, and you've been very cooperative. We know that."

Sam sighed—an all-body sigh that rounded his shoulders.

"I don't want to. I'm tired."

Sam's chin sunk into his chest, and he examined the locks that bound him to the table.

"In your own time," Stephen said. "We're not here to bring you any trouble. We're here to listen."

Sam turned his attention to me. His eyes had a yellowy cast.

"You're not police," he said. "Are you?"

"WPC Devon is an observer from our Care in the Community division," Stephen said. "I'll be asking the—"

"You're not," Sam said. "I don't think either of you are police."

Stephen produced his warrant card, opened it, and slid it across the table. Sam leaned forward to have a look at it.

"And where's hers?" Sam said.

"She doesn't carry one in her capacity," Stephen said smoothly.

"Why doesn't she talk?"

Sam had clearly figured me out. Of course I wasn't a cop. A small child or a dog could have figured that out. I guess I thought that since Stephen came up with the idea, it might actually work.

"She's an observer," Stephen said again. "If her presence upsets you, she can go into the hallway and we can talk alone."

"I want to know who she is," Sam said.

There didn't seem any point in playing this game any more.

"I'm Rory," I said.

"You're American," Sam replied.

Stephen didn't make a noise, but I could see the sigh shrugging through his frame.

"Who are you?" Sam asked. "How did you get in here?"

"I'm here because bad things have happened to me."

That got his interest.

"What kind of bad things?"

Stephen cleared his throat loudly. "I don't think this is—"

"What kind of bad things?" Sam said again. His eyes were locked on me. This man was supposed to have murdered someone with a hammer. Being here, talking . . . these were possibly not the best ideas I'd ever had. But talking is still my thing, and talking was better than not talking.

"I was stabbed," I said. "At Wexford."

"You're that Ripper girl," Sam said. "They said it was an American girl. She's the Ripper girl."

That last one was to Stephen, who was forced to nod.

"Why did you bring the Ripper girl here?"

We were so far off track now that Stephen had no immediate reply to this quite reasonable question.

"You saw the news reports," Stephen said, after a moment.

"Do you remember how the suspect was never caught on CCTV?"

These words had an immediate effect on Sam. His arms went slack, and the restraints clanked against the table. The rest of his body became more alert.

"I think something in that cellar wasn't quite right," Stephen said.

Sam shook his head, as if he had water in his ear that he needed to dislodge. "No," he said.

"Sam, I don't think you wanted to hurt Charlie. Did you hurt Charlie?"

"I already said I did!"

"But *did* you?"

Sam began to cry. Tears dribbled down his face, getting stuck in the stubble. He turned his head back and forth as if trying to shake his face dry.

"What was in that cellar, Sam?" Stephen pressed on. "Why did you call Charlie down there?"

"I did it . . ."

"Sam." Stephen's voice had taken on a deep, steady tone that was kind of hypnotic. "Sam, you called him downstairs. Why?"

"The floor. I just wanted to show him the floor . . ."

"What about the floor?"

"The cross," he said.

"What cross?"

"When I went down for the tonic water, there was no cross on the floor. But then when I went back down again for the crisps, there it was."

"The cross?"

"It was drawn in chalk," Sam said. "I thought there was something wrong with my head. And I got near it, and suddenly this glass came out of nowhere, like it had been thrown at me. I yelled for Charlie . . ."

I realized my nails were digging into my thighs.

"Charlie thought I was on something, but I wasn't. I didn't take nothing, I promise. And I was trying to tell him that . . ."

Sam had started to shake, an all-over quiver that rattled his arms and pulled on the restraints that bound him to the table. Tears trickled freely from his eyes.

"What happened next, Sam?" Stephen asked quietly.

Sam shook his head.

"Sam," he said, "we will *believe* you."

"I don't want you to believe me."

It was horrible to watch, this tormented man, chained into place.

"Charlie started to wipe the cross away," he said. "He was down on his knees and saying, 'We'll just clean this up and have a cup of tea and we'll talk . . .' He thought I was high and things were going bad in my head. And then, the hammer . . . It did it on its own. I promise you, it went right for him, on its own. Right through the air. I didn't believe what I was seeing. I would have stopped it, but I didn't understand what was going on . . . but that didn't happen, did it? The hammer didn't move by itself. I must've done it. It was just me and him, and I picked up the hammer when it fell to the floor, and . . . it must have been me. I must've killed him. I must have—"

He broke down entirely, his body shuddering. He was chained to the table and weeping in agony.

Stephen stood and indicated that I should as well.

"You've done the right thing, telling us. This is a good place. They'll look after you here."

Sam turned away from us to face the wall, and the tears streamed hard and fast again. His sobs filled the room, and the air got thick and humid. The horror of it all was in this room, in sweat and tears and adrenaline—the pain of a mind rejecting something that seemed unnatural, something that had no place in this world. Something violent that had no face or body.

"Sam." Stephen's voice had gone very soft, softer than I had imagined it could go. "You'll be looked after. You don't need to be afraid."

"I did it," Sam moaned. "I did it. I must have. Please tell me. Please. Please tell me what's happening . . ."

"What's happening . . ." Stephen paused and looked for something to say. But how did you explain a thing like this to a man who'd seen his boss die right in front of him? A man who believed he committed a murder, and was now in a hospital chained to a table?

"I'll speak to someone outside," Stephen said. "They'll give you something. It will be all right. You will get all the help you need. Thank you for talking to us."

He nodded to me, and I stood up slowly and we left the room.

14

I DIDN'T EXACTLY RUN OUT OF THE HOSPITAL WHEN WE finished, but I came pretty close. Once we were outside, I tipped back my head. The drizzle went up my nose, along with the smell of wet leaves in a parking lot. I loved everything about this wet parking lot. I loved the fog that smothered the landscape. It wasn't the hospital itself that was bad. It was a perfectly nice and modern hospital—it was that it made me feel like I couldn't breathe.

"I told you it wouldn't be pleasant," Stephen said.

"I'm fine," I replied.

Stephen took me at my word. We returned to the car, but he didn't start the engine right away.

"There are two possibilities here," Stephen said. "One, Sam beat his employer to death with a hammer. Or, two—"

"He saw an actual flying hammer beat his boss to death, and now he's in a hospital for the criminally insane."

"That's the other one."

"Which one do you think it is?" I asked.

"I don't know." He rubbed at his hairline. "The forensics fit. The blood splatter on his clothes and body indicated that he had been standing about two feet away from the victim at the time of the attack. The pattern on the hammer was a bit more confusing. His fingerprints were on it, but they seemed to be old prints—the blood was over the top of them. The way the blood ran down the handle, someone's fingers should have interrupted the stream, but they didn't. The best guess was that he held the handle very low, and possibly with something like a cloth, but that was never recovered. The oddities about the grip patterns on the weapon could be overlooked because he *said* he did it."

"So it could have been a flying hammer?" I said.

"So it could have been a flying hammer. Or it could have been a weird way of holding the hammer. And if you're bashing people's brains in with a hammer, you might hold said hammer in a strange way, because it's a strange activity . . . Are you sure you're all right?"

As far as I knew, I was being completely normal. I wasn't screaming or crying or twitching uncontrollably. And I was feeling increasingly better every second we were out of the hospital. Clearly, though, I was giving off a vibe that indicated I wasn't okay.

"Just, you know, being in there makes me feel like it might be me, you know? Weird in the head."

"You're not weird in the head."

"There's a giant talking chicken next to me that would say otherwise."

"You are not weird in the head," he said, more firmly. "You

went through something horrible, and you survived, and you've done amazingly well. You're strong. Stop making jokes about it. There is nothing wrong with you."

I wasn't expecting this little outburst, or the anger that edged his voice.

"Sorry," I said.

"Don't be sorry. Just don't do it. It's important. Because of what we do, it's important to always remember that there is nothing wrong with you. Don't make jokes about your own sanity. You didn't like being in there. Neither did I. It's scary because when you have the sight, you wonder if you're going to end up in one of these places."

"Who knows?" I said. "If I'd told Julia what really happened, maybe I would have. Maybe I would have liked it in there. I think you get to do a lot of crafts. I like crafts. Crafts are good. I can make a mean God's eye. And I bet you get to eat a lot of pudding. Give me pudding and give me crafts and I'm going to be content for a while . . ."

"They're not bad places. I liked my time in one better than school in many ways."

It's not a good feeling when you realize you've been making jokes about something that the person you're talking to has actually been through.

"I didn't mean . . ."

"I know you didn't. I'm just telling you. If someone needs mental health care, they belong in a facility like this. But what you have is not a mental illness. I didn't go into hospital because I saw ghosts; I went because I attempted suicide. And that suicide attempt had nothing to do with the sight."

I'd never heard someone just come out and talk about their

suicide attempt so matter-of-factly. Come to think of it, I'd never heard anyone talk about a suicide attempt at *all.* Something about the fact that we had just gone into that hospital together had opened a conversational door. I could feel his willingness to talk creeping out like a reluctant cat from under a sofa.

"It was because of your sister's death," I said.

"And my inability to deal with it. Or my family's refusal to do so. Whichever you like. Both apply."

"How long were you there?" I asked.

"Just over a month." He pinch-wiped his nose. "My parents sent me to the Priory. No NHS for me. Posh hospital, and as far away as possible. I don't know if they really thought I needed to go or if they were just trying to get rid of me for a while. I went to hospital. They went to Greece. There was a reason my sister did so many drugs."

He almost smiled.

"Were you and your sister close?" I asked.

"She was three years older. We both went to boarding schools, different ones. I didn't even see her that often. I mean, we cared for each other, but we weren't in each other's pockets. I had no idea about all the things she'd been doing. I think that was partly why I felt so guilty. She was taking massive amounts of drugs, really dangerous amounts, and I had no idea. None of her so-called friends were all that surprised when she overdosed. I was the only one who was shocked. I was fine for three years, and then . . ." He cut himself off and brushed some imaginary lint off his sleeve. He was drawing a line under this subject.

"These things," I said. "They keep happening. Murders."

"It's not that there are more things happening. It's that you're aware of them now."

"I think more things are *actually happening,*" I said.

"It's still a question of perception. When I did the training to become a police officer, I got to see crime reports. I worked a desk on a Saturday night and saw what came in to the station. I saw people beating each other and stabbing each other. You start to see violence everywhere."

"I can't go on like this," I said. "School's a joke. I lie to everyone. My friends think I'm pathological."

"That's why it's easier not to say anything at all."

"How do you *not say anything* to anyone?"

"When you have no friends, it makes it easier," he said, with that weird little half smile.

"Not helpful."

"No . . . but more to the point, is what Sam told us true?"

Sharing time was over, and we were back to the matter at hand.

"I think I believe him," I said.

"I'm not sure where I am with it, but it's worth a trip to the Royal Gunpowder, at least. Callum and Boo should be back from hospital soon. We can go over this evening or tomorrow."

"Or you can go now," I said. "With me."

"Rory."

"Because if there is something down there, what are you going to do about it?"

"The same thing I've been doing for the last few weeks—I'm going to talk to him or her."

"Yes, but he or she probably killed someone with a hammer, so maybe that's not a good idea. You need me with you."

"You need to understand," he said. "This is our job. I am glad you are back and that you want to help, but—"

"I'll go by myself, then."

"You really are difficult, aren't you?"

"This should not be news."

"This isn't a game," he said.

"When, at any point, has any of this been fun or gamelike to me?" I asked. "Getting stalked for weeks? Getting stabbed? Going into a deserted underground station in the dark to see a man who had murdered about a dozen people? Tell me which part was the game, because I'm missing it."

I had him there, and he rubbed his nose again.

"Same rules," he said. "Let me do the talking. And I *mean* it this time. Promise me, and keep your promise."

"I promise," I said. "But, you know, he talked to me—and my talking is the thing that got him to talk."

"We got away with it in there, but we won't get away with it in a more public setting. We'll say you're a social worker, victim services, just there to observe. Keep your head down and don't engage. And remember, the owners of this pub just lost a family member."

"I know."

"So a certain amount of—"

"I'll be quiet. You go first. I get it."

What mattered was that underneath all of this Stephen was saying yes.

The Royal Gunpowder was very crowded. It appeared that some kind of informal memorial gathering was going on. There were flowers on the bar, and the conversation was loud, but respectfully so. We got some looks when we came in—well, Stephen did. I had shed the police accessories and was now playing the part of a person who was not going to say anything. Stephen worked his way to the front in a practiced way. (I'd noticed that most English people knew how to get to the front of a crowded bar, that there was an understood way to shoulder slide to the front without actually cutting anyone else in line.)

There was a woman behind the bar in a plain black dress, deep in conversation with a group of men who were holding their AA chips. She nodded a lot and wiped her eyes a few times. Stephen interrupted as politely as possible and showed his warrant card. I stared into the back of Stephen's jacket as he introduced himself and made some polite inquiries about how things had gone with the reopening.

"Do you feel comfortable here?" he asked.

"What you mean, comfortable? My father-in-law was beaten to death with a hammer in the basement," she said. "So, no, I suppose you could say I don't feel *comfortable.*"

"I'm very sorry," Stephen said quickly. "Let me rephrase that. Has anyone been disturbing you? Any vandals? Anything we need to be aware of? Sometimes crime scenes get hangers-on, so we like to check up."

I peered around Stephen in what I hoped was a casual manner, to see how this was going.

"Oh," she said. "Course. I see. No, nothing like that."

"You don't seem sure. Really. If there's something, however small, we'll look into it."

"Well . . ." She considered for a moment. "After what happened, we hired a cleaning crew to come in and clear the place up. You can hire people for this sort of thing, you know. They came and scrubbed everything, even the ceiling. Made it perfectly neat and new down there. Then I went down for the first time. I took some of the flowers people had been leaving and put them on the spot where it happened. When I went down the next day to change the water in the vases, they were all in different places. I asked the staff if they done it, and they say they didn't. They swore they didn't. But it's just flowers. You can't call the police because someone moves your flowers. Anyway, I'm sure one of the staff did it, but maybe they didn't want to say when I asked. Maybe they thought I'd be angry."

"It would be helpful if I could go down and have a look," Stephen said. "Make sure everything's secure. It will only take a minute."

"Who's she?" the woman said, nodding at me.

"Victim relations," Stephen answered smoothly. "She does the paperwork to make sure everything's in order."

I feigned intense interest in a menu on the wall advertising a five-pound lunch special. The woman started to come down with us, but Stephen held up his hand.

"If you can just stay up here," he said. "It's procedure. Health and safety. Stupid, I know, but there you go."

To my surprise, the woman nodded again and went back up the stairs, shutting the door. This astonished me.

"I can't believe that worked," I said when we got downstairs. "Procedure? In my town, no one would just *let the law* into their basement to have a look around for seemingly no reason at all. They'd either get a lawyer or a gun. If uncertain, they'd get both."

"This is England," he explained. "Tell someone it's a procedure, and they'll believe you. The pointless procedure is one of our great natural resources."

There was a shelving unit directly at the bottom of the steps, which was full of toilet paper: rolls and rolls of the stuff. Someone liked buying in bulk. There was an open doorway to the right and the left of this.

"Is there anyone down here?" Stephen asked the dark. "We mean you no harm. Please make yourself known to us if you are here."

No answer.

"Here's what we are going to do," Stephen told me. "We go to the bottom of the stairs. You will look to the left, and I will look to the right."

This was real police stuff—going to the door, one person covering one direction, another covering the opposite. So we did that. I faced a room full of pipes and kegs with no hiding spaces and no ghosts.

"Nothing," I said.

"Can't see anything this way," Stephen said. "But this side goes on a bit and has another room beyond."

We proceeded cautiously to a narrow room that mostly housed broken-down boxes, then entered a much larger room, which seemed to be the main basement room. This had shelves all around and the barrels that led to the taps upstairs. The lingering scent of some strong chemical hung in the air. But there were no ghosts.

"No reception down here," Stephen said, looking at his phone before pocketing it. "Not good enough anyway. I can't access the files with the photos, but I've looked at them enough. This is clearly the attack room."

There was a vase of drooping daffodils on the floor by some beer kegs.

"So let's go through what we know," Stephen said. "Both

from what Sam said and the report taken at the scene. Sam said he arrived at work at approximately nine forty-five in the morning. Shortly after Sam's arrival, Charlie Strong left to purchase a bacon sandwich and a cup of tea. We have a record of him buying his sandwich; the cash register receipt is marked three minutes after ten. While Charlie was gone, Sam vacuumed the floor. Charlie returns. Sam goes to the basement for the first time to get tonic water. The notes say that when he came up, Charlie was watching *Morning with Michael and Alice.* They were on the cooking segment of the show—"

"I like that show," I said. "I watched it a lot at home."

"—and they were preparing a roast chicken. That segment aired from fourteen minutes after ten until seventeen minutes after ten. Somewhere in the middle of the segment, Charlie instructs Sam to go to the basement to get some nuts and crisps. So here's what that tells us: at some point shortly after 10:03, Sam goes to the basement for the first time. There is no cross on the floor. The cooking segment was running both when he went down and when he came back up, so we know that the second trip to the basement occurs between 10:14 and 10:17, and at that point, the cross has appeared."

"You memorized all this?"

"Yes. Anyway, at this point, something happens. The glass is broken, something Sam claims he didn't do. This suggests agitation on the part of—whatever he claims was down here. Sam yells for Charlie, and Charlie comes down. Charlie finds Sam in distress over this cross and presumably some flying glass. And Sam said Charlie got down on the floor to wipe away the cross."

Stephen got on his knees in the middle of the floor.

"So Charlie is on his knees. He's cleaning the floor. What's a cross? It's a burial marker. *X* marks the spot. Maybe whatever it was was marking where it was buried? And the flowers—flowers also mark graves. She just said the flowers down here were also moved, maybe to indicate the site . . . maybe it attacked because Charlie was interfering with his gravesite?"

While Stephen worked that out, I walked over to the wall that butted against Artillery Lane, where the crack met the outside of the building. There were shelving units all along that wall, full of glasses and boxes of snacks. I tried to look between the shelves to see the wall, but they were too full. I started to remove the items.

"What are you doing?" Stephen asked.

"The crack. I'm trying to see if it comes down this wall."

Stephen got up and helped me move the boxes and glasses away, and together we moved the metal unit away from the wall. Funny, I was certain what I would find there, and yet I was shocked to actually see it. The crack came from the ceiling, from street level, and extended to about midway down the wall, snaking along the mortar that bound the brick wall of the basement.

"It doesn't go to the floor," he said. "So presumably whatever escaped from here, if anything did in fact escape, came from whatever is beyond this wall, under the street."

"Weird to think of things being buried under the street," I said.

"There are so many bodies around here. Over sixty-eight thousand of them over by Spitalfields alone. It's not just a question of there being a body. There's always a body around in London. I think it's more of a change of state issue. Maybe there was always some lingering presence here, but the explosion at Wexford woke it? Upset it? Shook it in some way? And it reacted violently to the disruption? Anyone will be upset by a nearby explosion."

"So you think it was just pissed off?"

"*Pissed off* ghosts are called poltergeists in the common vernacular, and they do some very bad things."

I felt a lecture coming on and turned away for a second.

"Stephen," I said.

"The thing we need to remember—"

"Stephen." I tugged on his arm to make him turn and look.

The figure was in the doorway. I say "the figure" because I couldn't quite tell if it was a man or a woman or what age it was. It was a bundle of cloth, of watery features and gray air. I could tell where the eyes were supposed to be, but there were just deep spaces with no center. It rocked back and forth, as if moved by a breeze.

"Hello," Stephen said.

The figure moved forward a few feet, and not by any method that resembled walking. It just *moved* and continued quaking at us from a slightly closer location.

"We're not here to hurt you," Stephen said. "Can you understand us? Please indicate if you can understand us."

The figure remained exactly as it was.

"I take that as a no," Stephen said, mostly to me. "And I think—"

Our new friend took this moment to respond. It made a noise. It didn't speak or cry, but made a low, aching moan—a moan it refused to *stop* making.

"I think we can be reasonably sure your hypothesis was

correct," Stephen said, over the noise. "There was something down here."

"Yep," I said.

We were frozen against the shelving units, and I got the impression that this thing, whatever it was, had no intention of letting us out. It was *unhappy*, and presumably the last time it became unhappy it bashed a man's head in with a hammer.

"I think we should be very careful," Stephen said.

"You *think*?"

"I also think that I might be right about this particular entity not liking things moved around. If this is a Bedlam patient, it might suffer from some sort of OCD, or just a desire to have a consistent environment. Order and consistency—"

"It's upset."

"It appears upset, yes. But I think it is also listening. Are you listening to us? Can you understand."

The moan remained consistent.

"Right," Stephen said. "Well. I suppose it's trying to communicate in its own way."

"It communicates with hammers."

"Yes. It does."

"Which means I have to take care of it."

"I told you," he said, "you don't *have* to do anything."

"We have to get out of this basement. And it killed someone."

"We don't know that. But it is very likely."

"And it might kill someone else. I can't *not* do this."

"But I'm saying—"

I stopped listening. I was in the unusual position of holding all the cards. I had to decide what to do, and only I could do it.

And I was going to do it. I had faced frightening things before and had been powerless. But not this time. I extended my arm and stepped toward the figure. It moaned and quaked a bit more, but it didn't approach or retreat.

For a fleeting moment, I wondered what would happen if it didn't work—if whatever had been in me had simply gone away, and I was about to paw at a very temperamental creature who did its talking with tools and angry flailing. But as soon as I put my hand out, I knew. First my hand warmed and seemed to stick to the figure. It stopped quaking. I closed my eyes and felt a gentle falling. The thing and I, we were one now and tumbling together through some unknown landscape. And then, with a mild shock sort of like static electricity, the connection was broken, the smell of flowers was in the air, and the thing was gone.

15

EVEN THOUGH I WAS JUST STEPS AWAY FROM WEXFORD, Stephen thought it might be a good idea to take me back to the flat to decompress and debrief. I was fine with that. I don't know *how* he drove since he was giving me the side-eye the entire time. I guess it was one thing seeing me do my new party trick from a distance or by accident, and it was another thing entirely to see it up close, being used deliberately. I killed a *ghost.* With my *hand.*

That was *awesome.*

"You did the right thing," he said.

"I know."

"Are you all right?"

"I'm fine."

"Not going to vomit?"

"I'm completely fine," I said.

"Are you sure? You seem a bit manic."

"Look," I said, turning to him, "I'm fine. I was right. You didn't believe me, but I was right."

"If I didn't believe you, would I have gone to the trouble of arranging an interview at the hospital? That wasn't exactly easy. Are you *sure* you feel all right?"

"Are you going to stop asking me that?"

"I'll stop when I think I've got the real answer," he said.

"Oh. Fine then. No. I feel like death."

"Do you?" he said, almost eagerly.

"No. I feel great."

I leaned back in the seat and drummed my fingers on the window and tried to look like a cop. I made cop faces at the cars passing by—hard, long stares. Sometimes I'd give them a little nod, as if to say, "You're doing all right, law-abiding citizen." I liked being right, and I liked being powerful, and I liked the way I felt right now.

"When we get back to the flat, let me explain to Callum and Boo what's happened."

"You always want to do all the talking," I replied.

"Because it is my job. I am in charge. And I was trying not to get us both caught out today. It's a crime to impersonate a police officer."

"I mean in general. Even Callum says . . ."

Stephen jerked his head in my direction, and I knew I had overstepped. This is what happens when I feel too good. I talk and talk and talk and eventually I start saying things that are supposed to be in the secret file, the things other people told you that you were supposed to keep to yourself and then . . . boop! Out they come.

"Callum says what?"

"That you're . . . serious," I said. "About your job."

"Of course I'm serious about my job."

"That's what he says," I replied.

"Meaning what?"

"Meaning . . . you can tell them. And something I never understood . . . how does it work, you being a police officer, but not a police officer, or—"

There was every chance that Stephen knew I was trying to switch topics. He definitely wanted to know what Callum had said. But I understood Stephen enough now to know that he could always be relied on to talk about procedures and how things worked. He would be compelled to answer me.

"Technically," he said, "I am a sworn police officer. I'm just not assigned to any particular station or role, at least not as far as the Met is concerned. I went through the training. I did five weeks at Hendon, another four months or so at Bethnal Green, then in-person training out of Charing Cross police station, then back to Hendon. It took about eight months. On the side, I was given some bespoke training at the MI5 training academy, most of it on how to get into places where security clearance is needed. Oh, and management. They had me do some management training. All in all, it took about a year, but I'm still learning, every day. A lot of these jobs, they train you, but you really learn by doing it. Normal constables train with experienced people, but no one does my job. I have Thorpe, I suppose."

"He's scary," I said.

"He has to be like that. You can't let your emotions get in the way of what you need to do, and you can't have too much of a personality, at least on show. But he's all right. Every time I've needed something from him, he's been there. And, frankly, I don't think he knows what to make of us. Must have been a shock to get us as an assignment. He might be relieved if it all falls apart. He can go back to finding terrorists or whatever he did before."

"I guess that is kind of crazy," I said. "He doesn't have the sight. He just has to take your word for it that there are ghosts and that you're getting rid of them?"

"Basically. Now, what did Callum say?"

"Nothing," I said. He didn't press the matter.

The flat had the sour smell of day-old garbage. Some effort had been made to pick up the place. Dirty containers had been bagged up and left to ripen in the kitchen. In addition to that scent was a sharp, familiar fragrance that made me wildly hungry.

"Look who it is!" Callum said. He was on the sofa, eating something from a bowl. Presumably this was the source of the good smell. God, I was starving. Taking out the ghosts clearly took something out of me. Boo was walking around the room in a pair of yoga shorts, flexing and pivoting on her newly freed leg. She spun around when Callum spoke.

"What are you doing here?" she asked. "Come to see me, right? I have my leg back!"

"How does it feel?"

"Ready to kick something," she said. "Still itches. And I think it might've shrunk? That can happen, you know. The muscles lose tone."

"Looks the same size to me."

"Does it?"

She bent over and examined her leg for a moment. I would have been freezing in those shorts. The flat was hardly warm. But English people are hearty.

"What is that?" I asked Callum. "It smells *amazing.*"

"Jerk goat," he said. "Made by my mum last night."

"Can I try it?"

"This is the real thing. My mum's from Kingston. This is a family recipe."

"I can't eat that," Boo said. "And I can eat almost anything."

"I *can* eat anything," I said.

"Not joking," Callum said. "This stuff would actually kill you."

"I'm hard to kill."

"If you like." He held the bowl out to me. "But I'm warning you. Be careful."

The meat in the bowl was gray and cooked to soft pieces. I held the bowl up to my nose and inhaled the delicious, prickly aroma of things that were on the high end of the Scoville scale. My eyes watered very gently from the pepper oils. Spicy food and I have a close relationship—an obsessive one, in fact. If it's spicy, I want it. I want to sweat and shake and go half blind from the searing pain . . . which, now that I put it that way, seems really suggestive. But spicy stuff is addictive. That's a *known fact of science.* I shoveled in three forkfuls one right after the other. And then, after riding through the sweats and shakes, had another. Callum burst out laughing.

"Clearly you *are* fine," Stephen said.

"Why wouldn't she be?" Boo asked.

Boo had been eyeing Stephen for about a minute now. I noticed it through the waves of delicious pain. Considering how large and luminous and heavily lined her eyes were, it was remarkable how she had mastered the subtle stare. I'd only learned to see it because she had applied it to me for about a week straight when we first met.

"We need to talk to you about where we've been this morning," Stephen said.

And so, he told them. His account was all right. I would have added a lot more description and detail.

"One morning," Callum finally said. "We were gone for *one morning* and this happens?"

"It wasn't planned that way. We went to the hospital, and then we stopped into the pub on the way back to Wexford. It all happened quite quickly, and Rory handled it very well."

"Boom boom," I said to Callum, hoping that would bring some light to the room, but he didn't react. Boo flexed her long purple nails.

"So this will look good to Thorpe," Callum said. "At least we have that. They'll reward us with great riches. Or, maybe, a new sofa from IKEA."

"I'm not sure about that," Stephen said.

"Why not?" Boo asked.

"Well, this might cause him more problems. The case against Sam Worth is fairly damning, between the forensics and the confession. It's going to be difficult for them to make this one go away, especially with a grieving family. They can't say that there was a ghost going around beating people's brains in with a hammer, so Sam Worth has to be set free. Someone has to be seen to pay, just like in the Ripper case."

"So Sam goes down for it?" Boo said. "It's not right."

"We can only do our job. We leave it to other agencies to do the rest."

"But that's not right," Boo said. "He didn't do it."

"But he *confessed,*" Stephen said. "And the forensics back up his confession. Even *he* would rather think he did it than admit to himself that some terrible unseen thing was in the room."

"So he just stays in prison?" Boo said.

"Again, that's beyond our scope. But there's something else that isn't. On the night of the attack, the floor of the bathroom cracked open. Rory also found a crack—"

"I know about this," Callum said.

"And he told me," Boo added. "Wouldn't it be nice if we all got together to tell each other things?"

"Right," Stephen said, sidestepping this. "Well, the crack is also present in the basement wall of the Royal Gunpowder. It's now a safe working assumption that the crack is in some way connected to both the woman Rory saw in the bathroom and the murder in the pub. So we should find out exactly how far this crack extends. To that end . . . all around London, there are GPS stations, used to track location. Mobile phone towers are also GPS stations. Aside from being location trackers, they can monitor the movement of the earth to a very high and precise degree. They're used to monitor earthquake damage now. We could potentially use that information to determine the size and location of the crack. Once we know that, we can deal with the question of precisely what it's done."

"Can we access that information?" Callum asked.

"We can ask Thorpe about it," Stephen replied. "I can get that process started. In the meantime, you and Boo should cover the area, working in hundred-yard circles. Canvas everything. Check streets, go into shops, access as many basement levels as you can. I'll see if we can't get you both some British Gas uniforms right away."

"I can also check with the Tube engineers to see if there are any broken substructures in the Liverpool Street area," Callum said.

"Good."

"I can get into Wexford," Boo added. "Come for a visit, have a look around."

"What about me?" I asked.

All three of them looked over. While I realized I was not a member of the squad, I certainly felt like I was entitled to be a part of whatever happened next. I think Callum was about to say something along those lines, because he nodded and opened his mouth to speak, but Stephen reached over and smoothly picked up the car keys.

"You should probably get back," he said. "You've been gone most of the day."

Boo and Callum exchanged a look. Stephen was already moving toward the door. I took the hint and pulled myself off of the broken-down sofa.

"What did Callum say to you?" Stephen said when we were back in the car. "And don't say *nothing.*"

"He just . . . he kind of feels you try to do it all yourself."

"I don't." Stephen shifted his jaw. "I'm in charge. There's a difference. We work in a secret department. I can't just tell everyone everything."

"Not everyone. Callum and Boo. There's only three of you."

"It doesn't matter."

"I think it does," I said. "If you don't talk to them, who else are you going to talk to? They're the only other people who know what's going on."

"You don't know what you're talking about," he snapped. "You don't understand my job."

Well, that got a reaction. Interesting. I didn't mind the snapping, and I gave him time to work out his feelings on the car. He ground through a few gears and maneuvered around a bus a little faster than normal, gunning the engine a bit. I don't know how to drive a manual car, so all the gear changes fascinated me. He didn't hold the gearshift, either—he kept his fingers flat and straight and pushed on it with his palm. It was a relaxed stance, not a tense death grip.

"You like driving," I said.

"It's good for thinking," he said in a low voice.

"I like to sing and drive," I said. "I only sing in the car, but I tell you, I am good. But only when I drive. I suck otherwise. Do you ever sing in the car?"

"Generally not. But I am driving a police car."

"I think people would like a singing policeman. Makes life seem more like a musical. Everyone wants to live in a musical. Like *Foot-tastic.*"

"You can talk for a long time about nothing."

"I certainly can, you charming man!"

His arms and shoulders sagged a bit, and the car slowed.

"I'm sorry," he said. "I don't like keeping Callum and Boo in the dark about some things, but I barely know how to do my own job. It can be terrifying to tell them to do something when I don't even have the facts. This job is dangerous. Boo's been hurt. You've been hurt. I've been hurt. Callum was hurt before he was on the job. And if one of us was killed, would they even care? Or would they just tidy it away, like they did with the old squad? Bury our files and make it all disappear?"

"So why do it?" I asked.

Stephen exhaled slowly.

"Better than banking, I suppose."

"Did you just make a joke?"

"I *am* capable of that."

"You are?"

"I'm full of surprises," he said.

He pulled up by Spitalfields.

"I'll leave you by here," he said. "It's best not to keep to the same places all the time. You can get back from here all right?"

"I think I can walk two streets over."

"Of course. And, just so you know . . . the timing alone suggests that the situation is safe. The crack opened over three weeks ago. You found one person within a day, and another turned up within forty-eight hours. If more had come up, I'd like to think we would have seen some evidence by now. This could be the end of the matter. But we'll do all we can and I'll keep you informed. I just don't want you to worry."

"I'm not worried," I said, opening my door and getting out.

He leaned over to have a better look at me.

"You're not," he said, "are you?"

And I wasn't. I realized on some level that I definitely should be worried if there was, in fact, a raging tear of angry ghosts *under my building*. Perhaps being a terminus did something to the chemicals in my brain. Or maybe I was just nuts, burned out from all that had happened to me.

"Promise me," he said, "if you see something, anything, you'll phone us first. Don't try to deal with it alone."

"Like I'd do that," I said, smiling.

"I think you might. I mean it. Don't try to do it alone."

"That's been the message of today's session," I replied. "I'm glad you got it. I think we've accomplished a lot."

"Go."

But he smiled. He didn't want me to see, but I totally saw.

16

JAZZA WAS KNITTING A LARGE BLUE TUBE.

It seemed to fit in with the way my day was going. Spend the morning at a mental hospital. Blast a murderous ghost into oblivion. Come home, and the roommate is knitting some long tube. Why not?

"You're knitting a big tube," I said. "You knit?"

"When I'm nervous," she said.

The tube looked to be about four feet long and was pretty narrow. Jazza's German books were scattered all over her bed, partially obscured by wool. It looked like she was trying to read and knit at the same time.

"Is it . . . for a snake or something?"

"I just learned how to do sleeves for sweaters, and I can't stop making them. I'm going to fail German."

"You're going to be fine," I said automatically.

"I'm not," she said calmly. "Which is why I'm knitting. It's very meditative. Where have you been? You weren't answering your phone."

"Oh . . ." I quickly turned toward my closet and opened the door. "I was at the National Gallery. Doing research for an art history project."

I'd come up with that excuse when I was about three feet away from the door.

"Oh. Right. Is . . . that my skirt?"

"Oh. Yeah. I borrowed it. Is that okay?"

"Course," she said. "I was just wondering."

Jazza allowed me to borrow her clothes, although I usually asked before I did so. But being Jazza and a nice person, she didn't grill me on why I needed to wear her black skirt to go to the museum to do research. I slipped off the skirt and hung it up in her closet. Then I went into my own closet and needlessly busied myself going through my clothes, dragging the hangers across the rail with a terrible squeak that ate away at the edges of my nerves. I smelled of mental hospital. The tang of it was in my shirt. I pulled it off and threw it into my laundry bag.

Behind me, I heard the *clickclackclickclack* of Jazza's needles gently striking together. The light clinking of the radiators kicking into life. Everything was clicking and clanking. What was I doing all day? Oh, I just solved a murder, is all. Solved a murder, took out the murderer. What was the point of that, though, if you couldn't *tell your roommate*?

"Revision party tonight," she said.

I'd forgotten all about this. The revision party was just a long study session in the refractory. The school kept it open late and served snacks.

"I may not stay," she said. "I have to speak out loud to get ready for the German oral. Do you think you'll stay over there?"

"I . . . maybe?"

"Are you all right?" Jazza said. "You seem a bit . . ."

I guess she didn't know what I seemed like, which was fair. Neither did I.

"Headache," I said. "I'm going to shower. Warm up. My blood is too thin for this weather."

I scoured the hospital stink from my skin with copious squirts of body wash that slicked the shower stall tiles and caused me to slip twice and bang both my elbow and head into the wall. I cranked the water up to the maximum temperature, reveling in the great clouds of steam I created. The ghost destroyer in her robes of mist. Alone at last, warm at last. I closed my eyes and let the water pour over me, and I thought about everything that had happened in the basement. It had been so simple—I'd just reached out and destroyed. It was no more complicated than stepping on a bug.

I allowed myself the fantasy of confronting Newman again, but as I was now. I saw him coming at me with the knife, and I just reached out and touched him with the tips of my fingers—

Then someone opened the bathroom door and I jumped.

"Who's in there?" a voice called. Eloise's, I thought.

"Rory!"

"It's so steamy in here. I can't even see where I'm going!"

"Sorry!"

I wrapped myself in my towel and pushed back the curtain. I really had done a job on the bathroom. All the mirrors were completely fogged, and the floor had a shiny veneer of moisture.

I did a quick little run back to my room and got changed for dinner. Jazza had stopped muttering German and was now just knitting, waiting for me to get ready. We walked over with Gaenor and Angela, both of whom had gone deep into exam madness mode. They laughed at everything. They *cackled.* They may have been drunk. I wasn't sure.

We sat with Andrew and some other guys from Aldshot. When I asked where Jerome was, I got some not very specific replies about him being held up doing something. He finally came in during the last ten minutes of service, grabbed a plate, and sat down heavily. He made short work of a few pieces of pizza, and he didn't have much to say.

Mount Everest, our esteemed, massive, and always angry headmaster, took to the raised podium that used to be the altar back when the refectory was a chapel.

"Everyone," he began, "the dinner service will now be cleared for tonight's revision party. Please assist by clearing your trays and putting them on the racks. The refectory will be open until midnight. Make sure to check in with your assigned prefect and let him or her know when you return to your building. While you may talk during tonight's session, please remember to think of your neighbors and control your volume."

"I'm going back." Jazza stood up. "See you at home."

Angela left as well, leaving Gaenor, Andrew, Jerome, and me in a group. A few people came over to ask the guys questions or tell them where they were going to be, and Charlotte came to check on me to see if I was staying. I pulled my books out from under the bench and tried to pick the subject I might have a chance of making some progress on. I decided on further maths. I could do some problems. Math problems gave me a feeling of accomplishment.

I was quickly distracted when the kitchen staff started putting out the study snacks—bowls of potato chips, trays of cookies, pitchers of pale lemon and orange drink. I immediately got up to help myself, but then the guy in front of me sneezed into his hand and dug the same hand into the chip bowl. I returned to my seat and tried to do more problems. I was also trying to make eye contact with Jerome, who was working on Spanish. I tapped my leg against his under the table, then I rubbed my calf against his. He lifted his head partway, but kept looking down at the table.

I pushed my notebook toward him and wrote, *What's wrong?*

He scratched his nose, then wrote, *Nothing. Just trying to work.*

Which was fair. Everyone was working. I seemed to be the only one with her head on a swivel, unable to concentrate. I stayed for two hours, managing to get through about twenty problems. I poked through some pages of French as well.

"I may go back too," I said quietly.

"I can take you back," Jerome said. "I'll let you in."

I assumed this was Jerome saying he was ready for a study break in the form of face-sucking. I slapped my books closed and scooped them up.

When we stepped outside, I expected his arm to slip around my waist. That didn't happen. He did head toward the darkness of the green, though, to a bench. It was under the shadow of a tree, which blocked the streetlight. I sat down next to him. The cold of the bench immediately attached itself to my butt and crawled its little fingers up my back. I leaned into Jerome for warmth. This is where he should have turned and put his face next to mine. Instead, he just sat there, slightly slumped forward over his knees. I reached over and pushed aside one of his longer half curls that was just brushing his ear. I would start there. Jerome liked those little kisses around the ear.

He shifted away ever so slightly.

"What's up?" I asked.

"I just wanted some air."

There was no shortage of that—night offered all of the cold, wet air you could ever want.

"Okay," I said. "Air. We've got it."

"You missed art today," he said. There was no particular inflection behind it, just a statement of fact.

"I did," I said. "I was—"

I was about to say "not feeling well" when he cut me off.

"You were researching at the National Gallery?"

I hadn't told him this particular little fib. I'd told Jazza. When had they had time to exchange that information? And why had they exchanged it? And why hadn't I come up with something better to tell Jazza? Because I'd been *busy*, that's why. Okay, better question—when was I going to shut up and explain this?

"I . . . yes. I was doing my project? That Mark is having me do? Because I'm behind?"

"You missed art history to work on art history?"

"Well, it sounds stupid when you put it like that—"

"What's the project on?"

"What?"

"What were you doing research on?"

This took me completely by surprise. I couldn't think of any paintings. Any. In the entire world.

He knew. I had never gone to the museum. In the chill and the dark, with the damp creeping into my clothes, the world was suddenly very foreign and unfriendly. And when I didn't answer, he stood up and paced in front of the bench.

"I don't know how to do this," he said.

"Do what?"

He inhaled loudly through his nose and ground one of his heels slowly into the grass.

"On Wednesday night," he said, "where did you go?"

"What?"

"Wednesday?"

Wednesday . . . what had I been doing on Wednesday?

"You were with some guy," he prompted me.

Of course. On Wednesday I had gone out with Callum. Callum, he of the many muscles, who almost played professional soccer. The fact that Jerome knew who I was with made me . . . well, actually kind of furious.

"Did you *follow* me or something?"

"No, I didn't *follow* you. A few of the year elevens saw you."

I handled that badly. I raised my hands in apology.

"Sorry," I said. "I mean . . . he's a friend of mine. Just a friend. You're being paranoid."

That was probably the wrong thing to say. In fact, I was 100 percent certain that was the wrong thing to say, but I said it anyway.

"Paranoid?" he said. "You're lying to me."

Well, he was right about that. But all the things he was thinking, those were wrong. Which meant that I had to do some very fast talking. Where, where, where could I have been?

"I was at *therapy*!"

And I said it loudly. Really loudly. I startled him, I startled myself, and I startled some little creature crawling around near the trash next to the bench, because I heard it scurry off.

"Therapy?" he said.

"Therapy," I repeated.

"And that guy . . ."

"Is in my therapy group."

"So you've been going to therapy and you decided to . . ."

"Lie?" I said. "I said that to Jazza because she asked where I was and the museum was the first thing I could think of. I never said anything to you because I didn't want you to have the girlfriend who always talked about her therapy. I mean, I'm already American. That would make me *super* American. Don't you think we're *all* in therapy or something?"

I don't like admitting this about myself, but I lie well. I come from a long line of people who can tell a story, who can elaborate on reality. I can sound convincing. And my words were having the right effect. Jerome was finally looking at me.

"There's nothing wrong with therapy," he said.

"I never said there was. I just don't want to talk about it all the time. I don't always want to be the girl who got stabbed, okay?"

All that, perfectly true. In fact, so true that my eyes were watering a bit and my voice cracked a little.

"You can talk to me," he said. "You can tell me what's going on. That's kind of the point."

I hated this. I hated lies, and I hated pity. I think I hated pity more. I hated looking damaged and weird and Jerome wanting to talk about feelings. I was so sick of *feelings*.

"I want to help," he said. "I'm sorry. I'm really sorry—"

"Forget it," I said. "The point is, there's nothing going on. There's nothing to tell you."

Oh, except that I took down a murderous ghost today. And went to a mental institution to interview a murderer. Except for that.

"I can't believe I did this," he said.

Now his voice was honeyed with guilt, and my stomach was churning slowly, like a soft-serve ice cream machine.

That was what did it. The guilt. This emotional mess that I didn't want and I didn't need. I liked making out with Jerome and I liked that Jerome existed in the boyfriend sense, but I didn't want to deal with all of his feelings about my feelings.

"We shouldn't do this," I heard myself say.

"Do what? Fight?"

"This," I said again, and flopped my hands around in a way that was supposed to mean us. This thing that we were.

Amazingly, Jerome spoke hand-flop. I saw it hit him, and I saw him try to deflect it by quickly looking away, as if it didn't hurt.

"Break up," he said. "That's what you want."

This wasn't his fault. I had lied to him—not because I was evil, but because I had to. My life was a disaster and I was sick of problems and he was just one more. Breaking up made things simple. For me, anyway.

I felt queasy now, and I just wanted it all to stop. I wanted to go inside.

"I'm going in," I said.

He didn't reply. It seemed so harsh, what I was doing. I

hadn't planned it, and I seemed to be moving on autopilot, walking away, leaving him there on the bench.

Then there was Jazza. Jazza, I was certain, had asked me where I was for a reason. She had reported it to Jerome. My suspicion was confirmed when I stepped into the room and she immediately pulled off her headphones. German mumblings leaked into the air. She set the knitting aside like she might have to make a sudden leap out of the window.

"You're back early," she said, her voice wavering a bit.

I sat on the edge of my bed and faced her. Jazza was too compulsively honest to keep up any façade.

"Did you talk to Jerome?" she asked.

I nodded.

"Are things okay?"

"I wasn't cheating."

"I didn't think you were."

"But he did."

I could see her choosing her words carefully—plucking each one delicately out of the lexicon in her head, as if she were picking up tubes full of explosive chemicals.

"I don't know what he thought," she said. "But he was concerned. And confused. And . . . I think you've been coping with this, and no one knows what that's been like for you and we all respect that and . . . it's . . . it's hard to know? What you're thinking? But I told him to just talk to you and . . ."

"We broke up."

A widening of the eyes.

"Oh . . . but . . . no! But . . . nothing was . . ."

"I just can't do this right now."

"Oh."

A more final oh. An oh that sounded understanding. She got off her bed and came and sat next to me on mine.

"Are you all right?" she said.

"That's all anyone has asked me for weeks."

"Oh, I'm sorry . . . I . . ."

"I'm fine," I said. "I really am. I might even be too fine. I should be upset, but I'm not. I'm just . . . nothing. I just did it. I had to."

All of that was true. I didn't really know why I had done it—why I had just broken up with the only actual boyfriend I'd ever had. But I just knew I had to.

The radiator clanged and whistled, and Jazza and I sat there, both staring down at the floor. She was my friend, but she was Jerome's friend before she knew me.

"Do you hate me?" I asked.

"Do you know what I think?" she replied.

"Smarter and better things than me?"

"I think . . . we should go next door and see if Gaenor and Angela have any plonk."

"Plonk?"

"Wine. And I have chocolate. I say we wrap ourselves in our duvets and drink wine and eat chocolate."

I started to shake my head—I didn't want anyone to be nice to me—but Jazza was not taking any of that. She pulled me upright, yanked the cover from my bed, and wrapped it around my shoulders.

"This is not me asking," she said. "This is me telling you."

17

THE NEXT MORNING, I WOKE TO THE SOUND OF CHURCH bells. London is full of them, old bells in old stone towers, calling out through the gray December gloom. They continued to ring and vibrate in my head, each percussive blow bringing thoughts of nausea. I'd had one and a half mugs of the warm and cheap red wine Gaenor kept in the bottom of her closet, really not that much, but the effect was still seeping over me. My mouth felt like an acre of cotton field, and there was a vague and unspecified ache crawling up and down from my stomach to my head.

I liked it. I liked waking up like this. I'd had a good night. Everyone had rallied around me—Gaenor and Angela and Jazza. Eloise had come in and told us about all the French guys she'd dumped. No one seemed to think I was a monster—though I was sure Jazza was going to check on Jerome immediately and make sure he was okay. She was already awake, bundled in her robe, a cup of tea in her hand and the German book back in front of her face.

"Morning," she said. "Breakfast? I've been up for hours now and I'm starving."

Hours? A look at my watch (and the bong of the bells) told me it was only nine in the morning. She was making up for the time she'd lost on me last night.

Breakfast, of course, meant facing my now ex-boyfriend. It was going to be an issue, this eating business. I sat with Jerome and Jazza and Andrew. How would I ever eat again?

"Not for me," I said. "I think I'll stay here and die."

"Ill?"

"A little. I'll be fine. You go."

So Jazza got herself together and left, and I thought about the word *ex-boyfriend.*

How was this going to be, seeing him everywhere? What the hell had I done? A quick flush of terrible feelings came over me—guilt, sadness, shame—they were all in there. I shook them off. This morning I would find some money—I had to have a few pounds left—and get a muffin and a coffee for myself. I would deal.

I shabbily dressed myself in already worn sweatpants and a T-shirt, brushed my hair with my fingers, and rubbed some terrible crud from my eyes, then I scuffed down the steps. As I reached the bottom, Charlotte came out of Claudia's office.

"Oh," she said. "Here she is now. Rory? Claudia needs to see you."

"What for?" I mouthed.

Charlotte smiled a bit stiffly and gave a little shrug. I stepped around her and into the office.

"Please close the door," Claudia said. "I'll be just a moment."

She was typing away on her computer and didn't look up. Her office was icy cold and kind of dark. She had all the lights off except her desk lamp, and only a small electric heater by her desk. I huddled in the chair, pulling my fleece down over my hands.

"Aurora." She swung around to face me, and the effect was a bit disturbing, like I had been called into the office of the evil supervillain. "Tell me about how this week has gone for you."

"Oh. Well, it's been good, I think."

I was expecting that she would say something rote in return. "Good" or "glad to hear it" or "let's arm wrestle in celebration, for I am very strong." But she didn't. The high, red flush on her cheeks seemed a bit higher and redder than normal, and the cold crept up my sleeves and down my neck.

"Aurora," she said again. (It's never good when someone uses your name twice at the start of a conversation.) "I am aware . . ."

She let her open-ended awareness hang in the air for a moment.

"I am aware . . . you were a bit behind when you returned."

"Well," I said, "I did what I could. You know. I was . . ."

"Of course."

She adjusted something in the top drawer of her desk that must have prevented it from closing all the way and gave it a firm push.

"You have handled this situation very bravely. But there are some concerns. It's become fairly evident that you are falling behind academically, possibly to the point where you cannot catch up to the place you need to be."

She opened a folder on her desk, and I saw it contained my history pre-exam.

"I wasn't really ready for that one," I said.

"These are quite basic questions, and much of this was material you covered before your departure . . . though of course I understand that there were stressors then as well. But there are other things. I have reports of you using your phone in class, of sleeping in class, and even, just yesterday, of missing class."

Okay, so maybe they did track you at Wexford.

"And I do understand that these circumstances you are in are not normal," Claudia went on. "But you should know that anyone else would have already been disciplined for this. Anyone else at your level of progress would already be gone."

"The class I missed," I said. "I was at therapy. That's where I was."

"You had therapy? You haven't been to the sanatorium."

"With an outside person. Charlotte gave me her name."

That was possibly a misstep. If Claudia called Charlotte, Charlotte would give her Jane's name and number, and if Claudia called Jane, she would soon discover that I was a big fat liar. The lies, the problems, they seriously never ended.

"If you are going for treatment, we need to be informed—certainly if that means you won't be in class."

"I'm sorry," I said. "I thought it was okay for me to go."

Claudia pursed her lips and looked down at the desk drawer again. The room suddenly seemed very dark, and the orangey light from her desk lamp throbbed in my vision.

"Having you come back was an experiment," she said. "We've had a week to assess where you are. And I have to be honest, Aurora . . . I don't think it's quite fair to you to have you continue at Wexford. Perhaps this isn't the best place for you to regain your footing. Before you go through the stress and strain of exams, I want you to think carefully. I think you should consider departing early."

What was happening? This couldn't be what I thought it was. Because it *sounded* like I was being kicked out.

"Departing early?" I said.

"The exam process is quite arduous, and it was always a worry. There is no shame in any of this. You are not to blame for the events that led up to this moment. However, I don't see how you can recover academically, certainly not enough to participate in the exams. If you wish, you may remain for the exams. I am trying . . ."

And she was clearly trying. I didn't think this was comfortable for her at all. For all her meatiness and love of hockey violence, I never got the feeling that Claudia was an unkind person.

"I'm trying to give you the best way out. Go home for the holidays. Be with your family. Make a fresh start in the new year."

"But not here," I said.

"I think it's unlikely, Aurora."

I would not cry in Claudia's office. No. I would not. I looked up, because sometimes you can dry up your eyes that way, but all I saw were mounted hockey sticks. Hockey sticks are not calming.

"Have you talked to my parents?" I managed to ask.

"Not yet, no. And to be clear, this is not a punishment. This is just something very unfortunate, and I truly want what's best for you. If you really feel you can handle the exams, then by all means, stay on and take them. But if you don't . . . and there's no shame . . ."

Funny there being no shame, because all I felt at the moment was shame. Shame is like melting. You can actually feel your muscles sag and drop, as if your body is preparing you to crawl, or possibly ooze, to the nearest exit.

"Think it over and let me know what you would like to do," she said. "I don't want to make this harder on you than it already is. How about we speak again tomorrow?"

"Tomorrow," I said. "Sure."

I pushed back my chair, and it scraped loudly on the floor and wrinkled the oriental rug. In the lobby, I paused by the pigeonholes and listened to some screaming laughter from the common room. Someone dropped something in one of the rooms overhead, and it made a loud *thunk* on the ceiling. Hawthorne was full of life.

I climbed the stairs slowly, past the dozen or so framed and all slightly crooked photographs that lined the entire stairway. Sports day photos and team photos and class photos. I would not be a part of this place. My image wouldn't hang on the wall. Once the talk of the school, I'd quickly be forgotten, like Alistair, who died in his bed. The Ripper news wasn't even the biggest story in London anymore. That was over. A political scandal had taken its place.

I stopped in between the fire doors on the second floor and stared at my hall through the glass window. Today was Sunday. We had "reading days" through Monday, which just meant study days. Then the exams were Tuesday and Wednesday. I wasn't going to get anything accomplished today, and tomorrow wasn't looking so great either. Exams on Tuesday, and then

Tuesday night to scrape up whatever remnants of my brain were left and try to mold them back into a brainlike shape for the next two exams.

I stood there in the two feet of vestibule, the one that always stank so sharply of industrial carpeting. I probably would have stayed there all day, except that there were loud footsteps and Charlotte threw open the door behind me.

"Are you all right?" she asked.

That was all it took. I just started crying. Proper, full-on crying. I flowed like some kind of industrial hose. Charlotte instantly put an arm around me and walked me down to her room, pushing my face into her shoulder and her masses of red hair.

Charlotte had a single, much smaller than my room. But the smallness also made it feel more snug, and probably a lot warmer. Unlike me, she didn't store her partially worn clothes on the back of a desk chair. I had seen her room from the hallway many times, but never from the inside. On the wall where the door was, the entire thing, floor to ceiling, was a collage. We were allowed to Blu-Tack things to our walls. She had a carefully curated selection of tear-outs from fashion magazines of models reading books, posing with books, or generally standing near or approaching books. Glamour and brains, all glossy, all perfectly arranged on the wall. It must have taken her a long time to put them up, to make sure they lined up just right, neat and square to the edges of the wall.

It took me by such surprise that I stopped crying. I'm not sure why it came as such a shock to see that Charlotte had decorated her wall in this way.

"I'm failing," I said, wiping my nose with the sleeve of my fleece. There was a large floppy cushion on her floor, all ready to receive my butt, so I took advantage of it. "I missed too much. I'm too behind. Claudia said I could stay and take the exams, but there's kind of no point . . ."

To her credit, Charlotte didn't argue this. Nor did she try the Jazza way, telling me things would be fine when they clearly would not be fine.

"Have you discussed some other arrangement?" she asked. "Maybe you can take the exams at another time?"

"No." I shook my head. "They're sure I'm not going to catch up, not this year. And she's right. I'm not going to catch up."

"So you're going back to Bristol."

"I guess?"

"And go to school there?"

That's what my parents said *before* I returned to Wexford in this little experiment. That was before the experiment totally failed, and my parents were about to be told that this whole year was basically a bust. God only knew what would happen now.

I leaned back against the radiator and banged my head against it gently. It was much too hot to be leaning against, but better burning hot than cold. I didn't really care if it seared my back. I looked from picture to picture on her wall, my eyes twitching a bit as they took in the information. Books and brains. Successful girls.

I was not a successful girl.

"Jane," she said, handing me a box of tissues. "I think you should go talk to Jane. Today. Right now."

"There's nothing she can do," I said. "This is all academic stuff—"

"No," Charlotte said firmly. "She can help. And I know she'd see you."

There was a look to Charlotte—a bit of an evangelical glow. Jane was the magic problem solver as far as she was concerned. It must have been nice to have that kind of faith in therapy, or problems that could actually be solved.

"Jane's dealt with all kinds of people in crisis. Loads of people who have been expelled. I know she could help. Let me phone her. Please."

Charlotte made the call. I could tell from her end of the conversation that Jane was fine with me coming over.

This was one of those moments when I was excruciatingly aware that I was not at home. At home, I had friends at the other end of a phone, friends who were close by. I had friends here, but they were friends I'd been lying to almost as long as I'd known them. I'd had a boyfriend up until last night. He'd probably be glad this had happened . . .

No. He wouldn't. That was worse.

I had Stephen. I could call Stephen.

Except my being kicked out destroyed *everything*. All his work. The squad. Me gone from Wexford meant no terminus, no squad, nothing. How had so much come to rest on me? Me, the one who, given the opportunity, would wake up at three P.M. every afternoon and eat Cheez Whiz twice a day. I was not the kind of person on which the fate of police organizations should rest.

I just wanted to go back to bed and wake up when I was twenty-five.

"She says to come right over," Charlotte confirmed as she

hung up. "I told her the basics. And don't worry. I won't tell anyone. Not a word."

"Thanks," I said.

"You'll figure this out," Charlotte said. "It's going to be fine, no matter what happens."

Of course, Charlotte had a very limited knowledge of things that could happen.

18

JANE'S VIVID RED HAIR WAS ONE OF THE BRIGHTEST THINGS on the street. She was wearing an extraordinary dress—one with long flat shoulder pieces that raised up at the tips. The dress was both boxy, baggy, and form fitting and was made of an African-inspired print in orange and black and yellow.

"Cup of tea," she said, ushering me inside. "And a little something sweet."

"It's okay. I don't want anything."

"I have to insist. I don't problem solve on an empty stomach. Let's perk up your blood sugar a bit. You've had a shock. You look peaky."

It was very dim in the hallway. I caught just the tiniest glint of the strange silvery leopard over in the corner and the fans of gold on the wallpaper. She drew me deeper into the house, past the staircase, to the kitchen. The kitchen had a bit more light pouring in from the garden windows—not that there was much light to be had.

"Very interesting ones today," she said, pushing forward a container of baked goods. "This is an Earl Grey shortbread, and this brownie is made with orange and chili. Eat it. You'll feel better."

Jane's practical and positive manner was infectious. I did as I was told. I plucked out a brownie and ate it in three bites, crumbs falling from my mouth onto the counter. She nodded in satisfaction and went about filling the kettle and setting it to boil.

"Now," she said, "Charlotte told me the basics. What were you told, exactly?"

I recounted the conversation with Claudia, and Jane listened soberly.

"You could take the exams," she said.

"I could. But I have more or less no chance of passing."

"You're sure?"

"I'm sure," I said.

The kettle clicked off, and she filled the teapot and set out the mugs and milk and sugar.

"Let me ask you something," she said. "And I want you to really think about this question. Tell me truly. *Why did you come back?*"

"They sent me back," I said.

"Who did?"

"My . . . doctor."

Jane cocked her head at this answer.

"But you could have said no. Surely, you could have returned to America. But you came back here."

"I had to," I said.

"*Had* to?"

"It's complicated." The understatement of the year. "My shrink . . . sorry . . . thought it was a good idea. It was an experiment in making me normal again. And it failed."

"Now, now," Jane said sternly. "None of that. None of that. You've failed nothing."

"Besides school."

"You can hardly call what you've accomplished a *failure,* Rory. Think about it. How many people could come to a foreign country to do a year of school to begin with? And then continue with school after a brutal attack?"

"I kind of don't care," I said. "I'm tired of being different because something happened to me. I just want things to be regular. And nothing is ever regular now."

A cloud passed over whatever sun there was, and the kitchen dropped into shadow. She got up and turned on the overhead light, then filled our cups with tea. She put sugar in hers, and I was mesmerized by the gentle *tink tink tink* of the stirring spoon against the side of the cup.

"I told you what happened to me when I was your age," she said. "I told you about the man who chased me, how he hit me on the head and I ended up in that pond. I almost drowned that night. I touched death, and the experience left me a bit *changed.* And I have a feeling you know what I mean. It changed you too."

She couldn't be saying what I thought she was saying.

"It began with the Ripper," she said. "Those of us with the ability recognized the signs. A killer who never showed up on CCTV. Pops up all over the place. No physical evidence. This same person gets into the BBC and delivers a package with a human kidney in it, and again, no one sees a thing. And just as

mysteriously, he goes away. He turns out to be a person without a past? Without relations? No trace in the world? Not very likely, now, is it?"

She smiled, her mouth broad. She wore dark lipstick, a shade between red and orange. The color made my eyes throb. There was an unreality to all of this—the big kitchen, the high counter stools we sat on, the swirling oil painting by the window that I'd never noticed before. It was a painting of the sun, or maybe some snakes . . . how was I mistaking the sun for some snakes?

"Charlotte told me about the night you and she were attacked," she went on. Her voice was so low, so calming. "She saw and heard nothing until the lamp came down on her head. And you were found in the toilets down the hall, all the mirrors shattered, the window broken. The door had to be broken down. What was the story? That the killer escaped through that broken window and ran? But Charlotte told me the protective bars on that window had just been repaired, because they had been loose. No. No living person escaped from that room. What you saw and what was reported, those were very different things, weren't they?"

I could only nod. Jane let out a tiny, contented sigh.

"When did it happen?" she asked. "When did you get the sight?"

Ever realize you've been holding your breath? You think you're breathing normally and then you just become aware that you've clenched your abdomen and the space around your heart is full and your lungs are filled to bursting and you let go . . .

I let go. Of all of it. Well, mostly all of it. I began with the

night of the double event, when Jazza and I snuck through the bathroom window and went to Aldshot. How we ran back across the green in the middle of the night, and as we climbed back into Hawthorne, I saw a man that Jazza couldn't see. And the next morning, they found a girl's body on the green. When I got to the part where Stephen and Callum and Boo entered the picture, three words popped into my mind: Official Secrets Act. The terrible document I had to sign in the hospital, the one that made me promise that I would not talk about the squad under any circumstances. And while the Official Secrets Act might not have been written with people who saw ghosts in mind, it was still scary, and my signature was still on it. And I was pretty sure they were not joking when they said I *really* wasn't supposed to say anything.

"Right after I got to England," I said. "I choked at dinner. Stupid."

"Not stupid. It happens how it happens. But I suspected you were one of us. That's why I reached out to you. I wasn't certain, but I felt it was very likely."

"The trouble now," I said, "is that I lie all the time."

Jane nodded. "So tell me what *really* happened to you. Because I imagine this is what complicated your therapy before. You can tell me the whole story."

"I don't know how to talk about this," I said. "I broke up with my boyfriend yesterday because of this."

"I know the feeling. At first, I thought I was mad, so I lied to cover that up. But then, through some sheer effort of will, I convinced myself I was *not* mad. What I was seeing was real. Now, luckily for me, this was the late sixties—pretty much the best time to run away to London that there ever was. People were open then. There were squats to live in. The rock-and-roll world was vibrant, and yet strangely down to earth. If you hung out on the street long enough, you could meet pretty much anyone you wanted. And there were many mystics, and a lot of people on a lot of strange drugs. If you said you could see ghosts, well . . . people didn't look at you quite so strangely. They either believed you or thought you were as high as they were. I knew, if I looked long enough and asked around, I would find more people like me. And I did. I found friends. And that changed everything for me. Everything. Rory, the things you've been through, with no one to talk to. Unless you know people like us? Surely, you must have met someone?"

"No," I lied, again. "No one."

"No wonder you feel so alone," she said.

I started laughing—I mean, really laughing. I have no idea why, but I laughed until tears ran down my face.

"Why am I laughing?" I asked when I could catch my breath.

"Relief," Jane said, patting my hand. "It's relief. You're not alone anymore. You're one of us."

Relief. Such a nice word. Such a sweet word.

"Who is us?" I said. "There are others?"

"Oh, yes," Jane said. "Many others. And some live in this very house."

She held up a finger, indicating that I should wait, and slid off the chair. She opened the kitchen door and called into the dark.

"Devina! Are you here? Mags?"

There was a high-pitched reply from somewhere in the house.

"Come down for a moment, won't you?" She left the door cracked open and returned to her seat. I could hear a quick patter of footfall on the steps, and then a girl appeared in the door. She was very tall and very slender, with short silvery white-blond hair. Despite the chill, she wore a shift dress that exposed much of her very long legs. Her bony knees had scratches on them, like a little child's knees. As a concession to the weather, she wore a cropped denim jacket and a pair of short boots.

"This is Devina," Jane said.

"Hello." Devina's voice was high and light. Pixie-like.

"Is Mags in, darling? Or Jack?"

"Just me right now."

"Devina also lives here," Jane explained. "In fact, several people live here. The house has seven bedrooms and I find I can only sleep in one at a time. So I had the idea to share the house with people like us. Call it a home for the exceptionally sighted. Devina, be a dear and put that casserole in the oven? Rory needs a proper meal."

Devina went to the fridge and pulled out a big blue casserole dish. I was staying for lunch, apparently.

"You cannot go back to Bristol," Jane said, putting her hand on the table to mark her pronouncement. "You cannot go back to America. You need to be with people who understand, and people who can teach you. No one's even taught you about your ability, have they? No. You must stay here. There's another empty room upstairs. That one will be yours."

"I can't," I said. "My parents . . ."

"Don't know and won't understand. They certainly won't give permission for you to stay in a stranger's house after you've been asked to leave school. You need to do something a bit bold and brave. You need to take things into your own hands. You need to leave."

"You mean, like, run away?"

"I mean precisely that. It's the only way. These are exceptional circumstances, and this is the answer to your problem. Thank goodness you came here in time."

"It really is," Devina said, nodding in agreement.

When you hear about people running away, I always imagined it just like that . . . like, they take off physically running into the night. I hate running, and I never really wanted to leave home, so the concept was entirely foreign to me.

"I know this is quite a lot to take on board, Rory, but if you're brave and do this tonight, tomorrow will be the start of a wonderful new life. A life without lies. A life that makes sense."

"Tonight?"

"It has to be tonight," Jane said. "It sounds like they've already set the wheels in motion for you to be returned to your parents. It will be much harder after that. They've given you a night of freedom to think. You need to take advantage of it. And you'll have us helping you. You're not the first person I've helped."

"She helped me," Devina said. "Saved my life, coming here."

"It doesn't have to be permanent," Jane said. "But, Rory, believe me, it's easier when you're part of a group. When you're with people who understand. And we understand. It's up to you, of course, but I speak from experience. So does Devina."

It's possible that I have a higher tolerance for crazy talk than most people because of my background. I've channeled multicolored angels with my cousin and gone for discount waxes with my grandmother. I know *two* people who have started their own religions. One of my neighbors was arrested for sitting on top of the town equestrian statue dressed as Spider-Man. He just climbed up there with a few loaves of bread and tore them up and threw bread at anyone who got near him. Another neighbor puts up her Christmas decorations in August and goes caroling on Halloween to "fight the devil with song." That's just what things are like back home. While there were certain to be people back home who would fully accept my tales of seeing ghosts, they were also the same people who tended to see Jesus in their pancakes.

I could see this version of my future all too well. I would be fully absorbed into the crazy wavelength of Bénouville. Left to my native kind, I would get strange. But Jane was well-adjusted. She clearly had a happy and successful life. I didn't know much about Devina, but she looked happy too. They looked *normal.* And nothing, nothing was sweeter than that. Jane was right—there was no other solution. This was the juncture, and I had to make a decision. Home, where my brain would go soft and I would forever wonder about what I was . . . or here, where I could at least learn something. And I could stay around Stephen and Callum and Boo.

I could even join them, on their own terms.

The light seemed to grow warm around us at the table.

"How?" I said. "I don't know how to run away here, I mean, I know that sounds stupid, but . . . do I just not go back?"

"You don't go back," she said, "but we muddy your tracks. Who knew you came here?"

"Just Charlotte."

"Good. Now, did you use your Oyster card to get here?"

"Yes."

"Did you buy it with a credit card or cash?"

"My debit card . . ."

The Oyster card was the Tube pass. You put money on the card and then you just had to tap it on the reader when you got on and off at your stations so it knew how much to deduct. I saw what she was saying. It tracked your journey, and if you bought it on a credit card, there would be a record.

"I've done this before," Jane said. "Just a few commonsense steps we need to take. Here's what we will do . . ."

The plan crafted over the table was simple, and thorough. I would walk to the South Kensington Tube station and use the nearest ATM to withdraw all of the money in my account. It had to look like I needed it all. I would also be seen on the camera at the machine. Then I was to drop the Oyster card in front of the station. Someone would pick it up and use it, leaving a confusing trail on the Tube.

"Give your mobile to Devina," Jane said. "She'll take it and use it in a few locations around the city. Just drive around with it, D, then dispose of it."

Out of all of this, not having the phone made me the most uncomfortable. I didn't actually know anyone's phone number—not my parents in Bristol, not Jazza, not Stephen. They were on the phone.

"I won't be able to reach anyone," I said.

"You can't talk to anyone," Jane replied. "Not at first. You'll want to, but that puts the whole thing in jeopardy. We need the mobile."

I'd left my coat in the vestibule. The phone was in the pocket.

“I’ll get it,” I said, getting up from the table. I made my way through the dark hallway, my eyes struggling in the change in the light, my heart slamming in my chest. I had to do this. Jane was right. She was the one person with an actual plan. And doing this—terrifying as it was—was the right decision. It was the only thing that would make my life make sense again.

The room spun gently, and I realized I was smiling. I didn’t feel happy, did I?

I knocked into the silver leopard as I fumbled for my coat and retrieved the phone. Boo’s number was still on the display. Boo’s was a good number to keep. I stared at it, committing it to memory. At least, trying to . . . seven, seven, three, four . . .

“Here.”

Devina was behind me, and her hand was already on the phone.

“I’ll take care of this now,” she said. She grabbed a set of keys from a bowl on a little shelf by the door. And then my phone was gone.

I continued chanting the number in my head and reached into my coat pocket again. I’d shoved a colored lip gloss in there the other day. I rolled up my sleeve and used the sticky gloss to write the number on my arm. It was messy, but I had it. I had one link.

It felt like cheating, but Jane didn’t know about Stephen. I still had secrets to keep, even now, as my life collapsed around me and re-formed into something new and very unfamiliar.

And strangely, for the first time in what seemed like a very long time, I felt like I knew what the hell was going on.

NEW DAWN PSYCHIC PARLOR,
EAST LONDON
DECEMBER 9
11:47 P.M.

PAUL WAS A CHEATING BASTARD. HE WAS THE KING OF cheating bastards. He should wear a crown.

Oh, everyone had warned her. Her sister. Her friends. Her horoscope. Everyone said Paul was trouble, but Lydia had believed him. She had believed the stories of his weekends away with his mates, his overtime at Boots doing stock inventory. She believed him when his car didn't start and when he had a toothache. She was a trusting person, and everyone had warned her, and now it had come to this. The voice mail. The voice mail from some random slag that she heard when she accidentally but kind of on purpose got into his voice mail.

Okay, mostly on purpose. Paul was such an idiot. Only one password for everything. She'd seen him key it in dozens of times. All she had to do was ring the voice mail externally and put in the numbers, and there it was, the message from someone who just *sounded* orange. She was giggling away on his voice mail like a *Big Brother* reject.

Lydia wobbled on her heels as she hurried. It was hard to speed walk and cry. *Bastard!* Dawn would fix it. Dawn would tell her what to do. Dawn always knew what to do.

Dawn operated out of a third-story flat, which served as both home and office. She was there day and night. All you had to do was buzz up. It didn't matter what time. Dawn dozed between clients. And even at this hour, there could sometimes be a wait—people would sit on the floor of the hallway by the door. Everyone who went to Dawn knew she was good. But there was no one else there tonight, and Lydia was able to go right in. Dawn was sitting in her easy chair, dressed in a pair of jogging bottoms, a red jumper, slippers, and a dressing gown. Lydia carefully made her way over, her heels catching in the thick salmon-colored carpet.

"Hello, my love," Dawn said, setting down her magazine. "Come to see Dawn? Problems? I see all kinds of problems. Your aura is very dark, not like normal."

Lydia took a seat at the small card table Dawn used for business. Dawn got up from her easy chair and took a seat on the folding chair on the opposite side.

"I think my boyfriend is cheating," Lydia said tearfully. "What do I do?"

"Cheating? Well, we'll ask the cards, love. They never lie. We'll ask the cards and see what they say."

Dawn reached over and took a small blue velvet drawstring sack from the windowsill and pulled it open, exposing the tarot deck. She held the deck for a moment in both hands and closed her eyes. This part always calmed Lydia—you could almost feel Dawn reaching out, pulling energy closer. Dawn opened her eyes very slowly and, without another word, began laying the initial spread. When the spread was complete, she leaned back and examined it like a surgeon evaluating a complex injury.

"All right, all right. Let us see. I'm looking back now, here's your past. And right away, I'm seeing trouble with love. It's right there."

She pointed at the cards, and Lydia nodded.

"Present is the same. But the past . . . you're an honest person. That's what these cards are saying to me. You always try to tell the truth."

"That's true," Lydia said, nodding.

"But not everyone does. Because honest people, sometimes they are taken in by liars. And I'm seeing that here, even in the past. I don't think there was a lot of truth here."

Lydia started crying again.

"So he *is* cheating," she said.

"The cards say someone has not been telling you the truth for a long time."

"Do they say who he's cheating *with*?"

"Cards don't talk like that, my love. Cards speak bigger truths."

Dawn rocked to the side to adjust her dressing gown and continued.

"All right, my love. The cards are going to tell us what to do. The cards don't lie. Let's look and see what the future holds, yeah? Let's see."

Dawn laid down the remainder of the spread, topping it off with one final card. She placed the Tower down on the table and rocked back in her chair a bit.

"The cards are clear today," she said, her voice grim. "Tower always mean big change is coming. Look."

She pointed at the image of a tall stone tower being struck by lightning, causing it to explode and crumble.

"Always," she said. "Look at the people falling. Everything falls apart with the tower. Everything has to change."

"So, I have to . . . break up?"

"Something going to happen, love, something big. And I see lies. Someone was lying, and now everything going to change."

"So you're saying I should break up with him?"

"The cards say what they say. Somebody lying. Something is about to happen, something big."

Lydia paid Dawn her twenty pounds and thanked her profusely. Everything was always clearer after she talked to Dawn. She took the phone from her pocket and walked down the street, her steps firm and full of purpose. Paul was going to answer some questions. Paul was going to feel her wrath right now. He didn't pick up the first time she called, so she paused when she was almost at the corner and dialed again. And again. It took four tries before he answered.

"You cheating bastard," she began. "I know. . . . Yes, I know. I heard the message. . . . What do you mean, what message? Her voice mail. Yes, I listened to your voice mail. . . . Well, if you didn't do anything, then what's the problem with me listening, yeah?"

"No! No!"

Someone was screaming—it sounded like Dawn. Lydia spun around just in time to see Dawn leaning out of her window much, much too far. And then in the next, unreal moment, she tumbled from the open window, headfirst, toward the pavement.

THE

In a motion of night they massed nearer my post.
I hummed a short blues. When the stars went out
I studied my weapons system.

—*John Berryman,*
Dream Song 50,
"In a Motion of Night"

19

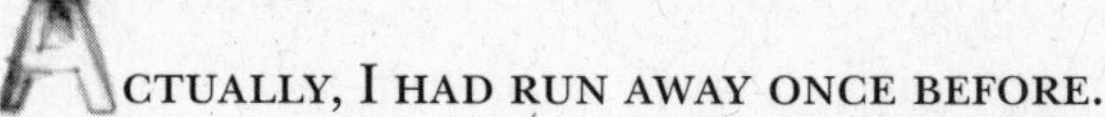

ACTUALLY, I HAD RUN AWAY ONCE BEFORE.

I must have been nine or so, and my parents wouldn't take me to some event at the mall or something, and I got mad. I ran out of the house and went to Kroger. Our family friend Miss Gina, the one my uncle Bick has been "courting" for the last nineteen years or so, is the manager. I had this idea that she might let me live in the office or something. She let me sit in there and gave me some juice and carrot sticks. After about two hours, I got bored and went home. My parents must have known—Miss Gina probably called them the minute I showed up. She walked me home, and I went inside, right up to my room. I kept expecting my parents to come to the door and start yelling, but they never said one word to me about it.

My parents are clever like that. They knew I would do a better job of berating myself for being an idiot than they ever could and that waiting for the punishment was much worse than the actual punishment. The *tick tick tick* is much worse than the *boom.*

I thought about this when I woke up in the guest room at Jane's and heard the *tick tick tick* of the bedside clock. Well, I thought about it after I figured out where the hell I was. It took me a few minutes to sort out which things in my head were reality and which were fantasy. The wallpaper, for example. In this room, it was a series of bronze circles that nested in each other. It was the kind of wallpaper that looked exciting and dramatic in the dark, because all you saw was the gold. In the morning, it was strange. And it was even on the ceiling. I had to stare at it for a while before I decided it went into the "real" column. I spent another few minutes considering the black lacquer bureau and the slightly gold-tinted mirror that rested on top of it. Also real.

And the heat. The house was warm. And also I was in a large bed, and yes, the blanket appeared to be some kind of fuzzy tiger print. I opened the (also black) curtains and some weak sunlight slithered in. I examined myself in the gold mirror. My eyes were bloodshot. My hair was a rat's nest on one side. A hair tumor. That's what I had.

"Awesome," I said.

I returned to the bed and lifted up the bedside clock. Right before I had gone to sleep, I had transferred Boo's number onto a piece of paper towel I'd snagged in the kitchen. There was a knock on my door, and a second later, it opened by itself. A dripping Devina stood there, dressed only in a towel. I balled the paper towel in my hand.

"I thought I heard you," she said. "I just woke up myself. We tend to sleep late here, don't worry. Jane'll be up, though."

"Is that you, Rory?" Jane called from downstairs.

"She's awake!" Devina yelled back.

"Good morning! Do come down for something to eat!"

"I'll see you down there," Devina said, continuing to her room, leaving a trail of wet footprints in the carpet.

I felt the need to secure the number—to keep it with me. I was wearing borrowed pajamas with no pocket, so I tucked the number into the side of my underwear at my hip. Stupid, but it made me feel secure, like I was keeping my friends close.

There was music coming from the kitchen, nothing I recognized. Some kind of rock, not recent, but not bad. Jane was wearing something approaching normal today—pants and a white blouse. It was still a funky pants and white blouse, puffy in all kinds of unexpected places, full of more folds I couldn't understand.

"Coffee or tea?" Jane asked pleasantly.

"Coffee, please."

She poured me a cup from a French press that was ready and waiting.

"How do you feel this morning?"

"Kind of shocked," I said.

"Yes, I remember the feeling. I ran away when I was your age. Took a night bus from up north. Slept on the bus. Woke up alone in London, ejected onto the streets in the pouring rain. I hope this was a slightly nicer way to face your first morning of freedom."

She offered me the usual plate of baked goods, but I shook my head.

"I'm not really hungry," I said. "I'm still kind of nervous."

"Sure? I can make you what you like. An egg, some toast . . . no? All right then."

"My parents," I said. "They're going to be really upset."

"Undoubtedly so." She nodded and leaned on the counter while she sipped her coffee. "But that will be temporary. And I have a recommendation. Write your parents a letter. Speaking to them on the phone will be too difficult right now. But you can express all you need to in a letter. Tell them you're fine, that you just need some time. A letter will put them at ease."

It sounded like good advice. I wrapped my hands around my mug and enjoyed the warmth.

"I've been thinking about our next steps," she said. "It might be good for you to get away from London, just for a bit. This is where they'll concentrate their search—not that it's easy to find people in London. Moreover, I think you could use a change of scene. I own a property out in the country. It's lovely this time of year. I was thinking we could drive there today. I'll have some of the others come along, and you can get to know everyone. We always have a good time in the country."

Running across London was one thing, but this idea of now running to the country seemed like . . . well, really running away.

"Darling, you've already done it," she said. I guess she saw my hesitation. "In for a penny, in for a pound. The house is exquisite. It belonged to the people who owned this house. It was their family seat. This was just their London residence."

"The people who owned this house?"

"Friends of mine," she said. "They died in the early seventies and left it to me. They made my entire lifestyle possible, which is why I, too, like to share the wealth. Finish up your coffee and have a nice shower. We'll leave whenever you're ready. Devina will show you where the towels are. You're just about Mags's size, so you can have some of her clothes."

The upstairs bathroom, like so much else in the house, was black. Shiny black tiles with shiny silver fixtures, a heated towel bar I burned my hand on, and a big, freestanding tub smack in the middle of the room, with a circular curtain to wrap around it. The showerhead was in the ceiling, so the water poured down on me like rain.

When I returned to my room in my towel, Devina was sitting in the middle of my bed reading a book. She was wearing a very long dress today, one that covered her feet. The denim jacket was back.

"Oh," I said. "Hi."

"Hi. Clothes for you."

A large pair of what seemed to be men's jeans and an oversized sweater had been provided.

She made no indication that she was about to leave. I wasn't sure what I was supposed to do—change here, or take my clothes back the bathroom. I decided to do that thing you do in gym (or, at least, the thing *I* do in gym) where you pull on your underwear under the towel. Then you maneuver into the bra with the towel on. Then you drop the towel and get into the rest of your clothes as quickly as possible.

"You going to be staying with us a while, then?" Devina asked.

"I don't really know what I'm doing," I said, fumbling on the bra.

"I didn't either when I showed up."

"How long ago was that?" The bra was being difficult and refusing to hook.

She stretched out and rolled onto her stomach.

"Oh . . . two years now? See, my mum had this boyfriend? Total bastard. Always creepy. Obviously creepy. A little too interested in me? And one night she went out and he started to get a little friendly. So I slapped him. And he slapped me back. I don't think he meant to do it so hard, but he was pissed. I fell down a flight of stairs. Almost broke my neck. I managed to get myself up and out of the house and walk to A and E. And my mum actually blamed *me,* even after they banged him up for it."

"Sorry," I said. Though sorry didn't seem to cover it.

"Don't be. I met Jane because of what happened to me. I'm glad it happened. It made me stronger, better in the end. And now I have a *real* family."

"You and Jane?"

"All of us," she said.

"Who is all of us?"

"Oh, you'll meet everyone. Jane's helped a lot of people. You'll see. She fixes people. She fixed me. I would have been a disaster if not for Jane. You'll see."

Devina smiled, and I noticed that she had extremely small teeth. Niblet teeth, like a child. I clutched the towel around my chest. Funny . . . I didn't really care that much if Devina saw me in my underwear, but the scar, that was private.

"So," I said, "I'll just finish getting ready and . . ."

I think she got the hint. She slid off the bed.

"See you downstairs," she said, wandering out of the room. I put on the jeans and sweater and sat on the end of the bed, kicking out my bare feet, trying to make sense of my life. If I was going to the country, it seemed wise to let someone know. I retrieved the phone number, which I had moved to the pocket of the jeans.

Boo was enough of a wild child to understand, and I felt certain that if I asked her to, she would keep the news to herself, or manage it in some way.

But I had no phone. The only one I had seen was in the kitchen. There wasn't one in this bedroom. I would need to find one. I poked my head out of my room and had a look around. All the doors on the second floor were closed but mine and the bathroom. It didn't seem right exactly to start poking into the bedrooms. The stairs went up to another floor. I decided to try that instead.

There were only three doors on the third floor, and the middle one was slightly open. I pushed it gently and stuck my head inside. This room was very large and, unlike the rest of the house, wasn't quite as starkly black or white or silver. This one was pretty much what I imagined an Arabian spice market to be like, or maybe the tent of a king in the deserts of Morocco. Or something. Really, the room had no precedent.

The floor was covered in multiple Persian carpets, overlapping each other to form a soft but uneven patchwork surface. There were several low octagonal tables inlaid with mother of pearl and ebony, others made of multicolored tiles. But there were also Victorian elements—a yellow chaise lounge, a rose conversation chair. There were mirrors as well, two massive ones, leaning against the wall. The walls were full of built-in shelving, mostly filled with books. One wall contained records. There was a large wooden cabinet that appeared to have built-in speakers, but not speakers like I had ever seen before. It had to be an antique. The table was covered in pots and bowls and ashtrays, dancing golden Shivas, and three alabaster chalices.

Despite the sensory overload, I managed to find a telephone.

A dial telephone, no less, and a receiver with a spiral cord. And it was heavy, some kind of special, fancy plastic that probably could have deflected a bullet. Dialing a phone is ridiculous. You have to spin the wheel for every number and wait until it rotates back into position before you can dial the next one. The receiver, along with being weighty, was also massive, easily as long as my head. The past, I decided, was a complicated place.

Boo answered on the first ring with a cautious and confused, "Hello?"

"It's me," I said.

"What number is this? It says blocked."

"Yeah," I said. "I kind of . . . left?"

She paused for a moment. Then it sounded like she was moving away and closing a door.

"Left?" she said.

"Ran away. Took off. You know."

"You didn't," Boo said. "Seriously?"

"Very seriously. They were going to kick me out, and I couldn't go to Bristol. I couldn't go home. So I left."

"My God, you don't do things by half, do you? We've been trying to call you all morning. Something's happened near your school."

"What? Is everyone okay? What happened?"

"It wasn't at your school," she said. "Just nearby. A woman died . . . it's a strange one."

"Is it related to the other thing?" I asked.

"We don't know yet. That's what we're trying to work out. Where are you? We'll come get you."

"I'll come to you," I said. "Just tell Stephen I was out and forgot my phone, okay? Don't tell him what I just told you. I'll tell him myself."

"Have you been taking Stephen lessons?"

"Seriously. Let me. I don't think he's going to take the news well."

"You're probably right," she said. "Fine. I'll cover, but get over here, yeah?"

As I replaced the extremely big receiver on its base, I heard someone in the doorway behind me.

"Oh, here you are," Jane said. "Phoning someone?"

"Sorry," I replied. It wasn't like I could deny it. "I know you said, but . . . it was just a friend."

"No need to apologize. I understand the impulse."

Her words said one thing, but her demeanor suggested another. Her face tightened a bit, like she was clenching her jaw a little. I understood why she would be mad. She was putting herself at risk to help me, and here I was breaking the rules and sneaking around her house. And I was about to break another of those rules.

"Before I go," I said, "there's just one thing I have to do. I have to meet someone."

"I don't want to tell you what to do," Jane said, "but in my experience, it's usually best not to do that, not at this juncture. Friends tend to report things back to authorities."

"Not these friends," I said. "I promise. They won't say a word. And I'll be careful. I just need a few hours."

"If you feel you have to," Jane said, her face relaxing into a reassuring smile, "then do what's right for you. I'm glad you came up here, actually. This is my favorite room. I wanted you to see it. This, as you can see, is the library. Lots of classic works of spiritualism, many not so classic works. And I keep the vinyl records up here, along with the turntable. As I told you, my friends and I were very involved with the rock-and-roll scene. We had just about every album that came out between the mid-sixties and the mid-seventies. It's quite a collection. I suppose they'd be worth something, as they're all original, but I'd never sell them. And they're not pristine. We played our albums until they wore out. We weren't gentle with them."

She smiled lightly at the memory, then went over to the shelves and fished something out of a bowl. She held up a silver Zippo lighter.

"Mick Jagger's cigarette lighter. He left it here one night. We have all sorts of things like that in here. I'll show them all to you when we get back—that's if you're interested. You probably wouldn't even know who most of the people are. I know this house must look odd to you. The early seventies were quite an unusual time."

"I like unusual," I said.

"That's an *excellent* quality, and one that will certainly help, considering who we are. Now, if you're going to go out, I think Mags has a coat that would fit you. And let's find a hat and sunglasses as well. Devina can drive you wherever you need to go."

In the end, I was outfitted in a red coat, something they called a "bobble hat," and a big pair of shades. When I looked at myself in the mirror by the door, I was greeted by a bright red buglike object in a big wool hat with a puff on the top. It was definitely not my usual look.

There were two cars in front of Jane's house—a buttery yellow Jaguar, clearly a classic from some other era, and a modern, more practical black car. We took the newer one.

"Where do you need to go?" Devina said.

I didn't want her to take me directly to the flat, so I asked her to drop me at Waterloo station. Devina didn't talk when she drove. She blasted music, and she drove fast. She tailgated, and she played chicken with every light, only screeching to a halt on red at the last moment. On the positive side, though, I did get there very quickly.

"I'll wait here," she said.

"I . . . um . . . It could be a while?"

"That's okay," she said. "I have a book."

"No, I mean, really a while? I can get back on my own. No one's going to recognize me in this."

Devina shrugged. As soon as I was out of the car, she sped off. I hurried over to the flat. I buzzed up and took the steps two at a time, slipping on some slick pizza menus and falling in the process.

"Where have you been all morning?" Stephen asked as he let me in. "We've been calling. And—"

"I was out," I said. "Forgot my phone."

"Isn't this exam week?"

"I don't have one now," I said. "Can you just tell me what's going on?"

Boo's eyes met mine from across the room. She took in the hat and the coat.

"There's been a death in the Wexford neighborhood," Callum said. "About a five-minute walk from your building."

"The facts are these," Stephen said, waving me to the sofa. I sat down as he picked up his computer. He clicked through a few documents. "Just before midnight last night, a woman named Lydia George went in to have her tarot cards read by a woman named Dawn Somner. Dawn was a psychic who operated out of her flat. The reading ended around quarter past. Lydia left Dawn's flat and proceeded down the street while making a phone call. She was just on the corner, about twenty yards from Dawn's door, when she heard Dawn scream 'no, no.' Immediately afterward, Dawn toppled headfirst out of the window. At this point, Lydia fainted. All of this is confirmed by a second witness, named Jack Brackell. He was standing there, directly opposite, waiting for a ride from a friend. It's when we get to Jack Brackell's story that it becomes of interest to us.

"Jack Brackell had the vantage point. He saw Dawn open the window and that she was acting like someone being *pushed or forced*—his words—but that there was no one behind her or next to her that he could see. He also reports that Dawn shouted 'no, no' and then fell from the window. He ran to her at once, but it appeared that she was dead. He phoned 999 and remained on the spot. No one emerged from the building. The ambulance arrived four minutes later, declaring Dawn dead at the scene; the police arrived two minutes after that. They secured the premises. No one else was home in the other two flats. Her flat was found to be absolutely in order, no signs of struggle or violence of any kind. The case isn't closed yet, but the notes indicate that it's believed to have been an accident—that what Jack Brackell saw was Dawn trying to stop herself from falling. They think she probably got her dressing gown caught on the radiator when she was opening the window. The gown was long and had holes at the bottom. She struggled to get it loose and lost her balance."

"But you think different?" I asked.

"Because of the proximity to Wexford and this detail of

Jack's, we think it's worth looking into. I made you a promise. I told you we would keep you informed."

"And if there *is* something in there," Callum added, "we need you."

We need you. Three little words.

"*If* you want to come," Boo added.

"Of course I want to come," I said automatically. There was no way I was going away with Jane until I found out what this was about.

20

Dawn's flat was indeed near Wexford, over by Goulston Street. It was on a street not often frequented by Wexford students, but I still hurried from the car to the door, well wrapped in my borrowed red coat and bobble hat.

We searched the building first. It wasn't a large building, so the checks were easy enough to do. Stephen gained admittance to the first apartment by showing his warrant card, while Boo jimmied open the locked door of another using a credit card. The basement was a storage area with no lock on the door. We found nothing—no ghosts.

Dawn's was the top-floor flat, the outside decorated with a doormat with a picture of the moon and stars and a piece of blue-and-white police tape. Stephen distributed latex gloves to Callum and Boo, but when he was about to hand me mine, both he and I seemed to realize the potential problem.

"I suppose," he said, "we don't know if you can have these, do we?"

"I don't know," I said.

"Well, the scene's been processed, and it's unlikely anyone is going to come back to have another look. Just be careful what you touch."

We ducked under the police tape one by one. The whole flat was thickly carpeted in a pinkish-salmon color and smelled of burning sage. The decorations were a bit wizardy—the walls had been papered in a pattern of white with small silver stars. The gauzy silver curtains, the small tables with hunks of crystals looking like strange moon fruit, the incense burners and framed pictures of astrological signs. Two widths of beaded curtain sealed off the rest of the flat—the kitchenette, bedroom, and bathroom. It was an all-in-one live and work space.

"Looks like my cousin's house," I said. "Except more weird. Which is saying something."

Pictures had been removed from their hooks and neatly set on the floor, facing the wall. Three of the chairs had been turned upside down—not as if knocked over, but neatly flipped and placed in a row. A small decorative table had been set on top of another, slightly larger decorative table. The gemstones were arranged in a triangular pattern on the floor.

"Is anyone in here?" Stephen called. "Anyone at all? Make yourself known."

That brought no response, not that I thought he was really expecting one.

We all stepped a bit further into the main room. Callum and Boo walked over to the beaded curtain. Boo drew them back and looked through the kitchen, then she and Callum stepped through and proceeded on to the bedroom. Stephen had a look at the window itself, looking at the radiator at the base, the locks, how it opened.

"No one here," Callum said, poking his head through the beaded curtain.

"Just have a look around," Stephen said. "See if there's anything in there that seems off."

I was just standing in the middle of the living room with nothing to do, so I went over to what I assumed was the reading table (it was covered in a purple velvet cloth). My cousin Diane, the one who operates the Healing Angel Ministry out of her house, loves tarot cards. She taught me to read them when I was twelve, when my parents had to go away to a seminar and I stayed with her for a week. While Cousin Diane was sure that the angels were speaking through the tarot cards, I was slightly more convinced that you just learn what the symbols are supposed to mean and make up a story. It's actually really easy. You start interpreting, and you watch people to see if they are responding. You normally say something like, "There are three things going on in your life right now that you need to deal with." There are always three things going on in people's lives that they have to deal with. People will fill in the blanks for you and tell you how amazing you are. I read cards at summer camp for two years in a row. I was so popular with the cards that I convinced my junior counselor to let me skip archery and gymnastics and sit in the games bunk and do readings. I am bad at cartwheels and shooting arrows, but I am good with tarot cards.

It was odd how these cards were spread out—the entire deck on display. And there was something odd about them that I couldn't place. Something was wrong with this deck.

"Didn't you say she had just done a reading?" I asked Stephen.

"She had, yes."

"How long before?"

"A few minutes."

This wasn't how you stored tarot cards. Usually card readers stack their cards carefully, and they often store them in special bags or boxes. They don't just drop them all over the table.

"Can I touch these?" I asked Stephen. "Everyone who has had a reading has touched this deck, so it's probably covered in fingerprints anyway."

"I suppose that's fine. Just be careful."

The sleeves of the coat were slightly too long for me and covered my hands, so I slipped it off and put it on the table. I used one finger to slide the cards around, sorting them into major and minor arcana. The minor arcana are the ones like normal playing cards, with suits (wands, swords, plates, and cups) and numbers, kings, queens, and princes. The major arcana are the ones with the titles and the more complicated meanings—Death, Love, the Star, the Sun, the Wheel of Fortune. The major arcana are all numbered, and they go in a certain order. Twelve, the Hanged Man. Thirteen, Death. Fourteen, Temperance. Fifteen, the Devil. Sixteen . . .

One was missing. The Tower.

A lot of people think that Death or the Hanged Man are the cards in tarot to watch out for, but the real baddie is the Tower. And even though I didn't believe in tarot cards, I took their significance seriously in order to do readings. The missing Tower gave me pause. I looked on the floor, the chairs. I looked on the chair and the shelves, anywhere a card may have been set down.

Boo and Callum had returned from their examinations of the kitchen and bedroom.

"Nothing," Boo said. "It's neat and tidy in there. This is the only room that's been disturbed."

"A card is missing," I said.

"She certainly could have caught her dressing gown on the valve here," Stephen said, pointing at the radiator. "Or she could have tripped over the cord of the floor lamp."

"A card is missing," I said again, louder.

"How do you know?" Callum asked.

"I read cards," I said.

"You what?" Stephen said.

"My cousin," I explained. "Owns an angel ministry? She taught me. And a card is missing. Not just any card either. The Tower."

"It can't be a coincidence that this woman is a psychic," Boo said.

Stephen got up and shook his head.

"What?" Boo said.

"I don't believe in psychics."

"You see ghosts, and yet you don't believe in psychics?" Boo asked.

"Correct."

"How does that work?"

"Because I have seen a ghost," he said. "I have abundant proof of their existence. Whereas I have no proof that any psychic, ever, has seen the future. They work through a series of suggestions and guesses."

"I had my cards read, and it was dead-on," Boo said.

"Which doesn't disprove my point."

I left them to debate the issue. People who do tarot often have books about tarot lying around. There were none in this room (which made sense—you don't want to keep a copy of *How to Read Tarot Cards* around if you're supposed to be an expert). No, you kept that stuff private. The bedroom maybe. I went through the beaded curtain, through the little hallway kitchen, into a very tight and dark bedroom with a claustrophobic floral wallpaper and a disturbing collection of stuffed animals lining all the surfaces. I found a pile of books by the side of the bed—books on crystal healing, color therapy, chakras. A bit more digging through the pile turned up books on popular psychology and reading body language. And sure enough, three books on tarot cards. I found the one with the best color reproductions of the cards and flipped through until I got to the Tower, and when I did, I actually let out a gasp.

Stephen and Boo were still having at it when I came back in with the book. It took me several tries and a progressively louder voice to get their attention.

"Listen," I said, holding up the book. "What does this look like to *you*?"

The Tower is an image of, as you might suspect, a tower. In many drawings, the tower is hit by lightning and is crumbling. But in almost every picture of the Tower, there is also the image of a person falling, usually headfirst. That's how it was depicted in this book.

"A woman falls headfirst out of a window," I said as they gathered around. "The one card missing is the one with a picture of a woman falling headfirst out of a window. What does that say to you?"

I was gratified by their stunned expressions.

"Definitely not good things," Callum said. "Nice one, Rory."

"And," Boo said, "another connection to the cards."

"This is no doubt important," Stephen said. "But I refuse to believe these cards are magic."

"Rory said she reads cards," Boo pointed out.

"Yeah, but I make it all up," I said. "The cards all have some meanings ascribed to them, but the way you do the reading is to make up a story based on what you see. The cards can mean a lot of different things, so you can go off of what people tell you. I mean, I don't know. Maybe some people have some ability, but I didn't. And I found all kinds of stuff in her room about reading body language and things like that."

Stephen held out his hands as if to say, "This is my point."

"All right," Boo said, holding up her hand. "Fine. Maybe whatever was in her flat takes offense to people who claim they are dealing with the spirit world when they aren't? Maybe it was looking for a way to communicate. If you're a ghost and you're afraid, you can't speak to anyone . . . maybe you look for someone who you think can see or hear you. You go to a psychic, and when the person can't help you, you get upset."

"And you fling her out the window," Callum said. "That does sound *possible,* at least."

"There is a logic to that," Stephen said, frowning. "Something to consider."

"But . . . ?" Boo said.

"But what bothers me is the *display,*" Stephen said. "It's so organized. The ghost we met in the basement was not organized."

"Different ghost," Callum said.

"Yes, but why go to all this trouble?" Stephen said. "The last one was, presumably, trying to protect its burial site. *If* this is a ghost, what's it trying to accomplish? What's it trying to say? Look at this. This isn't an angry scene. It's just a very odd one."

"Mental ghosts," Callum said. "Bound to be odd."

"But not all ghosts kill," Stephen said. "Before the Ripper, had we *ever* met one that killed?"

"We hadn't," Boo said. "It's true."

"But I've certainly met a *few* that could kill people," Callum said. "Even if they weren't successful, they were certainly capable. You forget I got this way because one tried to do me in with live electricity."

"I just think it's odd that we have two deaths resulting from what would clearly have to be two separate ghosts," Stephen said. "Given that the majority don't kill, to have two for two—"

"I'll say it again: *mental ghosts.* From Bedlam."

"Not all mental patients kill, either, you know. Homicide is not the inevitable outcome of all mental impairment. And this scene . . . it's just not *right* somehow. Why did this scene change *after* the police left?"

He went over to the window again and opened and closed it, looking for some kind of answer in the motion.

"Do you know Charles Manson?" he finally said. "American serial killer from the late nineteen sixties? He had a large group of followers called the Manson Family who murdered several people on his command—random people. Strangers. The scenes were famous for their brutality and strangeness, and Manson planned it that way. He told his followers to kill everyone in the houses they went into and to leave behind 'something witchy.' So they did things to deliberately make the scenes horrific and perverse. That's what this reminds me of. It's something *witchy.* The death of a psychic. A death that mirrors the image on a tarot card. A scene that changes like a magic trick after the police leave, as if whoever did this knew someone *else* was coming afterward."

His phone rang, and he took it from his pocket. His conversation was short and terse, with a few "yes, sir"s and "I see" and then a deeper "I *see.* Yes. I'll do that."

When he looked right at me, I knew.

"Boo, Callum, would you mind going to the car?" he said. "We'll meet you there in a minute. I have to speak to Rory for a moment."

There was an uncomfortable silence as Boo and Callum left us.

"That was Thorpe," Stephen said, holding up the phone, like Thorpe was actually inside and might reach out and wave to me.

"Wexford has reported you as missing," Stephen said. "You were last seen leaving with a bag at midnight by a prefect who is now, presumably, in a great deal of trouble."

"Funny story—"

"It's not a funny story. Rory, what the bloody hell are you thinking?"

"I'm thinking that they're kicking me out," I said. "I *told* you I was failing. Then it was back to Bristol and then back home, where I go insane."

"Where were you last night?"

"With a friend. I didn't have a choice. You yourself said I couldn't stay in Bristol. You know I can't go back. I need to be here, right? Especially, you know, since there's a big crack under the building that might be puking up dangerous ghosts, so . . ."

"I'm waiting for you to finish that sentence."

I swallowed before saying it.

"I should join you guys. Now."

"It's not something I can decide," he said quietly. "I don't get the final say."

"Yes you do. You said you do."

"I advise. Thorpe makes the call, along with his superiors."

"So tell *Thorpe* to hire me. I'm suited for it. Like, *more than anyone.*"

"I'm not sure anyone's *suited* to it," he said.

"But if you were going to hire anyone . . ."

"Why would you even want to do this job? Just because you're suited to something doesn't mean it's necessarily a good thing."

"So why do *you* do it?" I asked. "You went to Eton. You could have gone to university. You could do anything you wanted."

"It's not that simple."

"It *is* that simple. I just got booted from Wexford. My parents are never going to let me come back to London if I leave. Which means I am screwed and you are screwed, so really, when you think about it that way, it is *very, very simple.*"

"So," he said, "you think it's just like that? You think you just join because school isn't working out?"

"That's what I just said, basically. Yes."

"Do you realize what it entails?"

"Pretty much," I said. "I mean, it can't be much worse than what I've already experienced. I've been stabbed *by the Ripper* and turned into a terminus. Do you have some more surprises in store? More than that?"

"You need to go back. Right now. Before this gets any more serious."

"I'm not going back," I said. "You know I can't."

"You can. You can walk back there right now. They've already expelled you, so there's no harm done."

"Except my parents probably know I ran away."

"And they'll be *much* happier to know you've returned."

"Why are you being like this?" I asked. "If you hadn't listened to me, there would still be an insane ghost in the basement of the pub. And now a woman's been thrown out of a window."

"I know," he said. "I realize you were right. You don't need to keep reminding me."

"Are you angry because I was right about the last one?"

"Why would I be angry about that?"

"Because," I said, "I knew, and you didn't. I did something about it."

He started to laugh. Really, actually laugh. I had never seen Stephen just break down laughing before. It would have been great under any other circumstance, but not this one.

"What's so funny?" I asked.

"It's not funny."

"So why are you laughing?"

"Trust me, I find nothing funny about any of this."

I was filled with the urge to haul off and smack him—I mean really knock him across his face, just to make him stop. I even stepped closer to him, but I didn't swing, because I'm not like that. But I felt the impulse. Just to bring the flat of my palm against his face, those slightly hollowed-out cheeks. Put some life into that pale skin in the form of a big, red handprint.

"You don't think I'm capable?" I said.

"I never said you weren't capable."

My words were jumping around inside of me, bouncing around my veins, punching my heart, pressing at the backs of my eyes.

"I'm the one who can hold her own," I said. "That's why you brought me here. That's why you *tested* me. And now I'm here, and I'm willing to help, and you won't let me. I bet Thorpe would hire me. He knows what I can do. They need me more than they need *you*."

I said it because I was angry, not because I meant it. I said it because I knew that I had to get to him somehow, to make him react—but he didn't. He just made a slow circuit around Dawn's table, examining the cards. He leaned low over them for a moment, staring at them closely.

"It's time for us to go," he said, after a moment. "And it's time for you to go back to Wexford. That's the end of it."

I think he knew how keyed up I was and that the calmer his reply, the more the wiring in my head would fizz and burn until I just shorted out and did what he wanted. But I wasn't going to play that game. I took a deep breath, dug my nails hard into my palm, and said, "Sure."

He locked the door behind us, and we stepped over to the car, where Callum and Boo stared at us. Boo held up the missing card.

"Right," Stephen said. "We have work to do. Rory will be returning to school. Would you like us to take you back, or would you prefer to go yourself?"

There was an archness in his tone that infuriated me all over again. Callum looked understandably baffled, and Boo immediately turned her attention to the window of the car.

"I'm fine," I snapped. I tried to remain dignified as I walked off, but it was starting to wear on me, all of these arguments, all of the fighting. Jane had promised me the country, and now I was ready to go.

21

OF COURSE, I WASN'T GOING BACK TO SCHOOL. AND OF course, it rained. It always rained. And it was a particularly miserable December rain at that. Louisiana rain often cracks a day in half, bringing a welcome reprieve from the heat. Sometimes it rains on a sunny day, and sometimes it brings a dramatic storm that turns the sky green and splits it with lightning. English rain feels obligatory, like paperwork. It dampens already damp days and slicks the stones. I went to Liverpool Street and got one of the many cabs in the line. Cabs, as Jane had informed me yesterday, kept records of journeys, and some had cameras. I wore the hat and glasses and divided the journey into two sections, changing cabs at Leicester Square.

I tried to reason out Stephen's little tantrum. Stephen liked rules. He wanted to feel in control. Callum and Boo . . . they would welcome me with open arms. They would work on him. I'd bide my time for a bit, go with Jane to the country. I'd learn something about this condition I had. I'd come back even more valuable than when I left. Everything was going to be fine.

"There you are," Jane said, as she let me in. "We were worried you weren't going to come back. Is everything all right?"

"It's fine," I said.

"I'm glad to hear it. Come through to the kitchen. There's someone I'd like you to meet."

There was a guy in the kitchen, a little older than me, maybe in his twenties. To say that he was striking looking wouldn't quite have covered it. He was the human equivalent of Jane's décor. His hair was bright blond, like yellow gold, as artificially colored as Jane's and just as striking in its unnatural glow. And it was extremely well groomed in a sideways sweep, like some kind of old movie star. He wore a red dress shirt and a strangely wide tie in a bold red and silver stripe. I don't think that the color of someone's eyes tells you anything in particular about them, but Jack had cold, clear blue eyes. The blue was almost as unnatural as his hair. And his shoes were red with metallic silver stars worked into the leather. The entire effect was outlandish, costumish.

"Rory," Jane said, "I want you to meet Jack."

"Pleasure," Jack said, extending his hand. I shook it, and Jack smiled at me as if I was the punch line to a very funny, very private joke.

"Jack will be coming with us," Jane said.

"It's an amazing house," Jack said. He learned against the kitchen table, crossing one leg over the other and the ankle. Kind of a dancer's stance, or the kind of thing you see in old movie stills. A pose.

"Are you all right?" Jane said, leaning in to look at me. "You look pale. Have a little something to eat—you look like you might fall over."

She pushed forward the ubiquitous plate of baked goods. Jack's smile widened, and he looked at the floor, as if it might also find this funny.

"You have *quite* an interesting story," Jack said. "Jane's been telling us all about you."

"I think you all have interesting stories," Jane said. "We are all interesting people."

"True," Jack said, inclining his head in acceptance. He bit his lower lip just a little and looked up at me.

I can say this about myself—I don't often meet people and just not like them. That's not my way. But there was something about Jack I really didn't like, and it wasn't just that he seemed like some kind of costumed character from a weird play. He hadn't said or done much, but something about him was off and unpleasant, and the fact that he was coming to the country with us made the country considerably less appealing. This made no real sense, and I didn't really have much of a choice about the matter. It was just an immediate feeling, a bit of a chill.

"I just need to use the bathroom," I said. Which was true. I also wanted a moment to shake this feeling off.

I left the kitchen and went down the hall to the stairs. The house was encased in the thick afternoon gloom. The lack of hall windows meant it was very dark. I was about to turn to go up the stairs, and I guess I looked over at the silver leopard, when I noticed something else. I just caught it in the corner of my vision, and I had to stop myself and go into the vestibule to confirm what I'd seen. It was a Wexford blazer on a hook by the door. I'd seen so many Wexford blazers on so many hooks that now the shape of it was imprinted on my mind, and there was no mistake about this one. But I hadn't worn my blazer to Jane's.

I lifted it off the hook and examined it. Because of the laundry system, all of our uniforms were all labeled with our names. I looked inside the collar for the familiar white stripe of label.

The blazer was Charlotte's. And it was damp.

Which made sense. Charlotte came her for therapy. But Charlotte was, at this moment, in a Latin exam.

"Something wrong?"

Jane was in the hallway.

"Oh . . ." I didn't know what to say. Was something wrong? "It's just . . . Charlotte's blazer. Is here."

I lifted the sleeve as proof.

"Oh yes. She came by earlier. She must have left it."

"She has a Latin exam today," I said. "It's all exams today."

"I don't know about that," Jane said. "She was here, but she didn't stay, and she didn't say anything about her exams. I think she was a bit upset you didn't come back last night. You should get ready to go. We'll want to hurry. Miss the traffic."

That made sense. Charlotte turned to Jane for everything. I nodded and left the blazer and went upstairs.

But it wasn't okay. There was a flutter in my chest. My heart was skittering. Julia called this "victim's instinct." Once a really bad thing happens to you, your senses heighten. You become very attuned to things that aren't quite right, things that are potentially dangerous.

I went to the bathroom and locked the door. I needed to think.

Sure, Charlotte could have come here, but to miss an exam? And that blazer was wet, not damp. There was a radiator in the vestibule. Had the blazer been here for a while, it would have been warm and drier. And Charlotte wasn't the kind of person to just leave her blazer. Our blazers were the key part of the Wexford uniform. Putting them on—it was an automatic gesture.

But sure, she could have left it. It was possible.

What was the alternative?

The bathroom window was frosted for privacy. I unlocked it and tried to pull it up, but it made a very loud squeaking noise. I stopped, my nerves jangled. Then I turned on the faucet all the way and went back to the window, nudging it millimeter by millimeter until I had about three inches of room to peer out of. The bathroom faced the back and was a sheer drop down to the garden. There was certainly no way out through here. I could scream . . .

. . . .but there was no reason to scream, was there? Why did I want to scream?

Why had Jack smiled at me like that? It was just when Jane offered me the tray of cookies and brownies. That was normal. Jane always offered me that.

Then a thought came into my head that seemed both very, very paranoid and very, very logical. Every time I came to Jane's she insisted that I eat something. And every time I ate something, I started to feel lightheaded. I would talk a lot. Time seemed weird.

I don't take drugs myself, but I've heard stories from friends who'd had pot brownies, and it seemed like this was the kind of thing that happened. It didn't hit all at once—it took about a half an hour or so—but then the talking, the strange things I'd notice in the room. It wasn't like I was rendered unconscious, but I definitely relaxed to a degree that therapy had never before relaxed me.

Charlotte had that look when she came from Jane's as well. The glass-eyed stare . . .

If what I was thinking was correct, no wonder Jane seemed so amazingly good at her job. She had gotten us high as kites.

But *why*? This was insane. These thoughts were the thoughts of a crazy person.

But my life was not normal. *I* was not normal. And neither was Jane, or Devina, or Jack . . .

Jack had been the name of the witness in Dawn's murder.

Okay, that was a stupid connection. Loads of people are named Jack.

I flushed the toilet just for the noise. I exited the bathroom and went to the top of the stairs. Jane was waiting for me at the bottom.

"Rory," she said. "Ready to go? Why don't you come down?"

Why don't you come down?

Her words, her voice, they filled me with dread now—a dread I wanted so much to discount, but I just couldn't. I had absolutely no idea what was happening, but *something* was wrong. But I had to go downstairs. I couldn't leave from the second floor anyway unless I leapt from a window, like Dawn.

"Yeah," I said, trying to sound casual. "Sorry. I was drying myself off."

I don't think I sounded casual. Jack came around. He was next to the staircase, watching me descend as well.

My heartbeat was irregular, catching in my throat. I took each step at about half speed. This was wrong. Something was wrong. Everything was wrong. Something had to happen now, on these steps, at this second. Every fiber of my being screamed it to me.

So I listened.

When I reached the bottom step, I opened my mouth as if I were about to speak to Jane, then I broke toward the door. It's a strange thing to me, running. I only do it in my dreams, and I have often joked that I would only engage in the activity if being chased. This definitely had a dreamlike quality, running into the dark hall- way, feeling the arms grab me from behind. I landed face first on the floor, completely in someone's grip. My nose smashed into the floorboards, sending a singing pain throughout my face. My eyes welled up from the impact and tears flowed freely.

"Careful!" Jane said. "By God, Jack, don't hurt her. Get her up."

Two pairs of hands picked me up. Devina had come out of nowhere, and she and Jack got me off the floor.

"Now, Rory," Jane said, "don't struggle like that. Jack will have to use more force, and neither of us want that. Move her to the kitchen."

I was half-dragged, half-carried to the kitchen. And strangely, I relaxed a bit. There was a certain relief in just being right, the thing was now just happening. The tick tick had lead to the boom. I scanned the counter. There was nothing useful there. The knives were all the way on the other side of the kitchen. Unless I was going to beat Jack and Devina with a plate of baked goods or a magazine, I was stuck.

"Eat something," Jane said, presenting the plate once again. "It will make it easier."

"What's in there?"

"It's just a little hash, darling," she said. "You've been enjoying them so far. Perfectly harmless."

She held up the plate, and I shook my head. She shrugged and set it down.

"Up to you," she said. "It was for your benefit."

"What are you going to do to me?"

"No harm will come to you if you cooperate. I can promise that. Anyone with the sight is my brother or sister, and I take that very, very seriously. If you struggle, Jack will hurt you. But if you remain calm, you will be released."

That wasn't much of a choice, so I stopped struggling. Jane nodded and Devina released me at once.

"Jack," Jane said, "let her go."

The grip remained.

"Jack. I said *let her go.*"

My arms were released. Jane reached over and rubbed them. "My apologies," she said. "My apologies. Truly. The things that have happened in the last twenty-four hours, they were not part of the original plan. With the news that you would likely be departing soon, we had to work very quickly. I've always been honest with you, Rory, and I'll continue to be honest with you. Everything about your old life ends *right now.* The sooner you accept that, the easier things will be for you. But what happens next . . . that's really up to you. And I've come to explain the possibilities. The good news is, the possibilities are much, much better than your current state of affairs."

"Where's Charlotte?" I asked.

"Charlotte is in a safe place. She's already gone off to the country. You'll see her today. She's absolutely fine. She knew that you came here, and we couldn't have that knowledge getting around. So we had to take her along as well. But I assure you she'll remain safe as long as you remain with us. You're a terminus, the first instance of a human terminus that I've ever come across. We're all very excited about it."

"How do you know that?"

"Oh, Rory," she said. "We've been with you for weeks. We followed you to Bristol. We've seen how special you are. And now everything is coming together. You are the sign we've been waiting for. You'll help us, and we'll help you."

"I don't want to *help* you."

"You care about Charlotte, and those friends of yours in the flat near Waterloo, and . . . what's the address again, Jack?

"Seventy-seven Woodland Road," he said.

That was, in fact, my parents' address in Bristol. He then rattled off our home address in Louisiana, my Uncle Bick's address, my Aunt Diane's address, and my parents' work addresses, both in England and in America. And that's when everything got very cold.

"Which is why I say that everything is different now," Jane said. "We don't want to force you. Come of your own will. And once you come with us, you'll see. You'll see that what we're doing is right. You'll be glad. It's just an awkward adjustment period, but it won't last. Come now. It's time to go. Time to go to the country."

22

As it happens, I know a bit about survival. To a point, I know this because I come from Bénouville, Louisiana, where hurricane preparedness is a topic of conversation every summer. Did you stock up on bottled water? Batteries? Canned food and granola bars? Do you have bleach for when the water goes down and the mold comes? Do you have a radio? Flashlights?

But the nitty-gritty stuff I know because my neighbor is a nutjob. A nutjob with a lot of practical skills. I mean Billy Mack, who lives down the street.

Billy was never quite the same after Hurricane Katrina. A lot of people weren't the same after that. A lot of people went without food and water and help, and a lot of people developed an interest in survival skills. Billy Mack took this to an extreme. He has a boat on his porch roof, tethered to one of the second-story windows. Billy is also the founder of the People's Church of Universal People, a religion he runs out of his garage. As part of his mission, he sometimes goes up and down the street, handing out pamphlets. His religion is a kind of apocalypse-come-hither thing mixed with the Army Rangers field guide. He believes that the end times are coming, and people in his religion will not only be right with God, but they'll have the proper supplies on hand.

I don't spend a lot of time with Billy Mack, but we get the pamphlets. And right on the front they say things like, "A human being can survive for three to five days without food or water. Jesus needs you to be ready for His coming. Do YOU have the supplies you need?"

The pamphlets probably had all kinds of good tips for how to deal with situations like the one I was in now. But I'd never gotten past the front cover before I put them in the recycle bin. I was sorry for that now. Billy was the kind of person who always had a knife strapped to his shin. He would have had *ideas* about how to deal with this.

"This" was sitting in the back of the car with Devina on one side and Jack on the other. Jane was at the wheel, chatting merrily as if this was a perfectly normal trip, talking about "traffic problems on the A4."

As we went, everything seemed to slip away from me, like the buildings were fading from existence as I saw them for the last time. The roads were rolled up. The spare sky went into a box. Because, I felt sure, I would not come this way again. I looked at the names on the signs of places we were passing—Fulham, Hammersmith, Chiswick. I could try to fight, I could throw myself against the back window or grab Jane by the neck or do something . . . That something would only get me pushed down in the seat. It would get me hurt, and it would get people I love killed.

I was going to the country.

"We're coming up on Barnes, now," Jane said. "It's where Marc Bolan died. You probably have never heard of Marc Bolan, but he was one of my favorites. Crashed into a tree. Terrible and shocking. When we do our work, Marc is one person I'd love to help."

"What work?" I asked.

"We're going to defeat death," she said. It was very matter of fact, like she was saying, "We're going to have a bake sale."

"Oh," is all I could manage.

"Have you ever heard of the Eleusinian Mysteries, Rory?" Jane smoothly negotiated a roundabout. "In ancient Greece, it was understood that Persephone, the daughter of Demeter, presided over the fecundity of the earth. Persephone was kidnapped by Hades and taken to the underworld. Demeter forced him to return her daughter, but you see, Persephone had done the one thing that you shouldn't do in Hades—she had eaten the food of the dead—and was forced to return to the underworld part of each year. In their honor, the Greeks had the Eleusinian Mysteries, in which initiates were shown the real nature of life and death. Now, we think these things are just stories—except, of course, that the ancient Greeks were correct. Death, as you have noticed, is not the fixed state that most people believe it is. Do you agree?"

"Sure?" I said, because it seemed like the right thing to say to this terrifying speech that seemed to be going into a deeply bad place.

"They may have spun a colorful tale around it, but they were aware of the reality of life and death. Their mysteries, their rituals—they were experiments. And those experiments started to bring about changes. They made us, Rory. Those who achieved the highest of the mysteries, the hierophants and the initiates, they developed the sight. They began to perforate the wall between the living and the dead. Somewhere, far, far back in your family history, there was a great mystic, someone who achieved this wonderful state. We are all, in that sense, related."

"Family," Jack said.

"Family indeed," Jane replied.

"But the great work was destroyed. The Temple of Demeter was sacked. The Christians took over, and the mysteries were thought to be destroyed, the knowledge gone. But knowledge lives on. The rituals continue. Which is why we did what we did this morning. The psychic, of course."

"Why her? What did she do?"

"We needed a victim, someone in the right general area. Someone whose death would arouse suspicion. Someone we couldn't be linked to. A relatively insecure building where it was easy to get in and out. She was perfect. The death of a psychic so close to the Wexford grounds—we've put enough in play to keep your friends busy for a while. And Jack had a blood debt to pay. In the original mysteries, it was thought you had to be free of 'blood guilt,' that you couldn't have killed anyone. But we are performing the advanced mysteries now, and now a blood debt is required. You need to meet it in order to be initiated."

Jack reached into his pocket and pulled out a plastic bag. Inside was a piece of cloth, soaked in blood.

"Jack has proven himself ready," Jane said. "As has Devina."

"Mum's boyfriend," Devina said lightly.

"And you?" I asked Jane.

"The man in Yorkshire," she said. "The one I told you about, the one who attacked me. It may sound horrible, Rory, but we have all removed people from society who needed to be removed . . ."

"What did the psychic ever do?" I said. "She was innocent!"

"You think that's innocent? Someone who pretends to see into the future? Someone who tricks people for money? It's because of people like her that the good name of the true religion is sullied and lost."

I know a true believer when I see one—that high fervor, that total conviction, the calm that explodes into emotion in a moment. I was in a car full of conviction, full of belief in ancient Greek rituals and destroying death. And murderers.

The detour was taking us through a series of very tight lanes, barely wide enough to hold a car. Outside, England was normal and quiet, just living a December day. People would be getting ready for Christmas. Doing their jobs. Thinking about what to have for dinner. Cyclists rode past us on occasion. All that separated me from that world was a car door. But I could not get out.

"I would have fallen in with people like that," Jane finally went on, "New Agers, nonsense spiritualists, but I was lucky. I met my friends. They taught me about the true history of the sight. They had used their wealth to invest in knowledge. They traveled to India, to Egypt, to Greece. They collected books. They talked to seers. They brought the knowledge back to London, and they made the ultimate sacrifice to help us all, to gain control of our own destinies. It's been left to me to continue their work, to help them . . . and now . . . you. You are a transformed being. You are proof that what we believe is correct and possible."

"I'm not," I said. "I'm just . . ."

"You don't even know what you are," Jane said. "But we will show you your true potential. And then . . ."

And then we all jerked forward, all at once, with the impact.

We'd plowed directly into the side of a police car.

I suppose, on some level, I'd suspected it. Like everything else today, I hadn't really understood it fully—it made no sense—but it shouldn't have surprised me. I had reached the point where surprises were no longer really possible.

The police car had come shooting out of a small lane just as our car had approached it, and had taken a heavy impact in the passenger's side. Our car made a sickly sound, but was still running. The door of the police car opened, and Stephen stepped out, a trickle of blood running down the side of his face. At the same moment, there was a thud and a hiss on one side of the back of the car. Then a clank, then a similar thud and hiss on the other side. Boo and Callum then approached the back windows at the same moment. Boo had a crowbar in her hand. They had taken out the tires.

All of which would have attracted a lot of attention, but we were between two blind sides of buildings on a small street. The crash itself probably didn't make that much noise.

Stephen approached the driver's window like a policeman performing a normal traffic stop. He was walking stiffly, and he wiped away the blood on the side of his face.

Jane rolled down the window.

"Hello, Officer," she said politely. "You've ruined my car."

"I'd like Rory to get out," Stephen replied.

"And why should she do that? I don't think you have any legal right to remove her."

"She's a minor who's been reported missing. Either she gets out or I assure you that the full weight of the London police force will be brought to bear on this car."

"Well, I don't think Rory wants to leave, do you, Rory?"

I did not reply.

"This is all quite illegal," Jane said. "Police brutality doesn't even begin to cover it. We certainly won't be jailed for this."

"You're right," Stephen replied. "Now get out."

Boo was wedging the crowbar into the space between the door and the body of the car on Devina's side. She popped the door open, grabbed Devina, and pulled her out. Callum remained on Jack's side, his hands pressed against the glass of the window.

"Get out of the car, Rory," Stephen said. "This is over."

I slid over toward the open door. Boo pushed Devina aside and took me by the shoulders.

"You all right?"

"Fine."

Devina didn't move—she just stared at us both.

"Come on," Boo said, guiding me away. "Come on. We need to leave now."

But I stayed where I was.

"You are making a mistake," Jane said. "If you try to take me, that will be kidnapping. You will be prosecuted. I'm going to call my solicitor about this vandalization of my car and assault on my young friends. You'll never hear the end of this."

"I look forward to it," Stephen said. "You'll be walking

home. Which will be under surveillance. As will every vehicle registered to it, and every person known to have lived under its roof. Nothing you do from now on will be unobserved. On the street, cameras will turn and focus on you. And if anything happens to anyone connected with Rory's life, I'll personally see to it that every moment of what remains of your miserable life is spent in the maximum amount of suffering."

He said all of that as if rattling off a grocery list.

"Oh, you do go on, don't you?" Jane said.

"Come on," Boo said again. And this time, she wasn't taking no for an answer. Boo was strong. She could have thrown me over her shoulder if she felt like it.

The police car was clearly not drivable, so Boo hustled me away, back down the lane.

"I can't go," I said. "They know—"

"We can't stay, Ror. Come on, come on, we can't stay here."

Someone turned down the lane and saw the crash. She started to walk toward us. Boo pulled me harder, shoving the crowbar inside of her coat. Callum joined us in a few smooth strides.

"Just keep walking," he said, taking my arm on the other side. "Walk away. Let Stephen deal with this."

"How did you find me?" I asked.

"Stephen put his phone in your pocket when we were at Dawn's. It sounds like he didn't think you were going to listen to him and go back to school. We used it as a GPS. Who are those people?"

"That was my therapist," I said.

"And that's put me off therapy for life," Callum replied. "Do you have money? We know you emptied your bank account."

I had forgotten about the roll of fifties and twenties in my pocket. When I reached in for it, I felt the phone.

"That'll be enough," Callum said. "We'll find a taxi to take us back to the flat . . ."

"They know where the flat is," I said. "They know about you, where my parents live. They have Charlotte . . ."

That last one hit me all over again. Someone, somewhere had Charlotte.

"What do you mean?" Boo said.

"I mean, they had her. I saw her in the house. She was in the bedroom one minute, the next she was gone. They said I had to go with them or . . ."

"What?" Callum said. "How did we miss them getting her out of the house? We were parked up right outside."

"They kept talking about some house in the country. That's where they were taking me . . . Oh, my God. I'm sorry. This is my fault. They knew all this stuff, and I went . . . I listened to them . . ."

I started to shake, and Boo tightened her hold around my shoulders.

"Phone it in," she said to Callum.

Callum made the call to someone to report Charlotte's abduction. Boo stayed with me. Stephen came jogging along a few moments later, fast, if a little unsteady on his feet. Without a word, he reached into my pocket and took out the phone, then he stepped away from us and made a call. I just heard a few clipped words, like "cleanup" and a street name.

"You all right?" Boo asked, looking at the blood on Stephen's face.

"I played rugby. I've had worse. We need to get out of here."

"Flat's not safe," Callum said, coming back over. "They know the address. We could have more of them waiting for us there."

"Right," Stephen said. He wiped away a rivulet of blood that was creeping down his cheek. It left a streak on the side of his face.

"Does Thorpe want us to come in?" Boo asked.

"We can't walk into an MI5 building with a missing person. Rory's in the system now. She'll be caught on about a million cameras, and they do use facial recognition there, so no. We need to go somewhere and lay low and regroup . . ."

The blood trickled down again.

"Right. I know where we can go. It's in Maida Vale."

23

MAIDA VALE WAS A HEAVILY TREED AND DISCREET SECTION of northwest London, just above Paddington station. Quiet and secure brick houses with walled gardens and rows and rows of identical buildings in one solid block, side by side. There were commercial streets with pink and white cupcake shops and nonchain coffee places, stores where you could buy cashmere baby blankets, imported green tea from Japan, French cookware, and jeans so expensive one could only assume that they had been hand-sewn by monks who chanted prayers for the thighs of the would-be wearers. Stephen directed the cab to a series of golden brick apartments.

"What is this place?" Boo asked as Stephen punched in a code to gain access to the lobby.

"My father's flat. He uses it when he comes to London for work. I think he's in Switzerland right now. I hope he is, anyway."

"What exactly does your dad *do*?" Callum asked.

"Banking," Stephen said.

"Did he break all the money?" Boo said.

"Possibly. It's the sort of thing he might do."

We all crammed into a much-too-small elevator and rode to the fourth floor. Stephen led us down to one of the end apartments. He pulled back a framed photograph of a bridge that hung on the wall near the door and produced a key, which he used to open the door.

The flat was dark. The floor-length curtains were closed. He switched on just one light in the middle of the room. We were in a very tastefully, almost clinically decorated living room. There were two sofas facing each other, and between them, a long and low marble table that contained some books of art and photographs that looked like they had never been opened. There were no signs of life in the place, really. Just perfectly positioned vases and decorative bowls.

Stephen went into the other rooms, and I heard more curtains being closed. Callum, Boo, and I milled around. There was one family photograph, pushed back on an occasional table and mostly obscured by a yellow vase. It showed what was clearly Stephen's family, and it had been taken in someone's garden, possibly against their will. They all squinted a bit against the sun. His parents looked about how I expected them to look. His father wore a pinstriped suit, his mother a yellow dress and a very large yellow hat with a wide white band. And there was Stephen's sister, a girl with a surprisingly wide and open grin. Her hair was chestnut brown, and she was freckled. Her arm was looped through Stephen's. Stephen looked like he was maybe twelve or thirteen in the picture, a bit thin and very uncomfortable. He towered over his mother and sister and was as tall as his father. Even in this photo, it felt like there was something competitive about this, like his dad was standing as straight as he possibly could so his son wouldn't reach an inch past him.

"We need to get your head looked at," Boo said. "That's going to need some stitches."

"Head wounds always bleed a lot. We need to keep a low profile. I can stitch it myself if it comes to that."

"Well, let's clean it," Boo said.

"You know how to stitch your own head?" I said.

"There are probably instructions online. How hard could it be?"

While Boo helped Stephen clean the wound, Callum crafted a bandage by tearing an undershirt he found in the bedroom into strips, so the top of Stephen's head was now mummy-wrapped, with a shock of brown hair coming out of the top. Some blood was already leaching through. We gathered in the living room.

"When you were inside the house," Stephen said, pulling his notepad from his belt, "I pulled up some basic information on the owner. Her name is Jane Quaint, born Jane Anderson. Legally changed her name in 1972. Aside from working in a shop in Yorkshire around 1968, she has no employment history. She got the house in Chelsea from a brother and sister, twins, named Sidney and Sadie Smithfield-Wyatt."

"She told me about them," I said. "She said they had the sight. That they were doing some kind of experiment—that they died doing some kind of experiment."

"Sidney and Sadie committed suicide together in 1973. That's all I found at first glance, but we can find out more about them. As for Jane, her record is clean. She volunteers time to many victims' groups, gives substantial sums to charity. Overall, a model citizen."

"Who runs a cult," I said. "She said they were going to *defeat death.*"

"So these people wanted you because you're a terminus?" Boo said. "Did they say why, or what they planned on doing?"

"Just *defeating death.* And, I don't know, killing everyone I know if I didn't come with them. They know where my parents are."

"We'll get a car on their house," Stephen said. "Could one of you call Thorpe? Make sure that happens?"

He got up and went to the bedroom. Callum fished the phone out of the coat pocket.

"You would think he'd want to make this call," Callum said. "He always does the talking when it comes to Thorpe."

"Maybe he's finally delegating," Boo said. Then, turning to me, she explained, "We've been working on his control issues."

"So many issues," Callum said, going through the phone to find the number.

I got up and followed Stephen.. He was staring into the closet at a selection of three largely identical shirts. He had removed his own bloody dress shirt. Stephen had a chest. That should not have been a shock to me, but there it was. It wasn't as bulky as Callum's, but it had a shape. And it had hair on it—a thin, dark line of it, right at the top, making a V that thinned out about two-thirds of the way to his waist. He immediately slipped the old shirt on, but left it unbuttoned. There was something goofily gallant about that. Like it mattered if I saw him with his shirt off.

A car alarm went off outside. Stephen tightened the curtains, making sure there was no view of us from outside, though it was hardly possible to close them more than he already had.

"Can you really do all those things you said to Jane?" I asked. "Make cameras turn around when she walks down the street, stuff like that?"

"Maybe half of it. But your parents will be all right, I promise. And so will Charlotte. Our business can be unpredictable, but the police are good at preventing crime and finding kidnap victims. Their house is being turned over as we speak. She'll be found."

"Why didn't you *arrest* them?"

"Arresting them meant reporting you. And I'd just deliberately crashed into their car. We have to lay low until that mess is taken care of. I wish I could have come up with a more elegant solution, but there was no time. Thorpe already thinks I take too many risks . . ."

He sat on the end of the bed. I sat next to him. I meant to sit a bit further away, but the way I landed, I was right up against him. I expected him to shift over, but he didn't.

"I know you're angry at me," he said. "About what I said at Dawn's flat."

"Whatever," I said.

"No, not whatever. I want to explain. I don't want you to think it's because I think you can't do it, or that I'm upset that you can do more than I can. It's not that I don't think you're capable . . . I wasn't just going to let you sign up for this because your exams weren't going well and you had nothing else to do."

He shook his head.

"I didn't put that the way I wanted to," he said. "If you joined us, your family could never know what you were doing. Your relationship with them would be severed in many ways. I do this because I have nowhere else to go. My sister was my family, and I barely knew her. I had nothing. I've heard you talk about your family, your home. *You* have somewhere else to go. How would you really feel if you couldn't go home again?"

"I could go home . . ."

"No. You couldn't. Not easily. And everything your family knew about you would be a lie. You would never be able to tell them what was going on in your life. If I enlist you, if people higher up than Thorpe actually realize what you are and what you might be able to do, I don't think you would just be treated like a member of an agency. You'd be treated like an asset. And assets don't get to have lives."

"I never said I wanted to join," I pointed out. "But if I did, at least I'd be with you guys."

"And if something happened to us, you'd get whatever sad weirdos they managed to recruit after us. Or you'd have no one. If we were disbanded, this whole part of your life would be a big, blank space. You still have a chance to get out and do something else. I do this because it keeps me sane. I don't know if I *could* do anything else. But it's not easy. A big part of me wishes that I'd been given some other option, but I wasn't. I'm not saying that's easy. I'm not even saying that's what I want. I'm saying you have a chance to have some other kind of life."

"Maybe I need this life," I said.

"Has it really gone that well for you so far?"

I shrugged. "I've seen worse," I said.

That got a little smile from him.

"There you go," I said, elbowing him. "A little smile. I knew you could do it."

"I'm such a miserable sod."

"You're not *that* bad."

"I know I am. I don't want you to end up like me."

"Trust me," I said. "I am not going to end up like you."

His neck was long, and there was just a bit of stubble on it. His mouth, which was so often set in an expressionless straight line, there was a shape to that too. His nose had just a bit of a tiny downward turn. And his eyes, deep set, very tired, were fixed firmly on me.

"Everything is so messed up," I said. "My parents . . . I need to call them."

"That's not advisable right now. Just wait until we've gotten this mess cleared up, at least until morning."

"Why did I do it? Why did I listen to her?" I hung my head and rubbed my eyes, then pulled myself upright again. "They gave me some drugs. They put it in the food. No wonder the therapy always seemed so intense."

"Drugs make people suggestible," Stephen said.

"These people—they're a cult. I'm telling you. They were talking to me about these El . . . these mystery things in ancient Greece. Something about Demeter and Persephone and . . ."

"The Eleusinian Mysteries?" he said.

"That's the one. Of course you know it."

"Five years of Latin, four of Greek."

"God, what am I going to do? Do I go home?"

"We decide nothing tonight, all right? It will all be fine, I promise you. We'll make it fine."

He put his arm over my shoulders, which was understandable, because I was upset. But it also seemed very . . .

I wasn't sure what it was.

"How can you promise to make it fine?" I asked.

"You're alive. You're safe and with us. It's already fine. The rest is window dressing."

"You say that."

"Because it is."

The hand that rested on my shoulder rubbed it a bit, comfortingly. Then it gave my shoulder a little squeeze. I leaned into him.

Maybe it was that I was broken. Maybe it was just that I was out of my mind. But it occurred to me that I was going to kiss him. The thought just arrived, certain knowledge, delivered from some greater, more knowledgeable place. I was going to kiss him. Stephen would not want to kiss me. He would back up in horror. And yet, I was still going to do it. I reached over, and I put my hand against his chest, then I moved closer. I could feel just the very tips of the gentle stubble on his cheek brushing against my skin.

"Rory," he said. But it was a quiet protest, and it went nowhere.

For the first few seconds, he didn't move—he accepted the kiss like you might accept a spoonful of medicine. Then I heard it, a sigh, like he had finally set down a heavy weight.

I was pretty sure we were both kind of terrified, but I was completely sure that we were both doing this. We kissed slowly, very deliberately, coming together and then pulling apart and looking at each other. Then each kiss got longer, and then it didn't stop. Stephen put his hand just under the edge of my shirt, holding it on the spot where the scar was. Sometimes the skin around the scar got cold—now it was warm. Now it was alive.

"So Thorpe says that— Seriously?"

Callum was in the doorway.

Stephen mumbled what I think was a very obscene word right against my mouth.

"You realize I now owe Boo five pounds?" Callum said. "Boo! I owe you five pounds!"

"What?" Boo yelled. "In the toilet."

"She's in the toilet," Callum explained. "Can you not mention this? She said this would happen. She's going to lord this over me."

Stephen and I separated politely. I stared at my shoes, and Stephen buttoned his shirt.

"You were saying about Thorpe?"

"The freaks have cleared out of the house in Chelsea. Thorpe is having people pull records and look at CCTV. No hit on the house in the West Country yet. And someone's being dispatched to Rory's parents. Rory's parents have registered her as missing."

"Right," Stephen said. "It sounds like there's little we can do right now. We should try to rest. Tomorrow could be a very long day."

Boo had joined us by then.

"What were you yelling?" she asked Callum.

"Nothing," he said. "Just telling them what Thorpe said."

"And I said we should try to get some rest," Stephen replied.

Boo and I were given the bedroom. Neither of us was very tired. We flopped there, staring at the ceiling.

"My life is a mess," I said.

"Yeah," Boo agreed. "It is."

"Stephen says it's going to be fine."

"Probably will be."

She sounded less convinced.

"I broke up with Jerome. I left Jazza . . . I feel like I should . . ."

"Stay here and do nothing?" she suggested.

"I'm not going to call. I need to do something. Maybe . . . maybe I could write them letters? And then send them when it's okay?"

"That's all right," Boo said. "You could do that. But don't send them until things are fixed."

So Boo watched TV, and I found some paper in the desk drawer. I'd only ever written a letter once or twice in my life. I kept changing what I wanted to say and starting over. In the end, Boo was asleep, and I had two very short letters.

Jazzy,

You're mad at me for running away. Running away is stupid. I know. And nothing I can tell you is going to make what I did seem any less awful or nuts, so let me just say this . . . you're one of the best friends I've ever had. And if I could tell you all the messed up reasons I had to do this, I would. Just try to believe me when I say it was the best idea at the time. And that I miss you. And that I'm sorry I seem like such a freak and a liar and a weirdo. I think you knew all that and were friends with me anyway.

You're better than I am. You will not fail German. And you'll see me again, and I'll try to explain it all.

You can have whatever you want from my side of the room, including my alligator ashtray.

—Rory

Jerome's was shorter:

Jerome,

It wasn't you. It was me. I'm sorry. You deserve a better girlfriend, and you'll find one. And I promise to be jealous and know that it's all my fault.

I still think you are disgusting. You know what I mean. Maybe someday you'll come to America and see my town and then you'll realize what a narrow escape you made.

I crumpled that one up. It was too maudlin, and I didn't even know if I meant it. Because in my mind, I was still kissing Stephen.

That night, I had a dream I went home. Our house was flooded with sunlight, and all my family was there. Even our cat, Pow Pow, who died three years ago, and my aunt Sal, who died when I was twelve.

I'm home, I kept thinking. *But I can't stay. I need to tell them I can't stay.* So I went to each and every member of my family and started to explain to them the nature of life and love. I can't remember what I said, but I know it was awesome. I understood everything. The sight—it had given me knowledge as well, and I was able to reassure them all. "We're going to defeat death," I said.

I think I knew on some level I was parroting what Jane had said to me earlier, but I meant it. There was no death, which was why Aunt Sal and Pow Pow were there, and that was why it was so sunny. I told them about the sight, and everyone was so happy. Especially Cousin Diane, who went around telling everyone that she'd been right all along with her Healing Angel Ministry. And for some reason my cousin Diane also kept trying to give me some ham the whole time. I was having all of these meaningful conversations, and she kept popping up with this package of lunch meat, trying to force me to take slices of the stuff. So I took them to shut her up and flushed them down the toilet, one by one, and she kept turning up with more. It ruined an otherwise very deep and poignant dream. Everything had been so close to perfect except for all of that sliced ham.

I don't know what time it was when I felt the shaking.

"I don't want ham," I said.

"Rory."

There was light coming through the window, but not much. It was a weak and diluted sky, and Boo was standing over me. The look on her face was very odd, and she had no ham.

"What?" I asked, snorting awake.

"It's Stephen."

"What?"

"I can't wake him up," she said.

24

OF THE MANY THINGS THAT HAD HAPPENED TO ME IN those last few weeks, the wait for that ambulance was the most surreal.

It had turned into morning—very early morning from the looks of it, because the sky still had a pale cast. Stephen must have fallen asleep sitting on the sofa. His head was tipped back, one hand holding the makeshift bandage in place, the other hanging limply at his side. A fine coating of stubble had blossomed during the night, shadowing his chin. Without his glasses, without his look of constant worry . . . he looked happy, almost. There was panic at the edge of everything—in Callum and Boo's voices, in their eyes, in the air itself.

"He was fine," Boo said, her voice shaking. "He was fine earlier. I just woke up and came in and both of them were asleep, and I tried to wake them, and . . . Stephen didn't wake up."

"Siren," Callum said, hurrying to the window. "Hear it?"

I did. It was far off, but coming closer fast.

"I'll go to the gate," Boo said. "Let them in. What was that code? Do you need that code? What was it?"

"I think there's someone out there now," Callum said. "I see someone. You wait for them by the front door. I'll find the fire stairs, they'll never be able to get him into the lift. Rory, stay with him?"

"Yeah," I said, "I will."

Then it was just me and Stephen. I grabbed his hand. I pinched his arm.

"Wake up," I said. "Please wake up. Please."

He continued to rest there, his breath low and shallow, the rest of him unmoving. A few minutes later a male and female paramedic came clomping up the stairs and into the flat. They went right to work, setting down a heavy box of supplies and a backboard. The man checked Stephen's neck for a pulse and listened to his chest with a stethoscope.

"What happened to him?" the woman asked. "You found him like this this morning?"

"I found him," Boo said. "He just didn't wake up."

"Does he take drugs? Drink? Any medical conditions?"

"There was a car accident," Callum said. "He hit his head, but he was fine . . ."

"When?"

"Last night."

"Airway clear," the man said. "Pulse is forty-six. Pupils are uneven."

The blood pressure cuff went on. I listened to the pump and slow, disturbing hiss of the blood pressure cuff. The EMT ripped it off loudly.

"One eighty over sixty. How long ago did you find him like this?" the woman asked.

"I think, I don't know . . ." Boo looked to Callum for confirmation. "Fifteen minutes?"

She moved around Stephen, lifting his eyelids and shining a light into them, then she got on her radio.

"St. Mary's, I've got an unresponsive head trauma, GCS four. Pulse is forty-three and dropping."

There was an electronic hiss and a moment of silence.

"Team will be on standby," a voice crackled back.

"What does that mean?" I asked her. "What's a GCS?"

"Coma scale," she said.

"Coma scale? Is he in a coma? Is he . . ."

"Time to move," the woman said.

They were moving fast, but nothing seemed fast enough. The coffee table had to be moved. Stephen's neck was cuffed and secured, then he was moved to the board on the floor.

"Count of three. One, two, three . . ."

They lifted him up and carried him out, managing the stairs expertly. I followed as they carried him down and put him into the ambulance.

Another blur of activity as Stephen was expertly carried out of the apartment we had come to only hours before. He was put in the ambulance and we followed in a cab. Once at the hospital, we had to separate, with the ambulance going in its entrance. We were dropped off on the street by the A&E waiting room. Inside, there were people with bandages, bloody wounds, slings . . . all the usual emergency room nonsense. Just broken arms and broken noses and Stephen, unconscious, somewhere.

A man at a desk told us someone would come and speak to us and that we had to wait, so we stood in the waiting area, confused, staring between the desk, the television bolted to the wall, and the vending machine full of chocolate bars and bags of crisps.

"Thorpe," Boo finally said. "We should phone him. I'll do it. Give me your phone."

So she did that, and Callum and I continued to stand around, pacing the tiled floor. About a half an hour later, a young, red haired doctor with a carefully trimmed beard came out into the waiting area and asked who was here with Stephen Dene. We got up and hurried over.

"You're his friends?" he asked. "You found him unresponsive?"

We said that was us.

"We're going to need to speak to his relatives. Do you have contact information for his parents, or . . ."

"His parents are dead," Callum said quickly.

This surprised Boo and I, but we didn't contradict him.

"I see," the doctor said. "Is there someone else?"

"His . . . uncle," Boo said. "He's coming. But . . . what's going on? Please. We're the people he's closest to. Please."

After a moment of hesitation, the doctor nodded and took us to a small consulting room. "You stated he had been in a motor vehicle accident?" he asked, closing the door.

"Just a knock," Callum said. "He seemed fine."

The doctor nodded and leaned back against the door, looking down, as if thinking.

"In this kind of injury, that often happens. It's called a lucid interval. The injured person seems to have no symptoms. It's not the severity of the blow as much as how it occurs, which part of the head is hit. Maybe he complained of a headache, nausea?"

"A headache," Boo said. "But it didn't seem bad."

The doctor scratched at his eyebrow. Then he looked at us with the kind of directness that never means something good has happened.

"Stephen has suffered something called an epidural hematoma," he said. "The blow to the head caused a rupture, and he's bleeding between the skull and the dura matter. When this happens, pressure is put on the brain. We've attempted to relieve this pressure . . . the thing about an epidural hematoma is that it has to be treated immediately. This injury occurred somewhere around eleven or twelve hours ago. We've drained the blood, but his brain has suffered damage. He is comatose, and we've put him on life support."

"Life support?" Boo said. "But he'll be fine, right? You fixed it, yeah?"

There was a pause and in the pause, there was everything. All the air went out of the room, and nothing was real. I couldn't feel my hands and my head was tingling.

"We'll keep him comfortable," the doctor went on. "He'll be in no pain. But decisions need to be made by the family. Do you understand what I am saying?"

No, actually, what he was saying made no sense at all. But it didn't stop him from saying it. And then, we were moving again, into an elevator, down a hall.

Stephen had been moved to a room on the third floor. He was in a room by himself, much of which was taken up by a large piece of equipment. The window blinds were half-open, and slants of morning light cut across his bed. He was under a hospital blanket, which was tucked midway up his chest. He wore a blue hospital gown. Something about him being stripped out of his uniform, out of his serious sweaters or scarves, stripped bare of the things he wore in the normal world that gave him that appearance of authority, of seriousness . . . something about that papery gown stamped with the hospital name made it all true.

Boo made a sobbing gasp.

"Not this," Callum said. "Of all the things it could have been, you know? All of us . . . all the things that could have happened, and just some little knock in the car . . ."

"Callum." Boo was crying freely now, her voice thick. "Callum, don't."

"But of all the things that could happen to us . . . the Ripper. The things we see. The things we do. And some *car accident* . . . not even a bad one. It's just *stupid* . . ."

He started to laugh, and the laugh got stranger and louder. He sat down on the floor by the bed and put his head down and laughed. Boo sat with him, and he put his arm over her shoulder. I thought dimly how this was one of those moments Boo had been waiting for for so long, when she would just hug Callum and hold on. She could probably do anything she wanted. But that didn't matter anymore.

Stephen's glasses were off. His face was the most relaxed I'd ever seen it, the worried crease between his eyes finally relaxed. I could look at him now in a way I never could before—I could stare as long as I wanted. I had never noticed how high his forehead was, high and elegant, sloping down toward his nose, which was also long and fine. His eyes were darkly lashed, and his eyebrows thicker than I thought they were. The glasses had obscured much of his real aspect. There were the lips I had pressed against mine last night—a slender mouth, long, with a strong tendency to pull down at the corners. He was almost smiling now.

I remembered how, at first, I had felt the tension in his lips, as if he was trying to make a barrier between us—then they had relaxed, parted slightly. And that's when I had known he wanted to kiss me, wanted to give in. That little parting of the lips, the little sigh that came out . . .

I would hear that sigh forever. That little, little sound when the whole world seemed to open up.

"He told me if anything happened to him, he didn't want his family contacted," Callum said.

I had almost forgotten the two of them were there on the floor on the other side of the bed. They'd gone silent, and I had gone so deep in my thoughts that I was lost. Callum's hysterical outburst had calmed, and he was leaning forward over his knees, as if ready to spring straight up from the floor.

"We have to call them now, don't we?" Boo's voice was hoarse. "Don't we?"

"No. I think he meant it. It's about what he wants, not what they want."

"What *does* he want?" Boo asked.

"We should wait for Thorpe," I said. I didn't even mean to say it. The words came out, dry and automatic. Maybe I was channeling Stephen.

"Thorpe can't decide," Callum said. "Thorpe doesn't know him. We have to decide. *We* have to do it. Stephen needs us to take care of this for him, not some bureaucrat."

In the end, we took a vote.

I say that like it was possible. Like we could vote if Stephen lived or died. Like we were even thinking about this like it was really happening. It was more academic, like a question on an exam. If Stephen can't live without the machine, would he want to live? Would he want to go on, his body forced to breathe, his mind not present or active? It was obvious to all of us that no, he would not want that, but we couldn't quite say the words that followed. That the machine should go off. That he should be allowed to die. My head was feeling funny and light and my knees were shaking, and I got hiccups at one point and kept playing with the window blinds.

Then we talked to him. We told him stories. I told him about my grandmother's discount boob job. I told him stories I would never have wanted him to hear, in the hopes that he would suddenly wake up just because I was saying something horrible and embarrassing. Getting my first period. That kind of thing. I didn't care that Callum and Boo were there. They did the same thing. We told him jokes. Callum offered to show him paperwork to make him wake up.

Thorpe arrived, and brought the doctor back in with him. Every time I'd seen Thorpe before this he was just *some guy* from the government. The only thing I'd ever noticed about him was that his face looked too young for his white hair. This time, he didn't wear a suit or a dress shirt or a tie, but a polo neck and some fancy jeans and when he saw Stephen, he fell silent and put his hand over his mouth.

That's when I thought I was really going to lose it. That's when the bile came up the back of my throat and there was a roaring in my ears and I wanted to be anywhere but in this terrible room. I wanted to erase the last few months and run back to Louisiana and be back in my bed at home.

"What happens?" Thorpe asked the doctor. "When the machine is off?"

The doctor had positioned himself discreetly in the corner of the room, his arms folded in gentle, professional resignation.

"The body takes over. Things take their course. It can be minutes or hours."

Thorpe nodded and sniffed once, then looked at the rest of us.

"We'll need a few moments to talk," he said to the doctor.

The doctor excused himself again. Thorpe came to the foot of the bed and looked long and hard at Stephen.

"You've talked?" he asked us quietly. "I think we all know what he would say."

Our silence confirmed this.

"This should never have happened," Thorpe said. "I should never have allowed it to happen. It all went too fast. There should have been more time, more training . . ."

He trailed off, and shook his head once.

"I can speak to the doctor," he said. "I can . . ."

I missed the rest of what he said, though I got the gist that it was something about dealing with actually giving the order and saying he was Stephen's uncle. I was distracted by what I remembered. I remembered being on the floor of the bathroom, after the knife had gone in. I remembered the curious feeling of the wound. My body, unable to make tactile sense of the slash, told me it was an itch with a faint tingle. The blood was coming out so quickly—it couldn't possibly be mine. And through the roaring in my ears, I heard Newman explain to me what he was going to do. He gave me the terminus and he told me that he had a theory—a little theory—that people with the sight who died with a terminus might come back.

"I can fix this," I said. It was sudden. It just popped out of my mouth, and it got everyone's attention.

"What?" Thorpe said.

"I can fix this," I said again. "Newman . . . he had a theory . . . about people who had the sight. If they died in contact with a terminus they might . . ."

Callum stood, and the look on his face was like thunder.

"No," he said. "No."

Boo leapt up right after, but there was a very different expression on her face. Her face said yes.

"What are you saying?" Thorpe said. "You can keep him from dying? You can . . ."

"She's saying she wants to keep him here by making him some *thing* that isn't alive or dead," Callum replied. "And she's not doing it."

"You need to get over your prejudices, yeah?" Boo snapped.

Callum moved past Thorpe and came around to my side of the bed, and the way he was moving, I got the distinct impression that he would not hesitate to use force on me. I gripped the bedrail.

"You won't do this to him," he said to me. No one had ever quite spoken to me in this tone before, not even Newman. It was a clear threat, and the message was that I was the enemy. I would be stopped.

"Callum," Boo said. "Callum, she can *save* him."

"You don't *do* this!" Callum's voice was a roar, and he yelled right into my face. "You don't do this to my friend. You don't *touch* him."

He shoved the adjustable bed table, hard. He didn't shove it at me, but at the wall, as a warning. I became stone. I didn't care. As far as I was concerned, my hand was now welded to the bed.

"Callum." Thorpe's voice didn't have the anger, but the threat was no less serious. "Step away from her and leave the room."

"I'm not leaving." He was over me, looking down into my face.

"You're leaving now or you'll be removed."

"So remove me."

"Is that what Stephen would want? Now?" There was enough emotion in Thorpe's voice to make Callum turn and look at him. "Would he want you to be fighting over him?"

"He wouldn't want to come back like that," Callum said. "Maybe you want it, to study him or something. Maybe you want it"—this was to Boo—"because you think that would help. And *you* . . ."

He had nothing for me. "But he would want to just be allowed to go."

"You don't know that," Boo said. "You don't. You've always been angry at them. You think they're evil, that they don't belong. They're ghosts, not monsters, and they can be happy. They can be productive. You can't decide what he would want based on how *you* feel."

I took Stephen's hand. It was very cool. Not cold, but it was definitely not the hand of someone full of life. And already, I felt a kind of strange feeling. It wasn't like the times I would touch a ghost and feel myself being drawn in. This was a light sensation that started in the fingers and spread along the back of the hand, up the side of my arm, resting a moment at the pulse point inside of my elbow. It was a gentle numbness, like pins and needles, but without any discomfort. And my hand and arm grew warm as they touched his cold skin. In fact, I was starting to feel warm all over.

I looked at the machine that told me Stephen was still alive. The fight continued around me, but I was no longer part of it. I wasn't in this room at all. I was somewhere with Stephen that was entirely separate from the hospital or anything else I had known. It wasn't that I was certain of my decision. I wasn't really thinking anymore. I wasn't blind or deaf. I mean, I saw security come. I saw Callum deciding to leave rather than be pulled out. I saw Boo crying, and Thorpe shutting the door and putting a hand on her shoulder. I saw friendships being ripped apart and hearts broken, and it wasn't that I didn't care . . . it was just all happening behind some kind of pane of glass that kept me and Stephen separate.

It surprised me how clinical the next part was—how calm. The smoothness of it. I just watched and held on, and I thought about how there are systems for things, about how all things have happened before. People die every day, and there are systems for it. The doctor heard the decision and nodded and told us it was the right one. A few people came in, and we gathered around, and things were shut off. I hadn't noticed just how noisy the machine was until it was off.

The monitors were still plugged in, and they still beeped away, but slowly. And we were left in privacy.

• • •

It happened at nine forty-six in the morning.

Right before that, things had gotten very slow—the beeps and wiggles. People started to come in more often. I held his hand harder. The beeps became a flat, droning noise. I closed my eyes. Then *something* was pulling on me. Not something muscular, not something I could see, but something gentle yet unyielding. It reminded me of a science lesson in grade school when they gave us a box of magnets and let us play with them, and I made one tiny magnet pull another across a small distance and lock together.

You are not going anywhere, I said to him, in my mind. *You are not going anywhere. You are staying here. You are staying with me.*

I could still feel the activity around me. I was profoundly aware of Boo at my left side.

DO YOU HEAR ME? YOU ARE NOT…

It almost knocked me down. I was pulling on something, or it was pulling on me. And the space behind my eyes went white. The world went away entirely. Even the white went away, and everything was a bright nothing. Unlike the other times, it wasn't just a flash. I was calm and still and the world was gone, but that was fine. I had become something else, I had joined something larger. Maybe I was water. Maybe I was a drop of water in the ocean. Maybe I was a particle of light. I was the same as everything around me, and everything around me was peaceful.

I wanted to stay here.

There was whiteness. There was falling. I was falling a hundred feet, a thousand feet, but at no particular speed.

And then there were edges of things. Round things. A red line and a black lump. A face—Boo's. My head was forced between my knees, and when I opened my eyes, the hospital floor came back into violent, sudden focus.

"Sorry," I said. Because I knew what was coming next.

I threw up. A plastic basin was shoved in the approximately right spot and I did my best to aim for it. Someone helped me into a chair. I was put in a forward-facing position, slumped over my knees. Boo knelt down next to me.

"Is he—"

She nodded.

"Did it work?" she whispered, stroking my hair.

"I . . . don't know. Something happened."

"I'll look for him," she said. "You all right? I'll look."

Boo was gone for what seemed like forever. I finally lifted myself up and sat back normally. When I did that, I saw Stephen lying there, exactly as before. He looked no different, but all was silence, and his chest did not move.

Thorpe's eyes were red.

"How long does it take?" I asked when Boo returned. "Before they . . . you know. Appear."

"Jo said that when it happened to her, she thinks she woke up right after, but she was never sure," Boo said. "It could have been hours, or even a day or two."

"Alistair said it was right away," I added. "He was asleep, and then he was standing outside of himself. Do they always show up where they die?"

"He could be anywhere," she said. "It's often tied to the place of death, but not always. I've heard of other places people end up. He could be at the flat. He could be at his parents' house, though I doubt that. He's bound to be somewhere. We just have to find him."

"Unless it didn't work," I said.

"I know he's here," Boo said, nodding. "We need to start looking. We do the hospital. We do the flat, both the old one and the new one. And if that fails, we come back here and do it again. Yeah?"

It was then that I understood everything. There would be no train to Bristol. There might be no return to Wexford, or America. Life was being written, right now, in real time. I was not going home. I was staying here. I would find Charlotte. I was going to make Jane pay.

And I would find Stephen.

RORY'S STORY BEGAN IN . . .

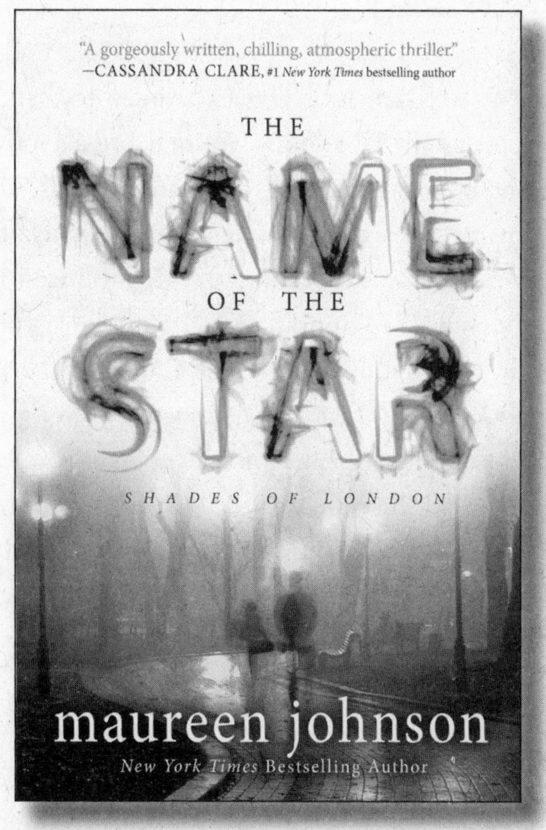

"A gorgeously written, chilling, atmospheric thriller."
—CASSANDRA CLARE, #1 New York Times bestselling author
THE
NAME
OF THE
STAR
SHADES OF LONDON
maureen johnson
New York Times Bestselling Author

1

If you live around New Orleans and they think a hurricane might be coming, all hell breaks loose. Not among the residents, really, but on the news. The news wants us to worry desperately about hurricanes. In my town, Bénouville, Louisiana (pronounced locally as Ben-ah-VEEL; population 1,700), hurricane preparations generally include buying more beer, and ice to keep that beer cold when the power goes out. We do have a neighbor with a two-man rowboat lashed on top of the porch roof, all ready to go if the water rises—but that's Billy Mack, and he started his own religion in the garage, so he's got a lot more going on than just an extreme concern for personal safety.

Anyway, Bénouville is an unstable place, built on a swamp. Everyone who lives there accepts that it was a terrible place to build a town, but since it's there, we just go on living in it. Every fifty years or so, everything but the old hotel gets wrecked by a flood or a hurricane—and the same bunch of lunatics comes back and builds new stuff. Many generations of the Deveaux family have lived in beautiful downtown Bénouville, largely because there is no other part to live in. I love where I'm from, don't get me wrong, but it's the kind of town that makes you a little crazy if you *never* leave, even for a little while.

My parents were the only ones in the family to leave to go to college and then law school. They became law professors at Tulane, in New Orleans. They had long since decided that it would be good for all three of us to spend a little time living outside of Louisiana. Four years ago, right before I started high school, they applied to do a year's sabbatical teaching American law at the University of Bristol in England. We made an agreement that I could take part in the decision about where I would spend that sabbatical year—it would be my senior year. I said I wanted to go to school in London.

Bristol and London are really far apart, by English standards. Bristol is in the middle of the country and far to the west, and London is way down south. But really far apart in England is only a few hours on the train. And London is *London.* So I had decided on a school called Wexford, located in the East End of London. The three of us were all going to fly over together and spend a few days in London, then I would go to school and my parents would go to Bristol, and I would travel back and forth every few weeks.

But then there was a hurricane warning, and everyone freaked out, and the airlines wiped the schedule. The hurricane teased everyone and rolled around the Gulf before turning into a rainstorm, but by that point our flight had been canceled and everything was a mess for a few days. Eventually, the airline managed to find one empty seat on a flight to New York, and another empty seat on a flight to London from there. Since I was scheduled to be at Wexford before my parents needed to be in Bristol, I got the seat and went by myself.

Which was fine, actually. It was a long trip—three hours to New York, two hours wandering the airport before taking a six-hour flight to London overnight—but I still liked it. I was awake all night on the flight watching English television and listening to all the English accents on the plane.

I made my way through the duty-free area right after customs, where they try to get you to buy a few last-minute gallons of perfume and crates of cigarettes. There was a man waiting for me just beyond the doors. He had completely white hair and wore a polo shirt with the name *Wexford* stitched on the breast. A shock of white chest hair popped out at the collar, and as I approached him, I caught the distinctive, spicy smell of men's cologne. Lots of cologne.

"Aurora?" he asked.

"Rory," I corrected him. I never use the name Aurora. It was my great-grandmother's name, and it was dropped on me as kind of a family obligation. Not even my parents use it.

"I'm Mr. Franks. I'll be taking you to Wexford. Let me help you with those."

I had two incredibly large suitcases, both of which were heavier than I was and were marked with big orange tags that said HEAVY. I needed to bring enough to live for nine months. Nine months in a place that had cold weather. So while I felt justified in bringing these extremely big and heavy bags, I didn't want someone who looked like a grandfather pulling them, but he insisted.

"You picked quite the day to arrive, you did," he said, grunting as he dragged the suitcases along. "Big news this morning. Some nutter's gone and pulled a Jack the Ripper."

I figured "pulled a Jack the Ripper" was one of those English expressions I'd need to learn. I'd been studying them online so I wouldn't get confused when people started talking to me about "quid" and "Jammy Dodgers" and things like that. This one had not crossed my electronic path.

"Oh," I said. "Sure."

He led me through the crowds of people trying to get into the elevators that took us up to the parking lot. As we left the building and walked into the lot, I felt the first blast of cool breeze. The London air smelled surprisingly clean and fresh, maybe a little metallic. The sky was an even, high gray. For August, it was ridiculously cold, but all around me I saw people in shorts and T-shirts. I was shivering in my jeans and sweatshirt, and I cursed my flip-flops—which some stupid site told me were good to wear for security reasons. No one mentioned they make your feet freeze on the plane and in England, where they mean something different when they say "summer."

We got to the school van, and Mr. Franks loaded the bags in. I tried to help, I really did, but he just said no, no, no. I was almost certain he was going to have a heart attack, but he survived.

"In you get," he said. "Door's open."

I remembered to get in on the left side, which made me feel very clever for someone who hadn't slept in twenty-four hours. Mr. Franks wheezed for a minute once he got into the driver's seat. I cracked my window to release some of the cologne into the wild.

"It's all over the news." Wheeze, wheeze. "Happened up near the Royal Hospital, right off the Whitechapel Road. Jack the Ripper, of all things. Mind you, tourists love old Jack. Going to cause lots of excitement, this. Wexford's in Jack the Ripper territory."

He switched on the radio. The news station was on, and I listened as he drove us down the spiral exit ramp.

"*. . . thirty-one-year-old Rachel Belanger, a commercial filmmaker with a studio on Whitechapel Road. Authorities say that she was killed in a manner emulating the first Jack the Ripper murder of 1888 . . .*"

Well, at least that cleared up what "pulling a Jack the Ripper" meant.

"*. . . body found on Durward Street, just after four this morning. In 1888, Durward Street was called Bucks Row. Last night's victim was found in the same location and position as Mary Ann Nichols, the first Ripper victim, with very similar injuries. Chief Inspector Simon Cole of Scotland Yard gave a brief statement saying that while there were similarities between this murder and the murder of Mary Ann Nichols on August 31, 1888, it is premature to say that this is anything other than a coincidence. For more on this, we go to senior correspondent Lois Carlisle . . .*"

Mr. Franks barely missed the walls as he wove the car down the spiral.

"*. . . Jack the Ripper struck on four conventionally agreed upon dates in 1888: August 31, September 8, the 'Double Event' of September 30—so called because there were two murders in the space of under an hour—and November 9. No one knows what became of the Ripper or why he stopped on that date . . .*"

"Nasty business," Mr. Franks said as we reached the exit. "Wexford is right in Jack's old hunting grounds. We're just five minutes from the Whitechapel Road. The Jack the Ripper tours come past all the time. I imagine there'll be twice as many now."

We took a highway for a while, and then we were suddenly in a populated area—long rows of houses, Indian restaurants, fish-and-chip shops. Then the roads got narrower and more crowded and we had clearly entered the city without my noticing. We wound along the south side of the Thames, then crossed it, all of London stretched around us.

I had seen a picture of Wexford a hundred times or more. I knew the history. Back in the mid-1800s, the East End of London was very poor. Dickens, pickpockets, selling children for bread, that kind of thing. Wexford was built by a charity. They bought all the land around a small square and built an entire complex. They constructed a home for women, a home for men, and a small Gothic revival church—everything necessary to provide food, shelter, and spiritual guidance. All the buildings were attractive, and they put some stone benches and a few trees in the tiny square so there was a pleasant atmosphere. Then they filled the buildings with poor men, women, and children and made them all work fifteen hours a day in the factories and workhouses that they also built around the square.

Somewhere around 1920, someone realized this was all kind of horrible, and the buildings were sold off. Someone had the bright idea that these Gothic and Georgian buildings arranged around a square kind of looked like a school, and bought them. The workhouses became classroom buildings. The church eventually became the refectory. The buildings were all made of brownstone or brick at a time when space in the East End came cheap, so they were large, with big windows and peaks and chimneys silhouetted against the sky.

FOLLOW MORE OF RORY'S ADVENTURES IN . . .

THE SHADOW CABINET

SHADES OF LONDON, BOOK THREE